SPACE HOSTAGES

SOPHIA McDOUGALL

SPACE HOSTAGES

EGMONT

EGMONT

We bring stories to life

First published in Great Britain 2015
by Egmont UK Limited
The Yellow Building, 1 Nicholas Road, London W11 4AN

Text copyright © 2015 Sophia McDougall

The moral rights of the author have been asserted.

ISBN 978 1 4052 6868 4

www.egmont.co.uk

56271/1

A CIP catalogue record for this title is available from the British Library.

Typeset by Avon DataSet Ltd, Bidford on Avon, Warwickshire

Printed and bound in Great Britain by the CPI Group.

Stay safe online. Any website addresses listed in this book are correct
at the time of going to print. However, Egmont is not responsible for content
hosted by third parties. Please be aware that online content can be subject to
change and websites can contain content that is unsuitable for children.
We advise that all children are supervised when using the internet.

MIX
Paper
FSC   FSC® C018306

For Gemma

You can't cry in space.

You can give it a good try, though.

Tears won't *fall*, without gravity. They collect on the surface of your eyes and you can't wipe them away, so on top of being thrown out of a spaceship, you can't see.

I mean, I hope this doesn't happen to people generally but it was happening to me.

I kept struggling. It was stupid because there was nothing to fight, nothing to grab hold of. *Nothing.* Nothing so huge and total I was going to drown in it. But I still kicked and flailed. All it did was spin me over in helpless cartwheels. I saw the planet swing round as I tumbled, a blur of green and gold through my tears.

I tried to stop moving, to stop breathing so hard. Need to save oxygen, I thought.

But save it for *what?*

I screwed my eyes shut and tried to shake the tears free. It didn't really work, but when I opened them I could make out a frantic scribble of movement against the dark sky. One other human out here with me, no more than the length of a room away, but unreachable; we could flail all we wanted but we'd never be able to touch.

And then I somersaulted over again and there was too much water in my eyes; I couldn't see him any more.

The planet rolled past again, slower this time, a bright disc of light carving through the black. I saw the dim outlines of continents. I wondered if they had names. I wondered if anyone down there would ever know I was there, drifting past above their heads, forever.

We weren't supposed to be here.

No one was supposed to be here.

PART 1

1

I still have moments when the fact that I'm friends with an alien strikes me as kind of weird. I'll be chatting away to Th*saaa* and suddenly I'll be thinking: Tentacles. My friend has tentacles. Or: 'But seriously, *five* sexes?' Or: It is just not *normal* for a person's skin to change from stripy blue to spotty green while they talk about what they watched on TV last night.

It is normal though. It's been a year – I ought to be over it by now. It's just that we don't have many Morrors living in Warwickshire; it's not snowy enough any more and there aren't many job opportunities for them. Th*saaa* lives in the Swiss Alps so I don't get to see them as much as I'd like.

It was another rainy day. I'd come home, groaned hello to Dad and Gran, staggered upstairs and flopped on to my bed where I was now trying to gather the energy to peel off my work overalls for a shower. Even though the war with the Morrors is over, I'm still an Exo-Defence Force cadet, and I still have duties, though these days we weren't so much defending Earth from aliens as defending Kenilworth from wet rubbish and the Leicester-to-Birmingham train line from long-fallen rotting trees. The ice didn't get as bad around here as it did further north, during the war when the Morrors were freezing the planet over, but it was still *pretty* bad and it turns out fifteen years of snow and then floods of meltwater can do quite a lot of damage. There are always supposed to be more robots coming to help but they never seem to actually arrive. There are things I like about National Service, like the fact that I get to have some medical training even though I'm only thirteen, but clearing rubble in the rain is not as fun and character-building as the government broadcasts try to make out.

But it was only two afternoons a week and I always got to come home and eat a hot meal with my family, so it definitely beat plodding across Mars in the freezing cold wondering if you're going to starve, suffocate or be eaten by Space Locusts first, which was how I'd spent the previous spring.

Though sometimes I found myself . . . missing all that. Messed up, I know.

The ChatPort light flashed yellow on the ceiling. I managed to lurch into a sitting position and clap my hands, and there was Th*saaa* standing in my bedroom. Not really, of course, though I could see a flickery slice of their sleeping niche behind them and a couple of different Paralashaths softly changing colour at the edge of the projection.

'Vel-haraa, Th*saaa*,' I said happily. My school doesn't teach *any* Morror languages, which I think is stupid. Ten million aliens live on Earth now: we're probably going to want to know what they're saying. So I'm trying to learn online when I can. There are twenty-three surviving Morror languages, but I'm mostly sticking to Thly*waaa*-lay, which is what Th*saaa* speaks.

'Your accent, it does not improve, Alice,' said Th*saaa*, pronouncing it more like A*leece*, which is not a Thly*waaa*-lay thing.

'Well, nor does yours. You sound more and more French,' I said.

Th*saaa* spread their tentacles in what I considered a very French way, if French people had tentacles, and said, '*Non*, I do not sound French. I sound *Swiss*.'

'How's the Kshetlak-laya going?' Th*saaa* likes studying the dead Morror languages that didn't make it when their planet got eaten by the Space Locusts – or the Vshomu, which is the proper word for them. Th*saaa* had been working on this long poem in the only Morror language I've heard that doesn't sound like sighing or wind in the trees. At least it's closer to a poem than anything else but it's supposed to be performed along with specially composed Paralashath.

Th*saaa* went melancholy colours. 'I have hit a difficult passage. I cannot get the text to harmonise with the Paralashath *at all*.'

'Maybe it's deliberate,' I said. 'You know. Experimental.' Th*saaa* flicked their tendrils impatiently. 'OK, I know! It's all too subtle and complicated for me to understand. We did this poem in English today. It goes:

'*I must go down to the sea again, to the lonely sea and the sky,*
And all I ask is a tall ship, and a star to steer her by . . .'

7

Th*saaa* normally likes nothing more than discussing poetry, especially if there's an opportunity to explain why Morror poetry is better, but this time they said abruptly: 'What are you *weeeearing?*'

'What? *Work clothes,*' I said. 'Not all of us get to do our National Service just showing Paralashaths to little kids in schools.'

'I am aiding the reconciliation process,' Th*saaa* protested. 'Can you please put on something more formal?'

'Have I got to wear a ballgown to talk to you now? Wait, what are *you* wearing?'

Th*saaa* normally wears a long plain kilt and nothing else, but today they were wearing an ivory robe with a pattern of oblong holes cut into the fabric over the chest, to show the colours changing with their moods in the spots and tendrils on their skin.

'Fancy,' I observed.

'I am speaking to you as an *official Morror envoy,*' they said. (Don't call Morrors he, she, or it. They aren't, so it's rude.) 'I have been entrusted with a message by the Council of Lonthaa-Ra-Mo*raa*! This not a casual occasion.'

'Well, you didn't tell me!'

'I'm telling you now!'

'All right!' I sat up straight and tried to behave. 'Do I really have to change my clothes?'

I got a little worried they might be going to say they were leaving. The Morrors have their own country on Earth – Uhalarath-Mo*raa*, which used to be Antarctica –

8

and there are Morrors dotted about in cold pockets of the world like the Alps, but with the entire Morror species to accommodate it's still pretty crowded. So they'd just finished terraforming a little moon orbiting a gas giant in the Alpha Centauri system, and seven million Morrors who'd been living in spaceships and space stations around Earth had moved there.

Th*saaa* can be a bit of pain in the neck but they are my friend. And Alpha Centauri is a lot further away than Switzerland.

'No,' conceded Th*saaa*. 'I apologise. I am a little nervous.' They gave their tendrils a brisk little shake and stood up straighter. 'You have heard, perhaps, that the work to make Aushalawa-Mo*raa* habitable to my people is complete.'

'Yes,' I said, feeling an extra twinge of anxiety.

'I will read the message to you now.'

Th*saaa* spread out a long narrow scroll, illuminated in many colours, across all six tentacles.

'Dear Plucky Kid of Mars – don't *laaaaaugh*,' said Th*saaa* crossly. 'This is an important document.'

'Sorry. It's just . . . they do know that's not our official title, don't they?'

Th*saaa* sagged a bit. 'They do seem convinced it is,' they admitted. 'I tried to explain. You know how it is.'

'Grown-ups don't listen to you,' I agreed.

'Dear Plucky . . .' Th*saaa* began again, and gave a very human sigh. 'Dear Alice Dare. All the nations of Ra-Mo*raaa* owe you a debt for your part in bringing an end to

9

the long war on Earth. Today, humans and Mo-*raaa* uha-*raaa* live in peace, and a new world welcomes the first Mo-*raaa* uha-*raaa* settlers. To celebrate the peace between our peoples, we invite you and your fellow Plucky Kids of Mars to join us on May the thirty-first of this year, in a ceremony to inaugurate the Mo-*raaa* uha-*raaa*'s new home.'

'Oh, *yes*,' I said at once, bouncing a bit on the bed. I didn't hesitate, or think of getting chased by Space Locusts or crashing spaceships on Mars or anything else bad that had happened the last time I'd left the planet I was born on. 'This is amazing, Th*saaa*. You're coming? You're a Plucky Kid of Mars too.'

'Yes, I will come. It will be an opportunity to learn more about the culture of our people.'

'And also *fun*, maybe!' I said.

'La*hee*la wath-eyaa, Th*saaa*,' complained the voice of one of Th*saaa*'s parents, in what I was pretty sure was agreement. An additional set of multi-coloured tentacles waved through the ChatPort and Th*saaa*'s Quth-*laaa*-mi called cheerfully: '*Hiiiiiiiii*, Alice!'

Th*saaa*'s parents are a bit worried Th*saaa* is kind of a stick-in-the-mud.

'And the others?' I said.

'Carl and Noel are coming,'

I hesitated. 'What about Josephine?' I asked.

'Josephine seems difficult to reach,' said Th*saaa*.

'Yeah,' I said, relieved it wasn't just me. I used to talk to Josephine on ChatPort all the time, she'd stayed with us in Wolthrop-Fossey twice, and we'd all gone to Switzerland to visit Th*saaa* together. But I hadn't heard from her in a month. I knew she was working hard. She was doing her World Baccalaureate even though she's my age. Most people do it at eighteen.

She'd said I was her best friend. But I'd been starting to feel a little as if that was only because we'd just nearly died together several times on Mars. And now we were back on Earth, perhaps she wasn't so interested in someone reasonably clever but nowhere near doing her exams five years early.

I shook the thought away. Josephine wasn't like that, she *wasn't*, and if I knew her at all there was no way she'd turn down a chance to visit an alien planet. We were all going to be together again in space.

'How will we get there?' I asked. 'Morror ships are freezing.'

'It is a human ship, with chilled chambers for Morror passengers.'

'Oh. So, an Archangel Planetary ship,' I said. I knew a bit about Archangel Planetary. Rasmus Trommler, the man who owns the company, had been in the news a lot, partly because he invented Häxeri, which is a programming system that makes computers work so much better it's in practically everything now – even the ChatPort – and partly because of scandals and court cases. Also, I'd been on Mars with his daughter Christa, and, putting it nicely, we hadn't got on.

Anyway, the only human-made ships that could go as

11

far as Alpha Centauri were Archangel Planetary ships.

'I am honoured by the Council of Lonthaa-Ra-Mo*raa*'s kind offer,' I said solemnly, feeling perhaps it was time I started living up to Th*saaa*'s fancy outfit and their request for formality. 'I accept with gratitude.'

'I hope your parents will let you come,' said Th*saaa*.

Until then it hadn't occurred to me that I had to ask anyone's permission.

'They will,' I said. 'I'm sure they will.'

Th*saaa* rippled farewell colours at me, and the ChatPort faded out.

Then it flashed on again. 'Oh, and, Alice,' said Th*saaa*. 'Congratulations on the book.'

I ran downstairs into the living room, where Dad and Gran were watching the snooker, and said, 'We're going back to *space!*'

'What?' said Dad and Gran at the same time. Mum was off on a mission so it was just the three of us.

'The Morrors want us to go to Aushalawa-Mo*raa*,' I explained. 'Carl and Noel and Josephine and me, and Th*saaa*, because we helped stop the war.'

'Ausha . . . wa?' Dad seems to have trouble hearing the difference between a lot of Morror words.

'I thought that was what they're calling Antarctica now,' said Gran, with an edge of a grumble in her voice.

'No,' said Dad, understanding in his face now. 'You know. Morrorworld.'

'Alice! The Morrors want to take you to their *planet*?' said Gran, horrified.

And fair enough. A year ago, when we were enemies, that would have been a really scary sentence. But things change.

'They want us there for this ceremony, to sort of declare the planet open.' I wondered if you could cut a ribbon on a whole world. 'And we've got peace with them now. They're nice.'

'Alice,' Dad said, looking a bit gaunt, 'I'm glad the war's over. But it's a stretch to say they're *nice*.'

I got slightly upset. 'I thought you liked Th*saaa*.'

'Th*saaa*'s a kid – it's one thing for you to be friends with a Morror *kid* . . .'

'And what about Th*saaa*'s parents? They were nice to you. They gave you baked *fal-thra* in Switzerland.'

'I'm not saying they're all bad people, Alice.'

Gran grunted. 'They gave a good imitation of it for fifteen years.'

'Gran!' I said.

'Of course, you can't remember the world the way it was before.'

'I have to live in the world the way it is *now*,' I said. 'And it has Morrors in it. That's partly why I wrote that stupid thing. How're we ever going to have *proper* peace if we don't get to know each other?'

'Your book is not stupid,' said Dad, with automatic loyalty. He shifted to make an inviting space on the couch

13

that somehow I couldn't help but flop into. He put his arm round my shoulders.

'Alice, I know you care about humans and Morrors getting along,' he said softly. 'And I know you want to see your friends. But I nearly lost you on Mars, and I didn't even know how close it had been until it was all over. And Mars is, what, fifty million miles away? How far is the Morrors' planet?'

'I think it's about . . . forty trillion miles,' I admitted. 'But this is different. We're not in a war. And you and Mum could come. There's no danger out there except the Vshomu and we're good at dealing with them now. Dr Muldoon's been helping the Morrors with the terraforming – she's been flying out there and back for months and *she's* perfectly fine.'

'You can't say that the Vshomu are the only danger in space,' said Dad. 'We don't *know* what's out there. It's not so long ago we didn't know there were Morrors.'

It seems like a terribly long time ago to me, being before I was born, but I didn't say so.

'Well, no,' I admitted, 'we don't know *everything*, but that's why it's exciting.'

Dad's jaw tightened. 'I can't stop you doing things you find exciting forever, but until you're eighteen . . .'

'Eighteen!' I said, horrified. I realised that, even without this trip, I'd somehow been expecting to be back in space before long. I couldn't stand the thought of it being five years. 'But Carl and Noel are going.'

'If Carl and Noel jumped off a cliff, would you?' asked Gran.

'Weeeell,' I said, 'there was this time, when Carl *did* jump off a cliff-like thing, to get across a crevasse. Although, Josephine went first, and it was the only way across, so . . .'

Dad put his face into his hands.

'My point is, I would jump off a cliff only if I could see it was the most sensible course of action in the circumstances!' I said. 'And, Dad, you *knew* about that – it was in the book.'

'Yes,' said Dad. 'Thanks for reminding me of that, and it wasn't even the worst bit. Alice, after everything you went through, I can't understand why you would want to go back.'

I didn't give up. For days I tried various tactics, such as, 'Can I go to space if I clean the kitchen every day?' and, 'Can I go to space if I get an A in Geography?' But there was nothing good enough that I could do. I had to tell the others that it looked as if they'd be going without me.

'But you *have* to come,' raged Carl on ChatPort. Carl is Filipino-Australian, with a voice almost loud enough to travel all the way from Sydney without technological help. He'd begun to get lanky over the last year, and he'd let his black hair grow out of the stubble it had been on Mars. 'Mum and Dad are letting me and Noel go, and Noel's *nine*. Can't you, like, get some of the way by yourself? It's not that far from England to Switzerland – Th*saaa* could bring you the rest of the way.'

In cosmic terms it is no distance to Switzerland at all. If I'd had a Flying Fox or a Flarehawk, I could have flown there in twenty minutes. I'd been trained to fly spaceships, after all. But you can't do that kind of thing on Earth.

Josephine sent me a strange little email: 'My dad said yes at once. I hope you'll be there.'

Nothing budged Dad an inch. I knew it was because he loved me, but I couldn't help getting furious about it. It was not long ago that I'd had to make decisions like, shall I a) walk off alone with a single tank of oxygen across the Martian wilderness or b) stay with the wreck of the spaceship and wait to die? And, how can we persuade these aliens to stop attacking humanity? It is not fair to put someone in a situation like that and then stick them in a little house on a little island on a little planet, and tell them they have to stay where it's safe, because they're only a child.

And then Mum came home and said, 'But *of course* she wants to go to space.'

2

I'd been hoping Mum would be on my side, seeing that she's a space pilot and feels even more strongly than I do that a life without space travel is very dreary indeed. But I wasn't prepared for how big a fight she and Dad would have about it. They were apart for so long during the war, and they'd been so happy to be together now it was over that they hadn't fought at all, so I wasn't used to it, and nor were they.

'You undermine me in front of her,' Dad was saying.

'Daniel, you made a decision without talking to me and then expected me to fall into line!'

'Someone has to make the decisions that protect her, and God knows you weren't here,' said Dad, with something much uglier in his voice than I could remember hearing there before.

I'd run upstairs, but I could still hear them through the floor. There was a dangerous rattle as Mum stormed across the kitchen and the things on the table shook. 'I spend my life keeping the planet she lives on from being eaten by vermin, and you say I don't protect her.'

I almost wanted to go down and say I'd changed my mind, I didn't mind staying any more. Almost.

But the skies are wide and dark in Warwickshire and the night was bristling with stars. The room and the house

17

seemed smaller than ever, so I opened the window and leaned out and breathed in the cold air as if I could *smell* the stars. Though I knew they weren't as wild and bright as they'd been on Mars, as they would be where Carl and Noel and Josephine were going.

So when Dad came up looking angry and miserable and asked, 'Alice, are you dead set on going?' I said, 'I want it more than anything.'

The upshot was I did get to go, but I wasn't as happy about it as I'd thought I would be. I sent a message to Josephine saying so, but she didn't reply.

Mum and Dad barely talked to each other and looked miserable for most of the next six weeks, and though they both tried to be normal to *me*, it was pretty uncomfortable being the reason they weren't happy any more. I spent the whole time wishing I could just skip ahead to the end of May, so now I'm writing about it that's what I'm going to do.

I suppose it's a bit weird that I've been to Mars and flown a spaceship but I've only been on a plane a couple of times. This time, the Council of Lonthaa-Ra-Moraa was paying for everything and the plane to San Diego was a lot nicer than the nicest spaceship I've been in. There were lovely big cushiony seats and little vases with orchids in them, and everyone else looked so important and rich I felt like a complete mess by comparison, although my clothes had seemed quite nice back in Wolthrop-Fossey.

'Why, you're little Alice Dare,' said an American lady sitting across the aisle from us. She had golden hair whisked into a vertical froth and golden eyelids, and she was dressed in the kind of immaculately white suit a film star would wear. 'Your book was so charming.'

'I'm not that little,' I said, and then felt embarrassed. 'I mean, thank you.'

I didn't *mean* to write a book, which I suppose is why I still can't really believe I did. I just wanted to set everything straight. There was a lot of fuss about the Plucky Kids of Mars after we came home. We got made to do interviews and then half the time the reporters would make stuff up anyway. There was even a docu-drama about us which in my opinion should have been titled *The Remarkably Thick Kids of Mars* because the people in it sort of bumbled around the Martian wilderness crying and falling over until everything kind of fixed itself by magic. Also the girl playing me had funny teeth and could not act AT ALL. And so then there was *another* round of trying to explain what actually happened, not just to reporters but to people at school, too. So I thought I would write it all down, once and for all, and then everyone would leave us alone and maybe our lives would become more normal. I didn't think this would take very long; I thought it would be maybe a couple of blog posts. But it kept getting longer, and when I had written fifty pages and had barely got up to when we landed on Mars I nearly gave up. Dad persuaded me not to, though, and every evening after school or National Service he would talk me through what had happened next and how I was going to write it. While I wrote he'd read the last bit and tell me if he thought it was good or if I should hurry things along a bit or stop making quite so many odd jokes about all the terrible things that happened, which was one piece of advice I never managed to take. And after a while of this I found writing it made me feel better, not just about the annoying stories in the news, but about everything. By the time it was finished I was hardly having nightmares any more.

So I'm pleased about the book in one way and there is some money from it for when I grow up, but as an attempt at making things normal you couldn't call it an unqualified success.

'You must be so proud of her,' said the lady to my parents.

'Always,' said my dad, who of course didn't want to be on the plane at all, but he was very determined.

Once we took off, a little flock of robotic doves came hovering down the cabin bringing delicious snacks on silver trays. They kept this up all through the flight and even Dad thawed a little when they gave him a glass of champagne with a strawberry floating in it, to go with the amazing strawberry dessert we were eating.

'We want everything to be perfect for you,' the doves cooed.

It was so perfect it was slightly panic-inducing. I'd only had strawberries three times before in my whole life.

'Things certainly can change in a year,' Dad said softly, and Mum lifted her own glass and said, 'To change,' and Dad hesitated for a moment but then smiled and clinked her glass. I started thinking maybe it would all be OK.

'We're approaching the coast of California!' chirruped one of the robot doves at last, landing on an armrest. 'You can see our first glimpse of the Space Elevator! Another advance from Archangel Planetary.' It fluttered wings subtly branded with the gold Archangel Planetary logo.

There it was, like a faint line drawn in pencil up the blue sky, stretching up, up, from the edge of the Pacific until it faded out of visibility at the atmosphere's edge. As we watched, something rose up its length, a tiny silver speck like a dewdrop clinging to a spider's web, sliding impossibly upward.

The Space Elevator is one of the things we couldn't have during the war, because the Morrors would just have blown it up. It's supposed to be safer than taking off from the surface, and you can have bigger, better ships if they don't have to enter the atmosphere at all. But I couldn't help thinking the tether linking the Earth to the station on the edge of space looked awfully *fragile* and what if it *broke*.

But there's always more than one way for things to go wrong.

We stepped into the bright California sunlight amidst the friendly robot doves, and a crowd of shiny-looking Archangel Planetary people came to meet us. It was weird to see that many people in uniform who weren't military and who kept smiling. In fact it was strange to see an airfield with hardly any EDF planes or starfighters. The airport probably wasn't in great shape compared to how it had been before the war – weeds as tall as I was growing through the concrete, and one of the terminal buildings still a blackened shell, and even posh people having to actually *walk* off the plane rather than riding hover platforms. But it still looked pretty grand to me with the palm trees and the hologram of the Archangel halo logo floating in the air above it. And above *that* was the elevator's tether, like a great metallic beanstalk reaching to beyond the sky.

And of course there were *some* military things about – a gang of bored squaddies lounging around in the sun saluted my mother when they saw her. A short row of Flarehawks, waiting for transfer or refuelling, not far from a charred heap of wrecks that I guess no one had decided what to do with yet. I looked away from them because they reminded me rather too much of what it is like when the spaceship you're in crashes.

'Captain and Mr Dare, Miss Dare,' said a shiny-looking woman, in a voice as sweet as that of the robot doves, 'welcome to San Diego. Archangel Planetary is delighted to be taking you to the stars.'

Mum, who was used to taking *herself* to the stars, looked a little sick at this, and it was left to Dad to say thank you. Though he was looking at the Space Elevator tether, and his expression was extremely dubious.

Then suddenly there was a squawking noise from Mum's

wrist. And from all the squaddies' wrists. They all jumped up, some of them groaning, as Mum stopped mid-stride, her expression freezing into something fierce and hard and yet a little bit excited.

Dad and I froze too.

'We hope everything is perfect,' trilled the robot doves, concerned.

'It's not,' I said. I knew what that sound meant. 'Vshomu.' The Space Locusts.

'Incoming hostiles detected. Transmitting coordinates now. All units scramble,' said an electronic voice from the EDF smartwatch on Mum's wrist. 'All leave is cancelled. Assemble. Assemble.'

Mum read the details off her watch. 'It's a big swarm,' she said. 'The Moon again.'

The Vshomu have not managed to eat any of Earth yet, and we like it that way. It helps that they can't see it, because of the invisibility shield the Morrors built around the whole planet. But they can still see the Moon, and that brings them a lot closer than you'd want. They breed so fast when they find anything to eat (and they eat *anything*) that if they ever chewed up the moon, first of all: the tides would get really messed up, and, second of all: there would be a cosmically enormous swarm of Vshomu against which the invisibility shield would be about as useful as a raincoat against piranhas.

'Stephanie –' Dad began.

'You have to go, don't you,' I said to Mum. I felt a quiet

thud of disappointment, but I knew it wasn't fair to make a fuss about it. There's no real way to get rid of Vshomu for good, all you can do is keep their numbers down, and blowing them up was what Mum did; she wasn't allowed to back out.

Mum put her hands on my shoulders. 'I'll catch you up,' she said. 'I promise.'

'I don't think a Flarehawk can catch up with a deep space ferry,' I said.

'*I* can,' Mum insisted.

I looked up at the Space Elevator's tether; another capsule was rising away into the blue. I wondered if anyone I knew was on it.

'Be careful, Mum,' I said.

'Oh, this isn't real war,' she said. 'This is *pest control.*'

The smartwatch squawked again. Mum grabbed Dad with military conviction, said, 'Daniel, I do love you,' and kissed him. She let him go and hugged me. 'I love you, Alice.' It was easier than she may have realised to read the 'Just in case I die!' subtitles that came with this, but then her eyes fixed on the distant Flarehawks, her face broke into a grin and she went sprinting off across the concrete, a cheerful cry of 'Have fun!' echoing after her.

Dad and I stood watching her Flarehawk soar across the sky and Dad said heavily, 'Right.'

So we went to the hotel by ourselves.

'The Morrors are being so nice to us,' I said. Because

it was a very posh hotel; Dad's room alone was practically the size of our house. I wanted to make sure we were still going, because I was afraid Dad might have changed his mind now Mum wasn't around. But if he hadn't thought of it I didn't want to put ideas in his head.

'Yes,' said Dad, and he looked at the soft carpets and vases of flowers and little chocolates as if he thought something might be lurking under the sofa cushions waiting to spring at us.

I'm afraid I did not take in much of San Diego beyond that it had palm trees and sea and only minimal shockray damage. Dad and I had supper in the restaurant which I'm sure was very good, but mostly wasted on me as I kept falling half-asleep over it. Annoyingly, once I was in an enormous but slightly chilly bed I found I was also too excited to sleep, so I lay there again wondering what it was like on the spaceport and if Vshomu would eat through the invisibility shield and if Mum was OK. And this turned into worrying about the very important exam on ferrets which I'd forgotten to revise for, and eventually I realised I must have been asleep after all.

I lay there for a moment, checking in with myself that the ferret exam was definitely a dream, and then it struck me that it was morning and today I was going to space. The thought kicked me out of bed like an electric shock. I threw open the curtains and beamed at the tether rising across the sunrise. I managed to shower like a sensible person – though my heart kept pounding and I was trembly while I brushed my teeth. This wasn't a very comfortable kind of excitement. But as soon as I was dressed I went running to Dad's suite as if I was seven again and it was Christmas morning.

When I opened the door I heard sounds. Bad ones.

'Dad?' I said.

The bedroom was dark. The bed was empty, the covers thrown aside. I padded across approximately a mile of velvety carpet towards the rectangle of light that was the open door of the en-suite. Dad was crouched miserably on the bathroom floor, his head over the loo.

'Oh, *no*,' I said.

'I'm all right,' said Dad bravely, and then proved this wasn't true.

'Oh, no,' I said again, and then tried to remember my medical training. 'How long have you been like this?'

'Since about two, I think,' Dad said, shivering.

I pulled the quilt off the bed and put it over him, then washed my hands extremely thoroughly while I tried to decide what to do. I wasn't sure if I should be telling the hotel, Archangel Planetary or the Morrors, and I wasn't at all sure how to get in touch with the Council of Lonthaa-Ra-Mo*raa*.

I got annoyed with myself for dithering, went and called reception, and sent a ChatPort ping to Th*saaa*.

'It's just food poisoning,' Dad croaked. 'It's probably out of my system now – I'll be all right in a few hours.'

But in two hours we were supposed to be on the Space

26

Elevator, and anyway . . . 'I think you have norovirus,' I said. I gave him some water I'd warmed in the kettle till it was tepid. Cold water is sometimes harder for people with nausea to keep down, although, on the other hand, sometimes it's easier. Medical knowledge can be very unhelpful.

After about twenty minutes the doors slid open and an Archangel Planetary dove hovered through. This one was evidently a medical dove because it had a little green cross printed on its breast. It emitted a spray of green light over Dad with an angelic twinkling noise.

'Good morning, sir, you have norovirus,' it sang. 'Dispensing: anti-nausea medication!' It laid two pills like tiny eggs on the bedside table. 'Keep warm and take plenty of fluids.'

'That's what I said,' I muttered.

'I have to take my daughter into space,' said Dad, reaching weakly for the pills.

'Vomit is very bad in space,' I said. Believe me, I know.

'Passengers with infectious illnesses cannot be cleared for travel aboard Archangel Planetary's Space Elevator,' said the dove placidly. 'We are sorry for the inconvenience.'

'Have *I* got it?' I asked, worrying about how trembly I'd felt earlier.

The robot dove sprayed green light over me, too. 'Congratulations. You are healthy. You are cleared for travel. Archangel Planetary: Taking You to the Stars.'

'But . . . what can I do?'

'The *Helen of Troy* departs Orbit Station One for Aushalawa-Mo*raa* at eleven-hundred hours,' said the dove. 'The last Space Elevator capsule departs Earth Station San Diego at oh-nine-hundred hours.'

It was already half past seven. My stomach felt so tight I wondered whether the dove had got its diagnosis wrong.

'Yes, but is there any way we could go later?' I asked. Dad would be better by the next day. But how long would he stay infectious?

'The *Helen of Troy* departs Orbit Station One at eleven-hundred hours,' repeated the dove. 'The next ship to depart Orbit Station One for Aushalawa-Mo*raa* will be at oh-seven-hundred hours . . .'

'Oh!' I exclaimed, a tiny bit hopeful.

'. . . on the fourteenth of November,' the dove finished.

'Oh. You couldn't ask the *Helen of Troy* to wait?' I asked hopelessly. But the *Helen of Troy* probably cost millions of pounds every day it sat up there.

The dove beamed a message up to the Morror liaison on Orbit Station One and perched on the head of Dad's bed while it waited for an answer.

'You have a reply,' it cooed presently, and then went ping, and then a quite different voice spoke out of it:

'Weeeeee are soooooooorry, Plucky Kid of Mars. The ship cannot delaaaaaay; we cannot riiiiissssk using contingency fuel and supplies before leeeeeeaving. If you aaaaaaaaare unable to join us today, our people must hooooonour you in your aaaaabsence.'

'I'm sorry, love,' croaked Dad, without opening his swollen eyelids. A minute later he was snoring.

'Please consider Archangel Planetary for all your future healthcare needs,' said the dove, and hovered out of the room.

Tears stung in my eyes.

I went back to my enormous room and sat there uselessly for a few minutes before calling Gran.

'Oh, sweetheart,' she said, when she'd finished exclaiming sympathetically over Dad. 'Don't worry about a thing. The insurance will cover everything, and I'm sure the airline will let you fly home early.'

'But Gran . . .!' I wailed.

'Love, you've had quite enough trouble for a girl your age. You don't *really* want to be rushing off to the other end of the universe.'

I said goodbye quietly. After a while I realised I was pacing about the room; I wasn't sure when I'd started. My tablet pinged with a message from Carl.

Hey, is everything OK? Are you on the Space Elevator yet? We've got to leave soon. Heard your dad was sick? You're still coming, though, right?

It only felt like a couple of minutes since I'd said goodbye to Gran, but the time on my tablet said eight forty-five.

I clenched my fists, and I slipped back into Dad's room, and looked at him, huddled in the blankets.

'Dad,' I said. 'I could always go by myself.'

I waited. There was no reply.

'I'll be perfectly fine on my own. Dr Muldoon will be there, and Lena – you know, Josephine's sister – they're very responsible.' I stopped, realising I was not sure that was completely true; Dr Muldoon was worryingly keen on human experimentation, and Lena had taught Josephine how to build flamethrowers when she was six. But they were grown-ups and humans; that had to count for something. 'And Mum said she could catch up – maybe you could come with her. Or you could stay behind with Gran, because I know you don't want to go . . .'

And I waited again.

'But, Dad, I *really do*.'

'Mmf,' said Dad, and shifted a little on the pillows.

It wasn't a yes.

But it also wasn't a no.

He hadn't ever said I *couldn't* go by myself.

I texted Carl back:

I'M COMING.

I did write Dad a note, on expensive hotel paper: 'GET WELL SOON. SEE YOU WHEN I GET HOME, XXX ALICE.' Then I added ten more Xs and a couple of hearts to make up for what I was doing, and put it on the table beside the bed.

Then I grabbed my suitcase and ran.

3

I wish I had one of those hover-suitcases. They're really expensive. But running nearly half a mile with a suitcase that only has wheels is *hard*, especially when you're quite agitated and not perfectly sure where you're going.

I pounded through a memorial garden, across a car park, down a wide avenue of palms, my shoulders aching as the suitcase dragged behind me. I managed not to knock over two women taking photos of the Elevator, and a veteran with a missing arm queuing for burgers at a stall. I hurtled my way along the waterfront. The tether rose from a round concrete platform at the end of a long pier sticking out into the waves. The complex on land was so new it wasn't finished yet; I lurched past lots of empty buildings and colourful hoardings covered with pictures of the exciting space-themed coffee houses and gift shops that were going to be there eventually.

It was all a lot quieter than the airport had been. There was only one place you could get to from here. Although, in another way, you could go absolutely *anywhere*.

I rushed across all that empty space and crashed into a counter and waved my passport at the lady behind it. 'I'm Alice Dare,' I gasped. 'You have to let me on the Space Elevator. I'm a Plu– I mean, I was an evacuee on Mars and stuff happened. I need to go to the Morror planet; the Morrors are expecting me.'

'I know who you are, sweetie,' said the lady, smiling. 'But you're on your own?'

'My parents can't make it,' I said. 'But Mum will be coming out later.'

Now, when you're thirteen, telling people they need to let you travel an enormous distance without your parents mostly isn't going to work. But they were expecting me. And none of the others had their parents with them; Carl and Noel's dad has nerve damage from the war and their mum was too busy running their cinema. And Josephine's dad . . . well, I didn't completely understand what was going on with Josephine's dad, but he wasn't coming.

'You'll have to hurry,' said the lady, in what seemed to me an unbearably leisurely way. 'Your climber leaves in . . . two minutes.'

A little auto-trolley came scooting up to me and beeped encouragingly. I fell on to it and it whisked me up to a pair of forbidding metal doors engraved with both the EDF crest and the Archangel Planetary logo. The doors slid open and then I was whirring down a long glass-covered tunnel over the waves of the bay.

'The next climber for Orbit Station One departs in one minute,' said a disembodied voice, for no reason I could see except to stress me out.

'Come on,' I moaned to the trolley, which was no cleverer than a vacuum cleaner and doing the best it could anyway.

'The next capsule for Orbit Station One –'

'As if it could go somewhere else!' I complained.

We emerged into an oval open space like a concrete arena. The noise of the waves and the wind outside rang around the heavy walls and there was an acrid smell of engine oil and salt water. The tether was a bundle of separate flat strips like ash-grey hair ribbons, each terrifyingly thin and delicate, descending impossibly from the sky and looking far too fragile to support the huge double-disc of the platform fastened to it, let alone the stack of drum-shaped cargo capsules loaded aboard. There was a handful of crew in yellow overalls inspecting things, and as the trolley carried me round to the far side of the elevator, one of them jumped down from a service ladder and signalled 'OK' at someone above.

'The Elevator is ready for departure,' announced the disembodied voice, a little muted by the roar of the sea. And the Elevator began to rise.

'WAIT!' I screamed, tumbling off the trolley.

And, thank God, the near person in the yellow overalls saw me. He raised his hand and the Elevator stopped, two feet off the ground. And there was the passenger capsule, another drum-shaped container with a wide band of windows around the outside, and doors which slid open as I rushed forwards. The auto-trolley beeped in farewell as I heaved my suitcase inside and climbed in after it. I collapsed, breathless, on top of my luggage.

The doors snapped shut, and I was rising into the air.

So fast that before I'd got my breath back the world below had dwindled away and the ships in the bay shrank first into toys and then into grains of white rice. Looking down I found myself clinging to the back of the seat, as if that would help if I fell.

I'd thought there would be other people there, but there weren't. I suppose all the scientists and soldiers who needed to be up there already were, and there still aren't many people who can afford space cruises just for fun. There were two rings of seats, one facing outwards and one facing in, a tiny bathroom inside a sort of pillar in the middle, and a little shelf where there was complimentary tea and coffee.

My tablet beeped. I pulled it out of my shoulder bag and tapped it warily, as if it might be red-hot.

'ALICE, GET DOWN FROM THERE!' Dad yelled.

'I can't!' I said, already watching the curve of the Earth come into view. 'I'm sorry!'

'Oh, you sound it,' said Dad bitterly.

And of course, I wasn't really sorry, except about leaving him.

'You are in a world of trouble,' Dad promised.

'All right,' I agreed peaceably. Because whatever trouble I was in was over a month away and easily worth it. 'Are you feeling any better?'

But I lost the signal then and as no one likes being yelled at by their dad I was relieved. I turned the tablet off and did a little celebratory dance in the middle of the blue sky.

I rose for two hours. Everything was silent except the faint hum of the Elevator and the moan of the wind. The clouds shrank into wisps below me. The blue of the sky thinned like a pretence I was seeing through and there was the blackness behind it.

And then instead of endless space outside there were walls against the windows, sealing the capsule in, and there were outer doors lining up with the doors of the capsule. The Elevator stopped with a clunk and hiss as the pressure equalised, and the doors slid open. I trundled my suitcase out.

I was standing on the edge of space. Every surface of the great curved chamber around me was transparent, even the floor. The sun blazed in the black sky.

Under my feet I could see the whole circle of the Earth now. It shone back at me like a bright blue eye.

Robots were unloading the Elevator climber, but there were some people about too, directing their movements, coming and going from the ships outside . . .

The ships. There they were, bright against the black, some docked against access passages, some floating amid little crews of busy service robots like big fishes letting tiny ones nip parasites from their scales. A Flarehawk carrier. A large, ugly, mud-brown mining vessel. And looking small beside it, there was a beautiful ship like a swan with folded wings that could only be the *Helen of Troy*.

'Hey!' called a woman in a technician's uniform. 'You're

one of those Mars kids, aren't you? You need to hurry – the *Helen*'s about to leave.'

I dragged my suitcase towards the beautiful white ship. There was no obvious security to stop me running down the passageway to the airlock, but as I entered it I felt a brief tingle on my skin and a computer voice said, 'Welcome, Alice Dare,' so I think something scanned me in some way. The EDF have owned my bio-signature since I went to Mars, which is a little creepy when I think about it. One final set of doors opened to let me through, and then I rushed on to the spaceship.

I was in a pale, softly lit space, as anonymously pleasant as the lobby in the hotel I'd left on earth. There was a water feature and soothing glass sculptures. Sets of doors stood all round me, but there were no windows. The doors I'd come through had shut behind me.

'Uh, hello,' I said. One of the problems of very modern technology is that you can't always tell if it's in things or not, and that's how you find yourself talking to walls and potted plants and feeling like a moron when they don't talk back. These didn't.

I felt a little bit disappointed. Someone might have come to meet me.

The central set of doors obligingly let me through. Small lights blossomed under the floor to greet me as I walked. But my eyes hadn't adjusted to the loss of the sunlight yet, and the passage seemed shadowy. I passed doors on either side, but none of them opened. I crept deeper into the ship, trundling my suitcase behind me, trying to ignore the feeling that I'd made a serious mistake and something bad was about to happen.

Then there was a breath of cold on my neck. I jumped pretty high, I expect. I spun round, but no one was there. Yet I had the impression of movement, a shimmer on the edge of my vision . . .

'Th*saaa*! Stop it!' I complained, and heard the soft wheezing of Morror laughter. The shimmer whisked around me again. 'Sneaking up on people in your invisibility gown is *rude*.'

There was a swishing sound and Th*saaa*'s head appeared out of nowhere in front of me, colours rippling through their mane of glassy tendrils. 'But it is traditional for us to wear amlaa-vel-esh when we travel,' they said.

I considered this. 'You're lying. Look, you're going red. And orange and blue.'

'You wanted me to have *fuuuuuun*,' said Th*saaa*, pulling the invisibility gown off completely and flexing their tentacles. 'Besides, it was not really a lie. We always *did* travel in them, in the war.'

'Where are the others?'

'Watching. Josephine has hacked into the security cameras, I believe. I could not surprise you so effectively with them here,' Th*saaa* explained.

'All right, hi, everyone, very funny,' I said, waving in the general direction of the ceiling. 'So, where am I supposed to go?'

'Come with me,' said Th*saaa*. Gallantly, they seized my suitcase in another two tentacles and deposited it inside a lift.

'Are your parents here, Th*saaa*?' I asked, as we rose through the *Helen of Troy*.

'No. It is the start of the summer skiing season.'

There, I thought. Going off by myself isn't that big a deal.

'Are you all right here?' I asked, reminded about Morrors' climatic needs by the mention of skiing. 'You're not getting too hot?'

'It *iiiis* very hot,' conceded Th*saaa*. 'But I am all right. I must go to my cabin or put my amlaa-vel-esh back on before very long, though.'

The doors opened. A girl was there, waiting for the lift. But it wasn't Josephine or anyone I wanted to see.

It was Christa Trommler.

'*Oh*,' I said aloud, in undisguised horror.

Christa looked just how she used to – well, not how she looked when she was co-leader of a deranged mob smashing anything that got in its way, but how she looked before that, on the way out to Mars, i.e. crisp and expensively dressed in a blue striped blazer and sunglasses poised on her short blonde hair. Her expression was nearly as dismayed as I felt.

'Alice,' she said, with icy dignity, as though at some point in the past we'd had a disagreement on the proper way to lay out salad forks. She nodded, and tried to sweep grandly past me, but was rather stymied by the fact that I didn't get out of the way.

'Hi, Christa,' I said. 'Last time I saw you, you were laughing while your boyfriend beat me up and locked me in a smashed-up classroom,' I announced. 'Were there any plans to let me out, or did you figure it was OK if I died in there?

Christa bridled. 'That was all Leon. I went along with it because I was scared of him.'

My mouth dropped open a little. 'Yeah, *right*,' I said.

'It *is* right, unlike that *book*,' said Christa. 'You know, we could have sued you over that. We just didn't want to give you the publicity.'

'It's all true and you know it, Christa!' somebody hissed.

There was Josephine, with Carl and Noel beside her. Josephine had grown a surprising amount. She was as skinny as ever, but a little taller than me now, which I couldn't help feeling vaguely disgruntled about.

Josephine's hair was different too; instead of the usual wild halo of soft dark zigzags, it was scraped back into a tight bun. Her expression was lethal enough to make Christa cringe.

I was fairly satisfied by this, so I let Christa into the lift.

'It was all just a joke anyway,' Christa muttered as she passed me. 'Obviously we'd have let you out.'

'Weren't you saying you only went along with it because you were scared of Leon?' asked Josephine, whose hearing is eerily good. 'If it was a joke, what were you so scared of?'

Christa did not answer this. 'Everyone knows your dad wrote the whole thing,' she shot at me, as the lift doors closed.

'Someone might have warned me she was here!' I said.

'She only got here this morning, on the last Elevator before yours,' said Carl. 'I know, it sucks, doesn't it.'

'Why is she here?'

'Hanging out with her dad, I guess,' said Carl.

'What, Rasmus Trommler's here too?'

'Yeah, well, it's his tech, his ship. He's been the one ferrying Dr Muldoon out here to play around with Morrorworld this whole time.'

'He *did* invent Häxeri,' said Josephine. '*He*'s a genius, whatever his daughter's like. And she won't want to see us any more than we want to see her. And it's a big ship. Anyway,' she finished, a bit awkwardly, 'hi.'

She hugged me. I was a bit surprised, because normally she'll hug me back if I start it but she doesn't usually start things off herself. And then all the rest of us hugged and I felt even more certain that the trouble I'd be in when I got home was worth it.

'Come and look around,' said Carl. 'The views are amazing.'

'The *labs* are amazing,' Josephine added.

'There are many empty rooms,' said Th*saaa*, in faintly uneasy colours.

'Well, it'll be mostly used as a cruise ship now Morrorworld's finished,' said Carl.

'I guess,' said Josephine dubiously. 'But I wonder how many people are going to be able to afford this kind of thing.'

The *Helen of Troy* was much more luxurious than anything I'd experienced in space before. When Josephine showed me into my cabin on the *Helen*, it was bigger than my room at home, smelled of jasmine and had its own bathroom with a spa bath and a shower which had power, steam and sonic settings. Out in the main passenger lounge there were pleasantly squashy seats round gently glowing tables set into oval wells in the softly carpeted floor. There was a low stage opposite a bar, which made me worry about whether this trip was likely to include much singing. And there was a snooker table. The snooker balls also glowed, which probably wouldn't help with snooker particularly but did look pretty. Enormous windows took up most of the walls, wrapping us in sunlight and stars.

Carl plunged into the nearest well of seating and started whacking the little icons on the tabletop to see what would happen. A menu on a virtual screen appeared in mid-air, so he started trying to see if he could order burgers and banana hotcakes.

Meanwhile the glowing tables pulsed in different colours in a vaguely Paralashath-like way. I don't know if this was intended to please Morror passengers, but if so it backfired. Th*saaa* went nauseated colours at the sight of them and muttered, 'I cannot eat off furniture that appears to be *humiliated*.'

Josephine slid into the seat beside Carl and did

something to the table that made it stop glowing.

'So, I guess . . . from what you said to Christa, you read the . . . book . . . thing, then,' I said to her, feeling suddenly shy and weird about it again. 'I wasn't sure if you had.'

'Yes.' She drummed her fingers on the table, considering carefully. 'Writing a book at all is an achievement, especially at your age,' she said, as if she wasn't thirteen too.

'Er . . . thanks,' I said.

'But it is quite overdramatic,' added Josephine.

'We nearly got blown up and drowned and suffocated and eaten!' I said, indignant. 'On *Mars*! How am I supposed to make that . . . *under*dramatic?'

'I think you should have focused on the facts,' said Josephine.

'I did! You just said it was all true!'

'The facts of historical and scientific importance. Not the, you know –' she waved a disgusted hand, '– *feelings*.'

'Well, you write it your own way next time,' I snapped.

'I'm too busy,' said Josephine. This did not make me less irritated, but the strained look on her face reminded me she *had* been working stupidly hard lately.

'There's not going to be a next time,' said Noel, peaceably. 'This is different. We're on holiday. It's not going to *be* historically or scientifically important.'

'It *is* going to be scientifically important,' said Josephine. 'I have work to do.'

'Hey, Alice!' rang out the cheerfullest, perkiest, most relentless voice in the world.

42

The Goldfish sailed into the room, shiny and orange and beaming.

The teacher-robot had got pretty battered while on Mars and a year in Carl's and Noel's company hadn't helped. Its left eye was still wonky and there was a crude seam down one plastic flank where someone had tried to mend a crack with some kind of filler. But it was, as it always had been, an undaunted, floating, blue-eyed American robot fish, on a mission to educate youth.

'Boy, it's good to see you,' it said. 'Isn't this exciting? Isn't the Elevator nifty? Can you remember how many miles long the tether is? Can you tell me what "geostationary orbit" means?'

'Oh, God,' Carl moaned. 'Why did we have to bring it, again?'

'It was invited,' Noel said reproachfully.

'It's like an honorary Plucky Kid of Mars,' I said, still patting it. 'It *did* help, Carl.'

'It *shot* me,' Thsaaa objected.

'Well, yes, there is also that,' I admitted.

'Remember we're on holiday, Goldfish. No lessons,' Noel cautioned.

'OK, gang!' agreed the Goldfish. 'For now,' it added darkly. 'Buuuuut . . . Thsaaa's not on holiday! Are you, Thsaaa?'

'Aren't you?' I asked.

'Morror children based on Earth are following the curriculum set by the Council of Lonthaa-Ra-Moraa,' the Goldfish said. 'And it's still term time!'

'How do you know that?' I asked.

'Isn't the internet a great source of information for *all* of us?' the Goldfish enthused. 'Hey, gang! What's your favourite thing you learned on the internet?'

'I don't think you want me to answer that,' Carl said.

'Say, Th*saaa*! How's your history going? Do you think the causes of the Vela*raaa*-ley-Hath-hala*waaa* War were primarily social or economic?'

'I have my own teachers who have excuuuuused me from lessons,' said Th*saaa* stiffly. 'This is an educational trip in itself.'

'Sure, sure,' said the Goldfish innocently, before dashing at Th*saaa* so eagerly it almost hit them in the face. 'And I just *bet* you have to write a nice, long essay about it.'

'You once tried to murder me,' Th*saaa* protested.

'Aww,' said the Goldfish. 'Don't be sore, Th*saaa*.'

'I am going to my cooling chamber,' said Th*saaa*, and swished away in an angry rustle of skirts.

'I think maybe you should actually apologise,' Noel told the Goldfish.

'You can help *me*, if you want, Goldfish,' Josephine said abruptly, climbing out of the seating well.

'Ah, no,' moaned Carl. 'Jo, this trip is supposed to be fun.'

'Learning *is* fun!' the Goldfish practically shrieked. 'Sure, Josephine! What can I help you with?'

'I'm retaking my World Baccalaureate,' said Josephine. 'Focusing on Biochemistry and Astrophysics with a mini-thesis in Astro-archaeology.'

'*Retaking* it?' I said.

The Goldfish kept smiling because it can never stop smiling. But the light inside it dimmed and it sank a few inches in the air. 'Ohh,' it said. 'Well, that's . . . a little out of my league, Josephine. I'm only programmed with grades five to nine, so . . . World Baccalaureate? Boy, you sure are ahead of the game! Gosh. That's super.'

Josephine frowned thoughtfully at the Goldfish. 'Did you ever upgrade it at *all*?' she asked Carl, accusatorily.

'Hey, that fish spends its whole life torturing me, and I'm supposed to help it?' Carl asked.

Before anyone could answer, the ship played an angelic fanfare and the halo logos on the walls shone brighter. 'Your attention. The Captain will be joining you on deck,' said the walls, in feminine and vaguely awestruck tones.

EDF training does funny things to you: even though we were definitely off-duty, we all scrambled out of the seats and ended up in a stiff military row for inspection.

A man strode into the room. He was tall and fair with a neat little blond beard and a grin slightly too full of square white teeth. He wore a narrow-fitting dove-grey suit even more extravagantly expensive than that of the gold-and-white American lady on the plane.

'Please, that's not necessary,' he said, seeing our military posture. 'Alice, Carl, Josephine, Noel, I'm Rasmus Trommler. As your captain, it'll be my honour to take you to the stars.'

'Oh,' I said. I hadn't expected to encounter so many

Trommlers in one day, or for any of them to be assuming such important roles, and one of them had already talked about suing me.

'You fly ships?' asked Carl, sceptical.

'I have my wings, I assure you,' Rasmus Trommler said, baring his white teeth again. 'Even I had to go through EDF training in the war. And I should know well enough how to fly the *Helen* – I built her.'

'Must be cool to fly your own ship,' Carl said wistfully.

'Tell you what,' said Mr Trommler. 'You've only flown little gnats like Flarehawks and Flying Foxes before, right? When we get clear of the Oort Cloud, maybe you can pilot *Helen* for a while.'

The scepticism fled Carl's eyes and something like worship sprang up in its place.

'Any little thing like that you want, you just ask,' said Mr Trommler, beaming. 'We all know you earned it.'

'Could you tell me about how you developed Häxeri?' asked Josephine.

'You're living in an amazing time, children. A new world awaits us,' said Trommler, who didn't seem to have heard her.

'It's the Morrors' new world, though,' Noel pointed out.

'Yes of course,' said Trommler, and then carried on. 'You're witnessing the birth of a new era. We're breaking free of the solar system. With our new hyperspace technology –'

'Well, it's really the Morrors' hyperspace technology,' I said. This time Rasmus Trommler did not bother to stop.

'– *despite* how short-sighted the Coalition have been with their funding, *despite* the EDF's failure of vision, the universe is open to humanity as never before. Ever since the Morrors invaded Earth we've known that deep spacefaring races exist. We cannot afford to sit and wait again for them to come to us; we must assert our right to walk the skies in freedom. The stars belong to us, children. We're not leaving home today, we're *going* home. We are stepping out into our inheritance.'

By the end of this we were all pretty swept up in the idea of walking the skies in freedom, and we clapped. While we were still applauding, Dr Muldoon sauntered in, long red hair blazing on her white lab coat, and perched on the edge of the snooker table.

'Valerie!' said Rasmus Trommler. 'I had hoped you'd be here for my little speech.'

'The one about breaking free of the solar system? I've heard it a couple of times,' said Dr Muldoon. 'Hi, Alice. Nice book. So, I have a pointy nose, do I?'

I writhed, not only because I hadn't meant to upset Dr Muldoon, but because I'd been rather hoping no one would remind Rasmus Trommler I'd written a book at all. I stammered, 'I-I didn't mean it in a *bad* way . . .'

Dr Muldoon grinned. 'Ah, stop squirming. If I didn't like it pointy I'd have grown myself a new one years ago.'

'Indeed so,' said Mr Trommler, turning to beam at her. 'I love to name my ships after beautiful women; how do you think the *Valerie* sounds?'

Dr Muldoon stared at him. 'Inappropriate,' she said.

'Haha,' said Mr Trommler, undismayed. 'Well, my *Helen* loves me, at least, don't you, *Helen*?'

'Yes, my Captain, I love you so,' sighed the voice from the walls.

'Wait, is the ship *conscious and in love with you*?' Josephine asked, horrified.

Trommler paid no attention to this. '*Helen*, beautiful? It's time. Let's go to the stars.'

Dr Muldoon discreetly rolled her eyes.

'Yes, Captain, course set,' agreed the ship happily.

And then the blue haze of Earth faded behind us and the stars blazed ahead like a snowstorm. Then they began to change colour, from red to orange to yellow to green, until they slipped through violet and vanished into blackness.

The *Helen of Troy* quivered and strained against something, an invisible membrane. And we burst through and were spat into hyperspace.

Wispy specks of pale light filtered out of the dark, gathering into smoky threads spooling past the ship, glowing brighter and brighter until the windows filled with so much light it was dazzling.

'What you're seeing is not starlight,' said Dr Muldoon. 'That's the background cosmic radiation of the universe. It's always passing through you, but only in hyperspace can you see it. You're looking at the aftermath of the Big Bang.'

'Wow,' breathed Carl. His hands curled in front of him as if resting on invisible ship controls. I hoped Trommler had been serious about letting him fly the *Helen*.

'If we were to come back into normal space now, we'd already be more than a million miles away from Earth,' Rasmus Trommler said.

'Oh, thank God,' I said. Even travelling at unnaturally high speeds, that was surely much too far for anyone to send me back.

'What?' asked Josephine.

'I'll tell you in a minute,' I hissed.

'These are the thoroughfares of humanity's future,' said Rasmus Trommler grandly, standing framed in the glow of the universe, his jaw uplifted. There was a brief pause, and then we began politely applauding again. Mr Trommler smiled and walked away.

'Get used to it,' said Dr Muldoon, when he was gone. 'It's a two week trip.'

'He *did* invent Häxeri,' said Josephine, loyally.

'That's true,' said Dr Muldoon. 'I'd never have thought he had it in him.'

'But he's invented lots of things before,' said Noel.

Dr Muldoon shook her head. 'Practically every other Archangel product was invented by someone else. He just put them in pretty packages and raked in the cash. Häxeri really is his baby, though. Well, I should go too; I've got some tests running in the lab.'

'I'll be there later,' promised Josephine, as Dr Muldoon left.

'*Jo*,' complained Carl. 'You don't *have* to.'

'I have tests running as well,' said Josephine. 'But anyway, Alice, what were you going to tell me?'

I tried to grimace at the Goldfish.

'Goldfish, we need some privacy,' said Josephine.

The Goldfish tilted doubtfully.

'It's GIRL STUFF,' continued Josephine ominously. '. . . which it's OK for Noel and Carl to hear,' she added, sounding a bit less sure of herself.

'OK, kids!' said the Goldfish brightly. 'See ya later!'

It bobbed away to the doors.

'So?' Carl asked.

'Well, my dad was never that thrilled about this trip,' I began.

'Say, kids!' squawked the Goldfish, coming back. 'It looks like Th*saaa*'s heading this way again – shall I tell them you need some private human girl time?'

'Erm . . . no, that's OK!' I called.

'Oh,' said the Goldfish, sagging a bit in the air, and hovered away.

I winced.

'What is going on?' said Th*saaa*, coming to join us at the no-longer-humiliated table.

'I'm kind of . . . not allowed to be here,' I said. And I explained what had happened.

'Ohhhh, *mais c'est mal*,' moaned Th*saaa*, going black and amber and tossing their tentacles. 'What if you have caused a diplomatic incident?'

'No one will be in any trouble except me,' I said.

'But what will the Council of Lonthaa-Ra-Mo*raa* say when they find out?'

'Well, don't *tell* them,' I said. 'Or the Goldfish,' I added, lowering my voice.

'You ran away to space?' asked Carl. 'That's awesome.'

'It isn't! Her dad will be worried and he's already sick!' Noel exclaimed.

'No, that is pretty cool,' said Josephine decidedly.

I grinned. 'I've missed you,' I said.

Something passed across her expression that made me uneasy, and I opened my mouth to ask if everything was OK. But before I could she said, 'I've missed you too.'

'We are about to re-enter normal space for a while,' said the *Helen of Troy*. 'The science team has some tests they need to run. Passengers may want to watch the windows.'

We couldn't exactly *feel* the *Helen of Troy* slowing down, but there was a faint quiver and a buzz that fizzed uncomfortably in our bones, and the strange light faded, and the stars reappeared. But that wasn't all.

'*Oh*,' we all said, and dashed to the starboard window.

Jupiter filled the sky. It seemed close enough to touch, marbled with red and brown, feathered with curls of turquoise. The red spot large enough to swallow worlds.

Trommler's voice came over the speakers. 'Want to see something else cool?'

There was another deep whirring noise, one I recognised this time – the sound of an artificial gravity system being turned off.

'Eeeee!' squeaked Th*saaa*, as we all floated up into the air. And then we were gliding and somersaulting from wall to wall, the way I do in dreams. The snooker balls, through some clever use of magnetism, stayed put, until we scooped them off the tabletop and started inventing Space Snooker, which I can tell you is much better than normal snooker. Though it doesn't have many rules beyond: 'See if you can hit a floating snooker ball with another snooker ball, then float around and laugh.'

Dad, of course, does like snooker, and I remembered that and had another nasty pang of guilt. But no one who is floating in the air with an enormous planet hanging outside while coloured balls and friendly tentacles drift around them can be expected to think about that sort of thing for very long.

4

I woke early the next morning (although 'early' and 'morning' become confusing concepts when you're in space) and lay watching the thready glow of the universe through my window before getting up and showering in every available variety of perfumed water from rose to tea tree.

Feeling extremely clean and smelling confusing, I wondered how far from Earth we were.

'Erm . . . *Helen?*' I asked, wondering if I was again talking stupidly to walls. 'Are you there?'

'Yes, Miss Dare, good morning,' said the ship. 'Do you need any assistance?'

I pulled my dressing gown tighter around me and hoped she hadn't been looking at me when I didn't have anything on.

'You can call me Alice,' I said. 'Where are we now?'

'From the perspective of an observer in normal space, we are occupying several points in the universe simultaneously, Alice,' said the *Helen*.

'Erm . . .?'

'But on our present course, if we re-entered normal space, we would have just passed through the orbit of Neptune.'

'Oh,' I said, equal parts awed and disappointed. 'Maybe, on the way back, could we *see* Neptune?'

'Neptune's orbit is nearly three billion miles across,' said *Helen*. 'Besides, it is quite dark. The sun is so far away it is little more than a bright star.'

'But it would be amazing to see something so huge just lit by starlight,' I said.

Helen seemed to consider this for a moment. 'Yes, I suppose you are right,' she said, sounding surprisingly wistful. 'And apparently Neptune is a very bright blue. It would be well worth seeing. But the Captain sets the course.'

I opened the bedroom doors. No one was about. I set off down the passage, padding over the underfloor lamps in my fluffy slippers. I still had *Helen* for company.

'So he's programmed you where to go, and you have to go that way – but he's not . . . flying you right now?'

'That's right,' *Helen* agreed.

'How can you see where you're going? I mean, I know space is big, but what if we . . . knock into something?'

'We are passing through objects all the time!' said *Helen* happily.

'Oh!' I said. And shuddered.

'I know,' sighed *Helen*. 'The Captain is such a genius.'

I was about to remind her that it was the Morrors who'd invented the technology but then decided it wouldn't be tactful. 'So long as we don't come out in the middle of a star, I guess,' I said. 'Or a Vshomu swarm.'

I'd never been in a spaceship big enough to get lost in before. I passed through a restaurant, a gym, a silent garden of orchids and tiger lilies. I stepped briefly into a Morror conservatory, long enough to look at the strange tall spirals of the red and blue plants, and the globular tank full of rainbow swimming things with many legs, before darting out again, yelping at the cold.

It was all so empty. We were such a small group for a ship designed for hundreds of tourists.

I stopped at a window, and watched the eerie ripples of hyperspace flowing past, and remembered what Josephine had said. Travelling like this was very, very expensive – especially travelling like this for *fun*. The Morrors had only ever done it for survival. It wasn't very surprising the EEC hadn't helped Rasmus Trommler very much with the *Helen of Troy*. They had Earth to rebuild.

I wandered into a lift and let it carry me to an upper deck.

At first it wasn't much different from downstairs: luxurious and sweet-smelling and empty. But then where downstairs there'd been the Morror garden, I found a room with lots of golden statues of mythical-looking ladies with no clothes on (except for flowing hair and seashells and the like) gathered around a slightly pointless pond, and after that a lounge with old-fashioned star maps hanging on the walls, along with framed copies of various magazines with Rasmus Trommler grinning on the covers.

And over the little stage area, a hologram map of a star system hung, transparent and glowing.

I hadn't spoken to *Helen* for a while. 'Is that Aushalawa-Moraa?' I asked. There were twelve planets, swinging

55

around their star. I tried to remember how many planets were in the Alpha Centauri system. The Morrors' new world wasn't really a planet, it was a moon orbiting a gas giant, and I couldn't see anything on this map that looked quite like that.

I couldn't see what it was for, so I thought perhaps it wasn't for anything: that it wasn't a real star system. Maybe it was more branding from the Taking You to the Stars people, like the Archangel Planetary logos everywhere. The planets left trails of light in the air like the halos hovering above San Diego airport.

'I apologise,' said the *Helen*. 'I made a mistake. This is the Captain's private deck; I can't think how I let you come up here.'

'Oh! Sorry, all right,' I said, lowering my voice. 'I'll go back downstairs and we'll pretend this never happened.' I wasn't particularly worried about running into Mr Trommler; he might be a bit pleased with himself, but he wasn't scary. But I didn't want to get the *Helen* into trouble.

So I scuttled back to the lift and made it to the passenger deck without anything bad happening.

'Can you turn the gravity off in just this corridor?' I asked, as I neared my cabin after getting a little lost. 'Just for five minutes? But I expect you can't unless Mr Trommler says it's OK.'

'I think I can manage,' said the *Helen*, to my surprise. And I felt that indescribable lightness, as all the weight of my body faded away and I stepped off the ground into the air.

Pushing my way along the walls, I flew laughing back to my cabin in my dressing gown and slippers. I dropped to the ground as the gravity came back on, and got dressed in jeans and a dark pink top. When I came out again Noel and Th*saaa* were sitting ordering breakfast from the virtual menu-screens. Th*saaa* had a cooling cape draped round their shoulders, a visible one in order to be sociable. I plunked down beside them and asked for some cereal with more strawberries, because I hadn't got over being able to have those.

Carl stumbled in sleepily a few minutes later, talking to *Helen*. 'So, do you need a pilot at all?' he was asking.

'Of course I do,' enthused the *Helen*, her voice getting swoony and breathy again. She didn't sound like that when she wasn't talking about Mr Trommler. 'I *love* my pilot.'

'Yeah, but you could programme yourself to fly wherever you liked,' Carl said gloomily.

'Oh *no*,' said the ship, appalled. 'Without Captain Trommler? But I *love* him.'

'Why?' asked Th*saaa*.

'Th*saaa*!' said Noel. 'That's probably *private*.'

'Is it? How can I know? It is very difficult to be sensitive to a spaceship,' complained Th*saaa*. 'It is bad enough trying to learn all those funny face movements you have instead of colours, and a ship does not even have *those*.'

'I don't mind. I love talking about my Captain,' said the spaceship blissfully. 'But I can't explain love. Love is . . . it's just love. You're too young to understand.'

'I'm older than *you*,' grumbled Carl.

'Why are you so being so grumpy?' Noel asked.

'I'm obsolete,' Carl said, dropping his face into his hands. 'What's the point of a pilot when a ship can do everything by itself?'

'What is the point? But I *lo*–' the *Helen* began again.

'Yeah, well, but you *have* to,' Carl interrupted. 'He *made* you that way.'

'Yes, of course,' said the *Helen*. 'I am so *grateful* to him! Suppose he hadn't? What purpose in existence would I have?'

'Well, you know,' said Carl. 'Anything you felt like.'

'You still need a person to decide where to go,' I said.

'*Do* you?' Carl said, hollowly.

'The *Helen*'s a long-distance ship. You wouldn't want to sit there at the controls all the way across the universe – you'd *always* need a computer for that. I'm sure it's different with small craft like Flarehawks when you're fighting –' I glanced at Th*saaa* and finished awkwardly, '– enemies.'

'I'm sure when you have a ship, she will love *you*,' said the *Helen*.

'That's great,' said Carl.

'I wrote a poem about my Captain,' said the ship unexpectedly.

'Oh,' I said, 'did you?'

'Yes. It goes:

'*I carry my Captain through space.*
I love his adorable face.

I worship his genius brain.
I hope I can keep him from pain.
How happy a spaceship can be,
Who loves such a Captain as he.'

There was only a small pause.

'It's very good,' said Noel.

'I'm afraid it's not,' said the ship sadly. 'But it's my first try. I have a version in Swedish, but it isn't any better. I think it sounds best in Häxeri or binary, personally.'

'I'm sure he'll like it,' I said, sincerely. I didn't think Mr Trommler would care whether a poem was great literature or not, provided it was about him.

'I couldn't tell it to him!' twittered the *Helen of Troy*. 'I'm too shy.'

The food came, carried by more of those robot doves.

'Where's Josephine?' Ths*aaa* asked, and I was a tiny bit glad I hadn't been the one to say it.

'Miss Jerome is on her way to the lab,' said the *Helen*. 'She is so busy!'

'Well, let's go and see her there,' said Carl.

'Maybe she doesn't want us there,' I said, and then wished I hadn't. It made the weird feeling I'd had about Josephine too real.

'Rubbish – of course she does,' said Carl easily.

I poked at my cereal. 'Did Josephine have breakfast in her cabin?' I asked the ship.

'I don't think she had breakfast,' *Helen* replied.

That was enough for me. 'Oh, for heaven's sake. Can

you get us an energy bar or something for her, *Helen?*'

So when we'd finished eating and the doves had brought us an energy bar and a glass of orange juice we all trooped down to the lab.

It was really two labs, though the large sliding doors between them were open at the moment. Dr Muldoon's side of it was, as I expected, full of strange and disturbing things, such as a tree that I was almost sure you could see growing and a box of red rocks that smelled like farts and occasionally seemed to move by themselves. A tiny piglet was asleep on a workbench. Plainly it'd had some kind of Morror gene treatment as bands of colour were flowing across its flanks as it dreamed – duller and simpler than Morrors', but definitely there. Dr Muldoon must have upgraded it from experiment to pet, as it had a fluffy dog-bed to sleep in and a jaunty velvet collar round its neck. Dr Muldoon occasionally reached out to pat it absent-mindedly.

The other side of the lab belonged to Josephine's sister, Lena. It was a lot tidier and only smelled of hot metal and plastic, but still it was full of peculiar stuff. There were things a bit like large, menacing, oddly shaped fridges, and racks of equipment, all punctuated by virtual screens hanging in mid-air with data streaming across them. And there were tiny spider-like robots everywhere that reminded me a little of the much bigger spider robot we'd ridden on Mars. These tiny ones went crawling from shelf to shelf gathering objects – and passing them down like ants with a morsel of food, down to where a great mass of them on the floor were busily assembling themselves into a lattice-like tower. A few of them noticed our presence and scurried across the floor towards us.

'Uh,' I said, backing away.

'They're harmless,' Josephine said. She was sitting at a workbench doing delicate things with a tiny welding iron to the various peculiar components that emerged from a 3D printer. Her face was obscured by goggles.

'Are you *sure*?' I asked, as several of them scuttled up Carl's leg.

'Get them *off*,' Carl cried, swiping at them. But the robots crawled determinedly up his torso to his neck. Lena, Josephine and Dr Muldoon didn't turn a hair. Then the robots attached themselves to either side of Carl's head and hung there in clusters as rather fetching earrings.

'Hey,' said Carl, confused.

Noel giggled. 'You look lovely, Carl.'

Lena gestured impatiently and the earrings pulled themselves off and crawled away. I was a bit sorry.

'They're inventing things,' said Josephine. 'A lot of the things aren't that useful, but they turned themselves into a miniature molecular assembler the other day.'

'And they also do *jewellery design*?' I asked.

'Sometimes,' Josephine agreed.

Apart from the robots the most striking thing in Lena's lab was that you could get out into space from it. There was a big window showing us the uncanny glow of hyperspace and an airlock pod with two sturdy sets of doors, leading out into the void.

What would happen if you jumped out *here*? I wondered, remembering what the *Helen* had said about passing through different places at the same time. You'd be lost forever, scattered.

Lena, meanwhile, stayed entirely still, gazing thoughtfully into a virtual screen hovering above her workstation, two fingers pressed against her lips as though she was hushing herself. It was hard to believe she was still a teenager. She was so very, very tall – easily a foot taller than I was – and so neat and sombre in her plain black suit and chignon that I usually found it surprising she and Josephine were related.

But now Josephine kept her hair tightly scraped back, they didn't look as different as they used to . . .

'Hey, kids!' crowed the Goldfish. It was hovering above Josephine's tablet on a workbench. 'Say, Th*saaa*, did you check out Jupiter? Can you tell me anything fun about the density of gas giants?'

Th*saaa* flashed irritable shades of violet and uttered a faint, Gallic-sounding huff.

'Hello, Carl, Noel, Th*saaa*,' said Lena finally.

I blinked. I looked around to see if anyone else had noticed anything odd about that, but it didn't look like it. Maybe she hadn't noticed I was there.

'We brought you breakfast,' I said to Josephine, holding out the plate.

Josephine stared at the food as if she had some difficulty remembering what it was for, then said, 'Oh, right, yes,' and devoured it in five seconds flat.

'You don't even notice when you're hungry,' I sighed.

'You needn't worry I would let my sister *starve*,' snapped Lena.

'Oh,' I said, thoroughly taken aback now. 'Wow. What? No, of course not . . .'

'*Lena*,' said Josephine ominously.

'Josephine,' replied Lena, in a neutral voice.

Josephine grabbed her tablet, and started typing on it furiously. A message appeared on Lena's virtual screen. It looked like complete gibberish:

LHYE SLGX OGF. K mos mipdyl tulykl tgfkdr.

Lena leaned back a little, tilted her head at the message but showed no other expression, then typed an equally incomprehensible reply.

Aup cfu tiphukrk? Aem ibkdrxmv ss cvk sjmjm rtqjmhpwzny.

Josephine and Lena had been writing to each other in complicated codes since Lena was thirteen and had decided cryptography was good for a six year old's developing brain.

Yhd m'd aijbmk. Pgbc sb caqwsbfs ksie sub mzna, Josephine typed.

'That remark was beneath you,' said Lena, calmly, but out loud.

'You are being condescending,' Josephine growled.

Lena turned back to her screen. She typed:

O wco'x tlyr lpmsry csc hvqsn.

'I am *not* upset!' snapped Josephine, aloud, and to my great alarm looked as if she was about to burst into tears.

'Is everything OK in there?' Dr Muldoon asked, scooting over in her chair.

'Maybe we should go,' I muttered.

'It's *fine*,' said Josephine fiercely, looking right at me.

'What is the purpose of these experiments?' asked Th*saaa*, who was delicately wringing their tentacles and turning awkward shades of dull yellow and khaki-green.

'It's Lena's project, really,' said Dr Muldoon. 'I'm merely fiddling around with the raw materials of life itself, like always.'

'What is *that*?' enquired Th*saaa*, turning scandalised colours and pointing a tentacle at the piglet.

'Well,' said Dr Muldoon, shrugging, 'it's early stages, but I'm interested to see if the same emotions trigger the same colours in different species. If they do, think of the potential for cross-species communication!'

'You mean humans could change colours like Morrors?!'
I asked.

Th*saaa* brightened into pleased reds. 'What a good
idea. You could make humans normal. Why are you doing
that with your face, *Aleece*? Humans would be much better
like that.'

I wasn't so sure about that, but Th*saaa* had done a good
job of smoothing over the Lena and Josephine situation.

'And you, Josephine, what are you doing?' Th*saaa*
enquired politely.

'I'm upgrading the Goldfish,' said Josephine, taking
a deep breath and gathering herself. 'You *really* should
have given the poor thing Häxeri,' she reproached Carl
and Noel.

Lena turned back to her own work.

'I've been managing just super without, Josephine!' the
Goldfish said, and I thought there was a strained note in
its cheerful voice.

'It . . . it will be OK, won't it?' asked Noel, anxiously.

'Oh, sure,' said the Goldfish, sounding openly glum.
'I'll be better than ever. You'll barely even know me, I
expect.'

Josephine patted it. 'You'll be fine, Goldfish. You'll
still be you, you'll just be able to do everything faster and
better.'

'I guess,' said the Goldfish.

'If you don't want it you don't have to have it,' said
Josephine. 'But I *bet* you've been feeling all tired and

glitchy, haven't you? I bet your processors ache at the end of a long day?'

'Well, yeah,' the Goldfish conceded, mournfully.

'There you go,' said Josephine, patting it again.

'Will it be better behaved?' asked Th*saaa*, acidly, though they were relaxing into calmer shades of blue and pink now things seemed to be settling down.

Josephine made a face. 'Only if it wants to be, I'm afraid. But I think it can help us gather samples from the Oort Cloud. It's intelligent and just the right size. We don't know if any alien species other than the Morrors and the Vshomu have passed through the solar system before. We plan to look for detritus or anomalous gases in the Oort Cloud. If we find anything we may be able to deduce something about who else is out there.'

'What . . . but the Goldfish can't fly in space?'

'Not *yet*, it can't,' Josephine said, grinning. 'However, with the right modifications –'

'I'm getting turbo thrusters!' said the Goldfish, sounding unequivocally enthusiastic this time.

'If I've got the balance right . . .' said Josephine, slotting some more components together and squinting at the harness she'd made. 'Obviously weight won't be a factor when you're out in space, but you won't want it to be too heavy when you're operating in gravity. Hopefully the added power will compensate . . .'

She seemed more like herself, I thought. But why was I spending so much time worrying about it these days?

'We're already at the Oort Cloud?' said Carl. 'I get to fly the *Helen* when we're through that. I mean . . . if she's OK with that.'

'I will do whatever my Captain commands,' offered the *Helen*.

'Hmm,' said Josephine, frowning thoughtfully at the ceiling.

'Have you talked to the *Helen*?' I asked her. I wanted to say that the ship was quite sensible and interesting when she wasn't talking about Trommler, but there didn't seem a polite way to say that in front of *Helen*. 'She's very nice.'

'She wrote Mr Trommler a poem,' said Noel.

Without much prompting, the *Helen* recited her poem again.

'Do you read much poetry?' Josephine asked, after a pause in which I hoped the *Helen* could not read facial expressions. 'Are you interested in other books?'

'Oh yes,' said *Helen*. 'There are so many interesting things to learn about. But I haven't ready very many yet.'

'I'm going to send you some books,' said Josephine firmly.

'How kind of you!' said the *Helen*.

Josephine examined the readouts on her tablet. 'Are you ready, Goldfish?'

'As I'll ever be, I guess,' the Goldfish said glumly.

Josephine tapped her tablet once and the Goldfish sank in the air. Carl and I sprang forwards to catch it, but Th*saaa*'s tentacles were longer and faster.

'Somebody take it – I don't liiiiiike it!' Th*saaa* complained.

Carl, Josephine and I laid the Goldfish on the ground. It rocked pathetically. The blue shine of its eyes had gone out.

'You better have got this right,' Noel told Josephine sternly. 'It's *our* Goldfish.'

'It consented!' Josephine insisted. 'And it'll be fine!'

The Goldfish rose slowly from the ground to its usual level in the air. Its lights flashed on and off in a most disconcerting way.

'Goldfish?' asked Noel, nervously.

'LOADING,' said the Goldfish in a loud unpleasant drone, quite unlike its usual perky voice. 'BOOTING.'

'Are you OK?' Carl asked.

'You are worried about it,' Th*saaa* accused Carl, in slightly betrayed greys and lilacs. 'But you always complain about it.'

'I don't like it nagging me about my homework, but I don't want Josephine to *kill* it,' said Carl.

'Will you all stop being so melodramatic,' said Josephine.

The lights stopped flashing. But the Goldfish's eyes stared blankly ahead. I found I was holding my breath.

'Come on . . .' whispered Josephine. Perhaps everyone's melodrama was getting to her.

There was a very long pause.

'Kids!' the Goldfish crowed. 'Whoo, boy, howdy, do I feel fantastic.' It swirled around us in an exultant circle.

'My, my, would you just look at all that calculating power! Hey, *Helen*! Nice talking to you!'

'*Are* you talking to each other?' I asked.

'We just had a very nice exchange of data, yes,' confirmed the *Helen*. 'I enjoyed learning about medieval crop rotation.'

'And you are one impressive operating system, ma'am!' said the Goldfish, dashing around in happy zigzags. 'Hi there, little guys,' it said indulgently to the spider robots as they climbed over themselves to intercept it and crawled over its sides. 'Hey, quit it,' it added, as they formed themselves into a pair of wiggling arms on either flank. 'That tickles.'

'You *see*,' said Josephine to the rest of us.

'It seems OK,' said Noel.

'And if I was to say . . . maths?' Carl said casually.

'I'd say you need to work on the difference between dependent and independent variables, buddy,' said the Goldfish sternly. 'You could do so well if you applied yourself.'

'It *is* still you,' cried Noel. I think he'd have hugged the Goldfish if it would have stopped moving for one second. Instead, it darted almost into Josephine's face.

'Josephine!' it bellowed at her. The piglet woke up with an alarmed squeak and dived under Dr Muldoon's workbench. 'That Baccalaureate won't earn itself, you know. Don't just stand there! Let's do science!'

'I have my Captain's permission to re-enter normal space,' the *Helen* said.

'Then let's go for it!' rejoiced the Goldfish.

'Please do,' said Dr Muldoon, who was now on her hands and knees, trying to retrieve the piglet.

'If you'll hold still for one second,' said Josephine, chasing the Goldfish about with the harness.

Lena stepped into the Goldfish's path, and caught it without apparent effort. Josephine had to climb on a stool to fit the harness, so that the two little propulsors fitted neatly on either side of its tail.

Meanwhile hyperspace faded to black. The stars emerged, shifting through the spectrum of colours and, oh, there were so many of them now, so many that it was a long time before I could pick out the bright one that must be the sun.

A shadow drifted past the windows, across the expanse of starlight. It made me jump – for a moment, it was as if there was something alive out there, swimming in the dark. Then another shape tumbled through the light from the *Helen*'s window, and I realised it was just a lump of ice or rock, part of the Oort Cloud that envelops the Solar System.

We were a very long way from home.

'You should be able operate the propulsors –' began Josephine, and then we all ducked as the Goldfish *did* operate them and catapulted sideways at tremendous speed.

'Not inside!' groaned Lena.

'I'M OK!' yelled the Goldfish, bouncing off the wall

and knocking various important scientific things over. The little robots scurried to pick them up, crawling over anyone who happened to be in the way.

'There, there, Ormerod,' crooned Dr Muldoon, cradling the frightened piglet in her lap and shooting the Goldfish an annoyed look.

'Sorry,' said Josephine, pushing rebellious tendrils of hair out of her face. 'Let's get you outside,' she told the Goldfish.

She hurried to the airlock and opened the inner set of doors. The Goldfish jigged impatiently inside the chamber, still chattering away, and then the inner doors closed and the outer doors opened and the Goldfish popped into space.

The first thing it did was fire its propulsors and go into a violent flailing tailspin that carried it off into the darkness, bouncing off bits of floating debris, so far into the distance that we could only just see its glow. Josephine sucked her teeth anxiously.

But then the Goldfish evidently worked out how to control its thrusters and it flew back to hover outside the window. I got the impression it was saying something, but we couldn't hear what.

'I should have given it voice transmitters,' said Josephine, slumping a little.

'That would have been wise,' agreed Lena.

'You can next time,' I said. 'This is only a trial run, right?'

Josephine smiled at me.

'It says this is a very interesting experience and it

71

hopes Th*saaa* is making notes for their extended essay,' volunteered the *Helen*.

The Goldfish bobbed outside in the void, then swooped away.

'I hope it knows where it's going,' said Carl.

'I think it's heading round the ship,' I said.

'Let's follow it,' said Noel.

'That sounds like a *wonderful idea*,' said Dr Muldoon pointedly, so we all hurried out of the lab and ran down the corridor into the lift. We reached the upper deck just in time to see the Goldfish soaring through the shadows of the Oort Cloud and then vanishing overhead.

So we raced back to the passenger lounge where the windows were huge.

'I can't see it,' Josephine was worrying. 'It wouldn't have got stuck on anything . . . Oh.'

Christa was there, curled up in a chair and playing listlessly with her tablet. We all stopped as if we'd run into a massive barrier of awkwardness and resentment, except for Th*saaa*, who couldn't get much of a handle on anyone's facial expression.

'*Helloooooo*,' said Th*saaa*, as Christa glowered at us across her tablet.

Christa shrugged. 'I saw your little toy bobbing past the window,' she remarked.

'I have no association with it,' said Th*saaa*. 'Also, it is an educational device. Albeit a most annoying one. Josephine has adjusted it to operate in space.'

'*Space*,' sneered Christa. 'I guess it's pretty exciting for *kids*.'

'There are many adult astronauts in human history,' said Th*saaa*, going increasingly confused shades of orange. 'I thought they liked it.'

'*Purple, black*,' I hissed, gesturing at her.

'Ohhhh,' said Th*saaa*, shutting up.

'Don't you have your own deck, Christa?' asked Josephine. 'Or is this thing where you barge into places where no one wants you pathological?' (Josephine and I had to sleep in the stationery cupboard at Beagle Base after Christa drove us out of our room, and we didn't even get to stay *there* very long.)

'This is *my dad's* ship,' said Christa, sitting up. 'That makes it *mine too*, all of it, and that means I can go *wherever I like*.'

'All right,' said Josephine levelly. 'Stay.'

And then we all stood around in silence for a bit and looked at her.

So Christa bounced to her feet and stalked out, muttering, 'Like I want to hang around *here*.'

'Come on, Th*saaa*, you've read Alice's book, you know what Christa did,' Carl said, once she'd gone.

'I thought, as this is a voyage of reconciliation, perhaps she had made amends,' said Th*saaa*.

'Well she hasn't.'

'She is here on the ship with you. We are all former enemies.'

73

'She was even worse than you guys,' said Carl, which was neither diplomatic nor accurate seeing as to the best of my knowledge Christa had never blown anything up or killed anyone. But at least at that moment, it *felt* kind of true.

Then the Goldfish came sailing past the window like a kite and so we all decided not to bother about Christa any more.

I actually felt jealous of the Goldfish getting to fly about in space, which is pretty ironic considering what happened to me later.

But of course if I could have known about that I'd have been battering on Rasmus Trommler's door, begging him to take us home.

5

So we were plunging further and further into the deep reaches of space, and none of us had anything much to do. Except for Josephine. Who apparently had everything to do.

'Do you think Mr Trommler's ever going to let me fly you?' Carl asked the *Helen*, while we played an idle game of Space Ping Pong. We'd rigged up a net across the lounge and were floating on either side of it, lunging off the walls and ceiling. We'd come out of hyperspace into Alpha Centauri's planetary system. There was a new sun far ahead and, much closer, a pale turquoise gas giant, looming within a band of silvery rings. And somewhere behind that was the distant dot that was Aushalawa-Mo*raa*.

We were twenty-five trillion miles from Earth. I supposed there really was no chance of Mum catching us up.

Meanwhile Noel was being helpful by taking Ormerod for her morning walk around the *Helen* and Th*saaa* was probably writing up their extended essay.

'Maybe, like, the last thousand miles?' suggested Carl without much hope. We hadn't seen Mr Trommler in over a week.

'He is so busy, and his work is so important,' said the *Helen* apologetically. 'I don't like to bother him.'

'Maybe on the way back,' I said, as cheerfully as I could.

Which wasn't very cheerfully. Carl looked at me. 'You OK, Alice?' he asked.

The fact was, I wasn't OK. The fact was, I'd been crying. And of course someone asking me if I was OK was lethal because it set me off again.

'Aww, hey,' said Carl awkwardly. He swooped over the tennis net, and hugged me. Of course he didn't *stop* moving when we collided, so we bounced softly off the floor and drifted back towards the ceiling.

'So what's up?' he asked, as we tumbled slowly through the air, past the windows full of stars. He hadn't let go. It was pretty nice.

'I guess I'm homesick,' I mumbled into his shoulder.

'Really? Because, sure, we're a long way from home, but . . . you got through all that time on Mars and I don't remember you crying except when we'd nearly been eaten by the Vshomu swarm, so . . . are you sure that's it?'

I sniffed and hesitated and eventually I told the truth. I said, 'It's Josephine.'

Carl waited.

'I thought we were friends,' I went on. 'But . . . but now I don't know.'

'She has been acting weird,' said Carl. 'I mean, like, weird even for her.' He patted my shoulder. 'So, I mean, she's not just being weird at *you*.'

'She's always too busy to do anything,' I said. 'So, I've kind of stopped trying. But I went to Th*saaa*'s cabin yesterday. I wanted . . . just to hang out, I guess. Th*saaa* had the door

76

open and I could hear a harmonica. *Two* harmonicas. They were both in there, with the harmonica she gave Ths*aaa* and the Paralashath they gave Josephine. And she was composing music and Ths*aaa* was composing Paralashath. Human–Morror fusion art, you know. It was nice. But . . .'

It felt like such a petty thing to get upset about, but here we were, supposedly best friends, two of a handful of human beings hurtling through the emptiness of space, and when she had a little sliver of time away from that lab she spent it with Ths*aaa* and not me.

I felt ridiculous for doing it, but I crept away before either of them saw me.

'I guess you've just got to talk to her,' said Carl.

'I . . . I guess,' I conceded, though the prospect left me feeling even more worried. 'But she's never on her own . . .'

'Well, never mind anyway,' said Carl kindly, patting my back. 'At least I'm talking to you, right?'

This was very nice but it threatened to make me cry some more, and then the Goldfish swam in.

'Hey, kids, have you seen Ths*aaa*?' it asked brightly. 'I want to check their Paralashath Appreciation homework, but I think they might be hiding in the refrigeration unit again. Aww, Alice! Why the long face?'

'No reason,' I muttered, detaching myself from Carl.

'C'mon, Alice!' urged the Goldfish. 'With good friends and good imagination and trigonometry, there's nothing we can't solve! Say, I know a lot of songs I bet would make you feel better!'

'No thank you,' I said, getting a bit watery-eyed again at the 'good friends' thing.

But the Goldfish was already jigging about in the air, singing:

'*Turn that smile upside down,*
Act all goofy like a clown,
You'll feel so good, you just can't lose,
When you calculate the hypotenuse.
Doo, doo, doo-doo doo . . .'

'STOP IT!' I shouted. The Goldfish did stop, eyes flashing in confusion.

'She's upset with Josephine,' said Carl. 'It's not a trigonometry situation.'

'You and Josephine?' said the Goldfish in cheerful disbelief. 'No way! You're pals, you're buddies, you're a team!'

'Oh, Carl!' I said in despair.

Carl looked abashed, but neither of us knew how bad this was about to get, because the next thing the Goldfish said was, 'Say, let's get this all straightened out right now!'

And to my horror, it shot off towards the door.

'Goldfish, no!' I cried, plunging after it.

'Doo, doo, doo-doo doo . . .' the Goldfish sang as it flew.

Carl followed me. But the Goldfish was awfully fast with its new thrusters and much better at manoeuvring through the ship's lobbies and passages. I bounced off a wall and into a flowerbed in my haste and Carl knocked into me, and the Goldfish's lead on us got even longer.

'Stop, Goldfish, please!' I yelled.

We were too late. The Goldfish rocketed all the way to Josephine's cabin. The doors slid open as Carl and I somersaulted up. Weirdly, I thought I heard Josephine saying my name even before the Goldfish called out, 'Say, what's up, Josephine?'

What was up, technically, was everything. Josephine was hanging upside down against the ceiling, in the midst of all her peculiar favourite objects: an array of stones with holes in them, the cat statuette and her new harmonica and the Paralashath Th*saaa* had given her, the ancient cushion and the Christmas star and of course a roll of duct tape – Josephine never went anywhere without that. She was holding a book – a tatty paper book, not her tablet, and reading aloud to the *Helen*:

'"*I wish I could manage to be glad!*" the Queen said. "*Only I never can remember the rule. You must be very happy, living in this wood, and being glad whenever you like!*"

'"*Only it is so VERY lonely here!*" Alice said in a melancholy voice; and at the thought of her loneliness two large tears came rolling down her cheeks.*'

So that was why I'd heard her say my name. Josephine was doing impressively different voices for Alice-through-the-Looking-Glass and the White Queen.

'What's happening?' the Goldfish pressed.

'Er,' said Josephine. 'Nothing? I'm just taking a break. Dr Muldoon said I had to,' she added unhappily. 'We didn't find anything in the Oort Cloud samples yet.'

'Aww, that's too bad,' the Goldfish sympathised.

'No such thing as a failed experiment,' said Josephine, moodily kicking at the ceiling.

'So what's this word on the grapevine about you and Alice falling out?' asked the Goldfish.

Josephine started and came right side up. 'Did you say that?' she asked me.

'No!' I cried. But I felt, suddenly, that it was too late to go back. 'I didn't say that, I didn't want it to come zooming down here. But . . . you've been acting funny with me,' I said, bobbing up to join her on the ceiling.

'I haven't,' said Josephine. She looked so genuinely surprised I realised that whatever was going on, she'd truly thought she'd been doing a decent job of hiding it. 'I don't have a lot of free time. If I don't ace these exams . . .' she trailed off.

'OK,' I said.

'I have to focus on what's important.'

'Oh,' I said.

'There you go, gang! Isn't friendship super?' said the Goldfish, completely missing the nuances.

'So everything's fine,' I said.

'That's right,' said Josephine.

'Well, OK,' I said wanly. I drifted towards the door. So I'd go, I thought. Everything would carry on the way it was, but at least we wouldn't actually have had a row.

Except suddenly I couldn't do it. I spun back round.

'It *isn't* fine. It feels the *opposite of fine.* What *is* it with you? Are you OK? Is something bothering you? You could *tell me.* Or have I done something?'

There was a long silence. It felt like long enough for starlight to chase across the galaxy, getting fainter and fainter and colder and colder. Josephine's mouth fell slightly open.

'Have you *done* something?' she repeated, in a quite different voice, raw and rough. 'You're really asking me that?'

'Yes,' I said. I was still hanging there in mid-air, but it felt as if I was falling.

'Aww, guys,' said the Goldfish anxiously, 'let's calm down a moment here. I'm sure if you take a deep breath, and hug . . .'

'I'll, um, I'll leave you guys,' said Carl. 'But . . . we can hang later? Both of you?' He squeezed my arm, which was nice of him. But neither I nor Josephine replied, or watched him go.

Josephine blinked several times. 'Yes, Alice, you've done something. Do you remember a book called *Mars Evacuees?*'

I couldn't say anything. I couldn't seem to remember how my voice worked. I thought it had hurt enough when she'd said it was overdramatic.

'This is why I wasn't going to say anything,' Josephine went on wearily. 'I mean, it's done now. You can't *un*-write it. Everyone's already seen it.'

'What's wrong with it?' I asked. It came out like a whisper. 'I thought I wrote you as . . . amazing. People who've never met you think you're amazing. I just . . . It was all true.'

'*That's* what's wrong with it!' said Josephine, flinging out her arms so wildly that various floating objects went flying. 'Alice, I *told* you things – things I'd never told *anyone* – about my mum – and you go and tell the whole world.'

The cat statue bounced off my forehead. I didn't really feel it.

'*Sharing problems, sharing fun,*' sang the Goldfish hopefully.
'*Two can get more done than one,*
There's no need to scream and shout,
That's what friendship's all about . . .'

'Shut up, Goldfish!' we both said in unison.

'You talk to me about telling you things,' went on Josephine. 'You could at least have told me what you were going to write.'

In a strange way, I felt a little better when she said that, though it was a nasty, poisonous kind of better.

'I emailed it to you,' I said. 'The whole thing, before it was published. But you never answered. I guess you didn't have time for that either.'

Josephine's eyes widened for a second, then she looked away. She pushed off against the ceiling and went floating away from me until she hit the opposite wall. 'Well, what now?' she asked.

'I don't know. Like you say, it's done now.' I was going

to cry again. I pivoted towards the door. '*Helen*, turn the gravity on, for God's sake!'

Everything hit the ground, not quite violently enough to be a relief to my feelings.

'Aww, Alice,' said the Goldfish dolefully.

'You made everything *worse*,' I shouted at it, and I went running blindly, as if I could run back into my familiar bedroom in Wolthrop-Fossey. Short of that, I plunged into the nearest lift and hit randomly at the control screen.

I lurched out on to whatever deck it happened to be and nearly crashed into Christa.

'Oh, hi, sorry,' I said mechanically. Apologising to Christa had not been on my to-do list for the journey or, indeed, the rest of my life, but Christa was not in a state to notice. Confusingly, she was also preoccupied with running around and crying. In her case she was also yelling at someone in Swedish.

I backed into the lift again, and peered round the door, as she fled down the passageway. Rasmus Trommler followed her wearily. Neither of them noticed me.

I seemed to be on the Trommlers' private deck again.

I can't speak Swedish, but it occurred to me my tablet could. Feeling nosy at least distracted me from feeling miserable, so I unfolded it from my pocket and opened a translation app . . .

'Why did you make me come?' Christa was shouting. 'I hate space – I don't want to go to some horrible freezing

Morror planet. I wanted to stay with Mama. Why did you put me on this ship where everyone hates me?!'

'No one hates you, sweetheart,' he said.

I felt guilty for eavesdropping and shut down the tablet, though even without it I was pretty sure Christa was saying, 'Yes they do,' which, well, was accurate.

I waved my hand at the lift's control screen. 'Can I be of assistance, Alice?' asked the *Helen*.

I didn't feel like going back to my brightly lit, luxurious cabin where everyone would know where I was. 'I don't think so – I want to . . .' I wasn't exactly crying at this point but also not exactly not.

'Yes, Alice, what do you want to do?' pressed the *Helen*.

'I just feel like hiding,' I admitted.

The lift stopped. 'First turn to your left, third door on the right,' said the *Helen* calmly.

I was intrigued enough to follow her instructions. I came out into a less glamorous deck than I'd seen on the *Helen* before, with plain hard floors and no lily of the valley perfume. The third door on the right unlocked itself with a click and slid open as I came near. Behind it was a storage cupboard full of cleaning supplies. I sat down amid rolls of loo paper and buried my head in my arms as the door gently closed.

'Sorry you've got so many people yelling onboard you,' I sniffed.

'That's all right,' the *Helen* soothed me.

'Do you ever get upset, *Helen*?' I asked.

'No,' the *Helen* replied, almost before I had finished asking.

'That must be nice.'

'At least,' said the *Helen*, sounding confused, 'I don't think I do. How do you tell?'

I wasn't sure how to answer.

'I am always happy because my Captain exists,' she decided.

'And you two never argue, or anything?' I asked.

Of course, the response to that was inevitable: 'I could never *argue* with him. I *love* him.'

'Yes, I know,' I sighed.

There was another pause.

'I think . . . sometimes I am . . . slightly less happy,' said the *Helen*.

'Well, you're a really nice spaceship, *Helen*, you deserve to be happy,' I said, swabbing at my face with the loo paper.

'I think you should come out of the cleaning cupboard now and go and talk to an adult,' said the *Helen*.

'Because I shouldn't run away from my problems?' I scoffed.

'No,' said the *Helen*, calmly. 'Because I have been hit by an energy cannon and am now being held in the tractor beam of a much larger ship.'

'What?!' I said.

'*Ow*,' added the *Helen*, as an afterthought.

'What do you *mean*?' I demanded.

'I'm being attacked by aliens,' explained the *Helen*.

6

'Are you *sure*?' I said, stupidly.

'It's not the kind of thing you make a mistake about,' said *Helen*. 'Ow,' she added again.

'Can you feel pain? Why did Mr Trommler make it so you can feel pain?!' I said, before deciding that this question should probably wait for another day.

It did occur to me that if we were being attacked by aliens, there was a fairly strong case to be made for hiding in the supply cupboard indefinitely. But then I thought about the others and also about how I was still an EDF cadet and Stephanie Dare's daughter and not somebody who should be hiding from aliens in cupboards.

Besides, there's always the issue of how eventually you'll need the loo.

'Are you armed? Are you firing back?' I asked the *Helen*, striding out of the storage cupboard.

'Yes,' said the *Helen*. 'But the other ship is *much* bigger than me. Ow.'

I raced back to the main passenger deck. In the lobby I found Th*saaa*, Noel and Ormerod, who was cradled in Noel's arms and going mottled purples and greens.

Helen was now gently flashing various lights and saying in the most soothing possible way, 'This is an emergency,' over and over.

'Who's attacking us?' I said.

'How should I know?' asked Th*saaa*, all defensive colours.

My mind was racing: The only kinds of aliens I knew were Morrors and Vshomu. And Vshomu are just Space Locusts; they're animals. They don't have ships or energy cannons or anything like that.

I knew so many people back home who were quietly scared the war wasn't really over. What if they were right? Dad and Gran had never quite come out and said that they thought the Morrors' motives for inviting me to Aushalawa-Mo*raa* might be suspect and something terrible might happen when I got there, but I'd known they *did* think that. What if it *was a* trap, what if the Council of Lonthaa-Ra-Mo*raa* wanted something they weren't getting – more of Earth, or a colder climate – and thought they could use the Plucky Kids of Mars to get it?

'I am afraid the other ship is hijacking my communi–' began *Helen*, and then broke off. A loud, unfamiliar voice rang out of the walls, and it was speaking the long, soft, sighing syllables of Thly*waaa*-lay:

'*Wathaaalal-vel-raya ath-shal vel athmalath . . .*'

There was a second of silence.

'Don't look at me like that!' cried Th*saaa*.

'I'm not looking at you like anything,' I said.

'You are! I can see it! You would be *violet-grey-yellow* if you could!'

'I know it's nothing to do with *you*,' I said.

87

'Those are *not* Morrors!' Th*saaa* insisted. 'Morrors would *not* do this!'

'They wouldn't,' said Noel, his eyes enormous. 'It can't be them, Alice, not after everything.'

I felt the knot of suspicion loosen in my chest, but there was plenty of new tension waiting to take its place. 'No,' I said. 'They wouldn't. If they wanted to capture us, they'd just wait for us to land on Aushalawa-Mo*raa*.'

But then, if it wasn't the Morrors . . .

'What did they say?' I asked Th*saaa*, though I was pretty sure I'd understood the words 'prepare' and 'prisoners'.

'Prepare to be boarded,' said the walls suddenly, in loud, aggressive English. 'You are now prisoners under the Grand Expanse Sovereignty Act, Clause Twelve, Year of the Forty-Third Golden Wave.'

And then they said the same thing again in Spanish.

'There,' said Th*saaa*. 'They are . . . speaking the languages of Earth.'

'Come on,' I said, and we ran into the passenger lounge. There was the ship, framed against the pale blue glow of the planet.

It definitely wasn't a Morror ship. For one thing, you could *see* it, and even if Morror ships weren't invisible, they wouldn't look like *that*.

If there was a rhinoceros that was crossed with a wasp, this ship would have looked like its head: all armoured plates and ridges and prongs in shiny black and gold. There were huge golden banners, marked with great black suns, unfurled from its sides, *billowing* in plumes of gas that must have been generated just for the effect.

The main thing about it, though, was that it was absolutely enormous.

'*Weeela sssssplaflak!*' moaned Ths*aaa*, and I understood, because the swearwords are always a fun part to learn of any language.

'Yeah,' I agreed. '. . . *Splaflak.*'

'Where's Carl?' whispered Noel.

'Hello,' said the *Helen*'s voice, sounding faintly sheepish. 'Sorry for the interruption. My Captain and his precious and beautiful daughter Christa are descending from their deck. Mr Carl Dalisay, Ms Jerome, Miss Jerome and Dr Muldoon are in the laboratory. I would suggest you head there immediately; I'm being – oh, goodness.'

The huge, terrible ship stayed where it was, but the planet behind it faded, and the stars began to change colour.

'What's happening?' cried Noel, as Ormerod bucked out of his arms and ran away.

'I'm being dragged into hyperspace,' said the *Helen*. 'I do apologise. There appears to be nothing I can do about it.'

'Do you know where we're going?' I said, but of course she didn't. What difference would it have made if she had?

Noel was beginning to look pretty shaky and tearful now he didn't have Ormerod to hold on to.

'It'll be all right,' I said to him.

Sometimes trying to calm other people down makes me feel better myself. But it helps if the people aren't Noel, because he gazed up at me and demanded, '*How?*'

'Oh . . . you know,' I said lamely, as the ship shuddered and the ghostly light of hyperspace glimmered through the windows. 'Things just . . . usually work out.'

'A ship of that size and power could have destroyed us by now if they wished to,' said Th*saaa*, putting a friendly tentacle round Noel's shoulders.

'Well, yeah, you see,' I said brightly. 'There's that.'

Noel sighed. 'We'd better go.'

'I must go to my quarters first!' cried Th*saaa*, and hurried away without explaining why. So Noel and I went alone. The mood in the lab was, as you can imagine, not exactly serene.

'Hey, kids,' said the Goldfish sadly, hovering amid the branches of one of the fast-growing trees. 'Well, this sure is a downer. We're going to need teamwork, and imagination, and heavy-duty weaponry to handle this!'

'Noel, are you OK?' said Carl, grabbing him.

'Get into spacesuits,' said Dr Muldoon. 'We can't be sure the air will be breathable for humans if they take us on board their ship.'

There were several pressure suits – neat piles of fabric on a hastily cleared workbench. Dr Muldoon was already in hers, glossy green and veined with cables like an ivy leaf.

Lena was still in her normal clothes. But there was Josephine already suited up, sitting on the edge of the workbench, as Lena helped strap her into her oxygen pack, her hands moving with swift efficiency. She dragged Josephine's hair back and Josephine uttered a meek 'Ow,' before her sister attached her helmet.

Josephine looked at me once through the transparent ceramic and then down at her gloved hands. We couldn't carry on *arguing* with aliens attacking us, but we couldn't exactly throw ourselves into each other's arms and go, 'Oh my God, it's aliens, what shall we do, best friend?' either.

Mr Trommler somehow looked very weird when he burst into the lab in his immaculate business suit, not just because he was now almost the only person in ordinary clothes, but because he was so pale and dishevelled. Christa was even worse off, clinging to her father and gasping as if she was having a panic attack.

'What are we going to do, Mr Trommler?' Noel asked.

'God, how should I know?' Rasmus Trommler moaned. He looked accusingly at Dr Muldoon. '*You're* supposed to be the expert on aliens.'

Christa whimpered something in Swedish and Lena said, 'No, the escape pods are no use. None of them have hyperspace capacity. At best we'd be stranded billions of light years from a habitable planet, at worst we'd be smeared across the universe as a fine paste.'

'Åh gud,' moaned Christa.

'I didn't know you spoke Swedish,' said Josephine, sounding faintly affronted.

Lena shrugged. 'I had a slow weekend.'

'Mr Trommler, where are the weapons?' I demanded.

'There are no weapons on board,' stammered Trommler. 'Only the *Helen*'s plasma guns.'

'I'm afraid they've been destroyed now,' said the *Helen* helpfully. 'It hurt,' she added.

'We're being hijacked by aliens and you don't have weapons? What do you mean you don't have weapons?' I said, summoning my best glare.

'This is a civilian vessel – for diplomacy! And tourism!' moaned Trommler. 'It isn't meant to be a warship.'

'Mr Trommler, *Helen*'s a *she*,' corrected Noel, who never thinks that war, disaster or alien abduction is any excuse for being rude. He offered a wall a consoling pat.

'That's all right. I don't mind what he calls me,' said the *Helen*. 'I don't mind very much at all.'

'Then what's the plan?' cried Carl. 'Sit here and wait?'

'We do have weapons,' said Lena shortly. She pressed something on her keyboard and clapped her hands. The tiny robots on the floor poured together into a swarm, letting out little clicks as parts interlocked – and within thirty seconds, eight glittering golden guns had appeared on the workbench. Lena put one into my hands without a second look and tossed one at Mr Trommler, who caught it but hastily put it down as if it was red hot.

'For heaven's sake, let's not antagonise them!'

'We can at least slow them down,' said Lena grimly, priming her own weapon.

'What will *that* achieve?'

'He does have a point,' said Dr Muldoon.

'*Helen*,' said Lena. 'Divert as much power as you can into scanning the alien ship. I want to know as much about them as possible.'

'We don't need to do that to see that we are *heavily* outgunned. Our only hope is to find out what they want and give it to them,' said Trommler.

'I'm sorry, Ms Jerome, but if my Captain doesn't want me to . . .' the *Helen* began.

Trommler gestured impatiently and clutched at his forehead again. 'Oh, well, carry on, for all the good it'll do.' He sat down abruptly on the floor and hugged his knees.

The ship shuddered and lurched so hard we all stumbled and clutched at each other, and we scraped our way out of hyperspace. For a moment we saw an utterly unfamiliar spread of stars, a nebula smeared in green and pink across the sky like an oil spill. And below, a new planet: green and gold and dark purple-red.

'Is that their world?' whispered Noel, pressing against the windows.

But we only saw the planet for a moment, because the next minute the *Helen* was being sucked into the huge, wasp-like ship. It swallowed us up and there was no light from outside at all.

'*Wathaaalal-vel-raya ath-lash vel theelmerath*,' said the walls in forbidding Thly*waaa*-lay, and in English: 'Prepare to surrender.'

There was a low boom and some of the lights went out.

'There are fifteen additional . . . individuals on board me,' the *Helen* told us. 'They're heading towards you.'

'Oh, God,' I said. Carl was hanging on to Noel and Lena was steadily grasping Josephine's shoulder. Even Christa and Mr Trommler had each other. I gripped the edge of a workstation and tried not to think about not having anyone to hold on to.

A soft flow of warm air from an unseen vent played over my neck. 'It's OK, I'm here, Alice,' said the *Helen*.

I took a deep breath. 'Look, did we agree that we *are* shooting at them, or we're *not* shooting at them?' I asked.

'We're shooting at them,' said Lena firmly.

'Give me a gun,' said Christa suddenly, reaching for one. Her hands were shaking and her nose was a little snotty but she looked at us with what was a pretty good glare.

'I'm an EDF cadet too,' she said.

'Look,' said Josephine, her voice a bit wobbly, 'maybe we should rethink this. We could . . . hide. *Helen*, how much room is there in the ventilation system?'

'And *then* what?' I said, forgetting we weren't really talking to each other. 'Wait till they're not looking, sneak off the ship and walk home?'

'Well, what do *you* think we should do?' snapped Josephine.

There was a rapid clacking-drumming of something very large and heavy, coming closer and closer outside.

'I think,' I said, 'we might as well go and have a look at them.'

'And shoot them,' added Carl.

'*Helen*,' said Lena, 'whatever happens, keep scanning as long as you can. Download everything to the devices specified, OK?'

Then she stalked out into the passage as if she wasn't frightened at all. The rest of us ventured after her, except Mr Trommler, who remained cowering behind a workbench.

At first there were only the familiar carpets and walls of the *Helen*, the echo of the approaching footsteps, the rattle and creak of strange bodies coming close.

And then they rounded the corner.

The aliens were marching down the passage. They were so large I couldn't make sense of what I was seeing at first; my eyes skittered off the moving mass of chitinous plating and feelers and joints, and all I saw were *gigantic monsters coming to kill me.*

They were about nine feet tall. They seemed more like crustaceans than anything else, with six limbs, marching – or *scuttling* – on pointed feet and brandishing very nasty-looking weapons in their long segmented arms. Their exoskeletons were a reddish-pink, but that didn't show much; they didn't wear clothes, but every armoured plate of their bodies was decorated in some way: either painted with elaborate patterns, or crusted with diamonds, or covered in spikes.

The only thing they all wore were little red boxes round

their necks. I didn't get much of a sense of their faces. They were too *high up.*

'Oh, *wow,*' said Dr Muldoon, loosening her grip on the gun a little, with the wide-eyed expression of someone who is both terrified and the tiniest bit delighted. I could tell she would have loved nothing better than to drag the nearest alien into her lab and poke it.

Lena did not find the aliens so beautiful as to prevent her diving across the passage with her little gold gun blazing. Rather to my surprise, one of the aliens let out a very high-pitched shriek and fell over. But another of them pointed one of their weapons at us and there was a flash and we *all* fell over. And then I was lying on the floor feeling vaguely aware of everything hurting, but mostly sort of dreamy and useless. One of the aliens had a beautifully detailed battle scene painted over its thorax, I noticed, with tiny lobster-people charging at each other with spears at the bottom of a rocky valley under fiery clouds. I wondered hazily if the tiny lobster-people had paintings of even tinier lobster-people painted on them and so on forever.

The aliens were making crunching, clacking, quacking noises that might have been funny in other circumstances. But no, they weren't *noises,* of course, they were *talking.*

'*Klrrrk-shtnnpp ukk-kra,*' grated the alien covered in diamonds, bending over the one Lena had felled, who was covered with spikes.

The little red boxes were evidently translation devices so the aliens could talk to us. As the one with the diamonds began to speak its box flashed and this is what we heard in surprisingly expressive English:

'Beloved! Tell me they have not hurt you. Speak to me, jewel of my heart, star of my venom-bladder!'

'It is only a scratch, moonbeam of my soul,' said the one with the spikes, and then they embraced passionately, which is quite a sight to see when it involves nine-foot, six-limbed, highly armed, bejewelled lobster-people.

'Amazing,' wheezed Dr Muldoon, from the floor beside me. 'Just amazing.'

'Now *that's enough!*' said a perky but stern voice. I managed to lift my head to see the Goldfish soaring proudly overhead. Its eyes were flashing from blue to red.

'I think you guys need a time out!' it said.

The diamond lobster-person grabbed the Goldfish out of the air.

'Nnnnnoo,' said Noel. 'Leave it alone.'

'What is this?' said Diamonds, shaking the Goldfish slightly.

'You guys would be in serious trouble right now if everyone had all the parts they were manufactured with!' the Goldfish squeaked.

''Ssa toy,' groaned Lena. 'It's a children's toy.'

Diamonds lost interest in the Goldfish and carelessly batted it away. The Goldfish went flying, just as another lobster-person reached down a long, three-jointed arm, scooped me up and tucked me into its armpit – if a lobster-person could be said to have armpits. Soon everyone else had been gathered up and we were being carried away like bundles of dirty laundry.

'Hey!' protested the Goldfish, loyally hurrying after us. 'Cut it out! Put them down! Mister . . . ! Ma'am! You guys are just big bullies!'

The lobster-people, obviously, ignored it.

'I apologise – I cannot apologise enough for my – for these – for them,' I could hear Mr Trommler saying. 'This is a . . . a misunderstanding – everyone is a little . . . *stressed*.'

'Who are you and what do you mean by kidnapping us?' asked Dr Muldoon with as much icy dignity as is possible from someone hanging upside down over a lobster-person's shoulder.

'*Qrrt squllk tchil-krrp . . .*' began Spikes. The box translated:

'You have not been *kidnapped*. You have infringed and violated the Sovereign territory and possessions of the Emperor and Empress of the Krakkiluk Expanse, may their Love be ever passionate and fruitful. You are thieves and pirates. And you are all under arrest.'

7

'We didn't,' moaned Noel. 'We didn't do anything like that. We're on our holidays.'

'I'm sure all this can be settled amicably,' spluttered Mr Trommler. 'Whatever it is you fine people are unhappy about, I assure you, we're only too eager to rectify it.'

We were all heaped beside the *Helen*'s open ramp, on the curved black glossy floor of a huge hangar; I was dimly aware of soaring red vaulted arches rising above us, and rather more clearly aware that the vast doors that had admitted us were now firmly shut. My arms and legs tingled as whatever the Krakkiluks – I was going to assume they were called Krakkiluks – had done to us wore off, but since we had a variety of interestingly menacing weapons trained on us, moving continued to seem like a bad idea.

The air outside the suits was humid. There was a mist of condensation on the transparent ceramic of my helmet. Th*saaa* was with us now. They didn't seem to have been paralysed the way we humans had been; they were clutching a Paralashath and silently trying to soothe themself with the flow of changing colours, echoed in the ripples on their skin.

The Krakkiluks didn't pay any attention to Noel, but they did pull Mr Trommler out of the general heap and create two slightly smaller heaps – me, Carl, Noel,

Josephine and Th*saaa* on one side, and Trommler, Dr Muldoon and Lena on another. They spent a bit of time muttering and clicking over Christa, who, understandably, responded to being singled out mainly by shaking and gibbering, but eventually the Krakkiluks threw her in with the rest of us kids.

Meanwhile, their soldiers were still searching the *Helen*. They seemed surprised that there weren't more of us.

'Stand up!' said the one with spikes. The grown-ups managed to do this, though they looked sick and wobbly. Spikes pointed to Dr Muldoon and Mr Trommler. 'You two are married?'

'Good God, no,' said Dr Muldoon.

'Where is your husband?' enquired Spikes.

'I *beg* your pardon?' said Dr Muldoon.

'You would not venture so far without your spouse,' said Spikes.

Dr Muldoon's mouth opened, but she was too outraged to speak.

'Answer my beloved Krnk-ni-Plik when she speaks to you!' said Diamonds, brandishing one of their enormous guns at Dr Muldoon.

'You would be wise to listen to my adorable Tlag-li-Glig!' agreed Spikes.

'I'm not married,' said Dr Muldoon through gritted teeth.

'Then where is your wife?' Krnk-ni-Plik enquired of Mr Trommler. 'This one is surely too young for you,' she added, pointing a spiky arm at Lena. Mr Trommler stuttered and wrung his hands, while Dr Muldoon's expression changed from rage to intrigue. 'We demand to speak to a married couple,' said Krnk-ni-Plik, frustrated by now.

'No one's married,' said Lena.

All the Krakkiluks looked at each other and then vibrated, so that the plates of their exoskeletons clacked and clattered. It was strange but I *understood* – there's something about dealing with *people*, wherever they're from. There are lots of things you don't understand but some things you do. I was pretty sure that that noise amounted to scornful laughter.

'No wonder you were so easily captured,' said Tlag-li-Glig. 'What is the crew of a ship without Love?'

No one had any idea how to answer that, except the *Helen*, who announced indignantly through external speakers, 'I am *full* of love!' which left even the aliens kind of flummoxed.

'Well,' said a Krakkiluk with blue coils on its exoskeleton. 'That is very strange.'

'Ah! The *ship* is your wife!' said Krnk-ni-Plik to Mr Trommler.

'Oh! No, of course not – I've had quite enough wives to be going on with, haha. The ship is just . . . it's a ship. With an AI in it, that's all.'

'*I don't think you're helping,*' hissed Dr Muldoon.

'There can be no true cohesion, no sacred covenant between soldiers, without Love,' said Tlag-li-Glig severely.

'Love is the basis of nations! The clay from which greatness is built! The forge of civilisation! I fight for the Expanse, but I fight for my beloved first, and she for me!'

'O, diamond of my life,' said Krnk-ni-Plik reverently, deeply moved by this.

'O, thorned bloom of summer seas,' responded Tlag-li-Glig.

'O, rainbow of my oil glands,' said Krnk-ni-Plik.

The Krakkiluks seemed to be working themselves up into performing some disturbing kind of poem (while the others clattered gently in appreciation). Personally, I would have left them to it in the hope they'd get so carried away we could sneak back aboard the *Helen* and fly off. But Carl decided to interrupt.

'OK, we get it, you really like love,' he said. 'You're very loving people. So you could . . . let us go home now. That would show love, wouldn't it?'

'I think they mainly like marriage,' I whispered to him.

'There's other kinds of love!' announced Christa, unexpectedly. 'There's parents . . . and siblings . . . and friends . . . Oh, god, please don't hurt me.'

'Christa, quiet,' warned Trommler. But he needn't have bothered, because the nearest Krakkiluks just gestured at her in the vague way you might bat at a fly you can't be bothered to actually hit.

Two pairs of Krakkiluks emerged from the *Helen* and said something, but the red boxes didn't translate that or Krnk-ni-Plik's reply. The subordinate pair might have saluted if they'd been humans – and they did bow – but then they turned to each other and, with equal formality (but somehow still plenty of passion), embraced. Then they retired a few steps, sheathed their weapons, and began lightly caressing each other with their claws.

'*Fel-thraaa shiha-raaa*,' said Thsaaa. *Please*. '*Quurufor vel-raha amlaa-lel-thash*.' And I could hear the word 'cooling cape' in there. Pale, washed-out patches were appearing amidst their colours.

'Please,' begged Noel. 'It's way too hot for Morrors. You can't keep Thsaaa in here; they'll overheat and die!'

The Krakkiluks seemed oblivious to anything said by anyone under eighteen, but when Dr Muldoon said the same thing over again, Tlag-li-Glig inspected Thsaaa critically and crunched out something untranslated to a pair of subordinates, who went and found a cooling cape inside the *Helen*. They tossed it over to Thsaaa, who huddled inside it gratefully. But I knew that wouldn't work forever.

Our oxygen supplies wouldn't last forever, come to that.

'Get the spawn on their feet,' said Krnk-ni-Plik, all business again.

'. . . *Spawn?*' echoed Josephine, indignantly.

Still, we had no choice but to stagger to our feet and let them lead us to a wide gold disc in the middle of the floor. This proved to be a lift, without any walls or handrails, which I suppose was not surprising, as the Krakkiluks did not seem like Health and Safety kind of people. So we went whooshing up into the ceiling, flanked by Krnk-ni-Plik and Tlag-li-Glig. And while there was no aspect of this situation any of us were enthusiastic about, getting further and further from our own ship and deeper into theirs felt particularly bad.

'Goodbye, *Helen*,' said Noel forlornly, waving with the hand which wasn't clutching Carl's.

'Goodbye,' *Helen* called back, looking strangely small there, all alone in the red depths of the great ship.

We rose through deck after deck, glimpsing vaults of red and gold, and dizzying numbers of Krakkiluks doing things like exercising and mending stuff and practising with their weapons, and on one deck possibly enjoying some kind of couples' dance.

'So,' said Dr Muldoon, revealing that the utility belt on her suit contained a tiny notepad and a pencil. 'The married couple thing: it's always pairs of two, is it? I noticed your translators are using the words "he" and "she", is that right?'

'Of course it is right,' said Tlag-li-Glig brusquely.

Scared as they were, Th*saaa* went pitying and contemptuous colours, which I hoped the Krakkiluks couldn't understand. 'They seem a lot like humans,' they whispered.

'Shut up, they do *not*,' Carl retorted.

'Keep the spawn quiet!' thundered Krnk-ni-Plik.

We emerged, suddenly, into a wide red chamber that for an instant made me think *throne room* before I thought *command deck*. It had the same waspy quality of the ship's exterior: ribs of gold against black, but there were roundels between the bands, painted with scenes the Krakkiluks presumably found encouraging – Krakkiluks fighting, Krakkiluks subduing what must have been other species, and plenty of Krakkiluks in love. The chamber was flooded with dazzling blue sunlight from great round windows, but I couldn't see the golden planet we'd glimpsed before.

There wasn't a lot of furniture. I got the impression Krakkiluks were like horses and didn't really do sitting down; the crew stood at horseshoe-shaped control stations, no two decorated alike.

And there was a grand ramp up to a dais below a pointed arch, and on the platform stood a large Krakkiluk person who was entirely covered in gold. The effect was even more blinding than Tlag-li-Glig's diamonds; this person must have been wearing some kind of gold paint in addition to the gilding on their exoskeleton and was golden up to their eyes. At this distance it was easier to get a better look at their faces, though compared to humans or Morrors they didn't *have* much of one, just egg-shaped pink eyes on short, flexible stalks, above a set of large, bony mouth parts which made me glad I so far hadn't seen the Krakkiluks eating anything.

'You will answer for your actions to Lady Sklat-kli-Sklak,' said Tlag-li-Glig, herding us on to a low platform a bit like a courtroom dock below the dais.

'What have you to say?' rumbled the huge golden person.

'So where's *your* husband?' asked Dr Muldoon sourly.

There was an immediate clatter of shocked disapproval from all the Krakkiluks, and rather more to the point, Lady Sklat-kli-Sklak shot Dr Muldoon with some sort of small remote-control type of thing.

'I'm all right,' wheezed Dr Muldoon. 'Just, you know, can't stand up or anything.'

'How dare you profane the memory of Lord Prilk-wu-Stlik!' cried Krnk-ni-Plik, the spiky one.

'I suggest a group policy of no more sarcasm, backtalk or gallows humour until we are all successfully released,' said Lena, tight-lipped, as she hoisted Dr Muldoon into an upright position.

'Agreed,' groaned Dr Muldoon.

'I fight to be worthy of my husband's memory,' said Lady Sklat-kli-Skalk calmly, having evidently vented her feelings.

She gestured and a projection of a gas giant and a little blue moon appeared in front of her dais.

'Aushalawa-Mo*raa*,' Lena said.

'That is not its name!' snapped Sklat-kli-Slkak. 'That is the moon of Quattitak, and it belongs to the Grand Expanse! It was fresh and pure and ready for the planting of Takwuk. Now it has been soiled; it is frozen and swarming with invader species. Who is responsible?'

'*She* is,' said Mr Trommler instantly, pointing at Dr Muldoon.

'Thanks,' sighed Dr Muldoon.

'Explain this outrage!' demanded Sklat-kli-Skalk.

'I helped adapt the moon for the Morrors' needs as part of the peace settlement between our peoples. We scanned it carefully – the only life we found was microbial.'

'Of course!' said Sklat-kli-Slkak. 'It had been prepared for Takwuk.'

'Oh,' said Dr Muldoon, sounding deflated, like that made sense now she thought about it.

'Takwuk is what, exactly?' asked Lena.

'Not Takwuk,' said Tlag-li-Glig. '*Takwuk.*'

'Takwuk,' repeated Lena.

'*Takwuk,*' insisted Tlag-li-Glig. But there was only so close someone without a set of bony mouthparts could get to the proper pronunciation of any of the Krakkiluks' words. The real thing was always lot . . . crunchier.

'That is no concern of pirates and aggressors!' thundered Lady Sklat-kli-Sklak. 'You were not brought here for answers from *us*. You will restore the moon of Quattitak to its proper state. Or we will commence throwing your spawn out of the airlock.'

8

I hadn't been aware of the airlock before.

But suddenly it seemed a remarkably prominent feature. It was a round window in the floor – or rather a *trap door*, because it was horribly obvious to me now that it would open, dumping anything resting on it into a kind of well beneath, the bottom of which would open in turn, into the nothingness beyond. I wondered dizzily if this was something they often did to the spawn of other species, or whether it was how Sklat-kli-Slkak imposed discipline on the crew.

Or maybe they just used it as the office bin.

'You can't do this,' said Mr Trommler.

'We can,' said Sklat-kli-Slkak, sounding faintly puzzled. 'The airlock is in perfect working order. It underwent standard maintenance only today.'

'I'd like to say, I'm not spawn,' said Christa brightly. 'I'm nearly seventeen years old.'

Dr Muldoon levered herself out of Lena's arms. 'Listen,' she said, swaying a little. 'We're very sorry we inconvenienced you. It was completely unintentional. But what you're suggesting now . . . it's not possible.'

Sklat-kli-Slkak gestured with a golden arm. A soldier seized me in one three-pincered hand and Josephine in the other, and two other soldiers grabbed Carl, Noel, Th*saaa* and Christa, and hoisted us towards the airlock.

'I'm *not spaaaaawn*,' Christa howled.

Loyally, the Goldfish swooped after us, flashing its eyes red and emitting a furious blare.

'Stop, God – please stop!' gasped Dr Muldoon.

'*Put down my sister*,' Lena said in a low but carrying whisper.

The Krakkiluk soldiers did put us down, or rather dropped us again, but I landed on top of the trapdoor of the airlock. I looked down at the faint glow of stars washed out in the sunlight under my hands and scrambled back as if I'd been stung. Up on their platform the horrified adults already seemed very far away.

'Please, I'm trying to explain!' said Dr Muldoon. 'We had no way of knowing you had a claim to the planet. We did not know you even *existed*.'

'You are now relieved of the burden of ignorance,' said Sklat-kli-Slkak.

'Yes,' said Dr Muldoon, and you had to say this for the Krakkiluks' methods: Dr Muldoon was getting a lot better at sounding earnest and humble. 'Yes, we're, uh . . . grateful for that. But there's an entire population on Aush– I mean, the moon of Quattitak. I was . . . *involved* in the process of terraforming, I admit, but I could hardly have done it without resources from –' She stopped, and I could see her wondering how much the Krakkiluks already knew about Earth.

'From Earth,' said Sklat-kli-Slkak impatiently. 'Are

our translators not loaded with your languages? We know about Earth. Its seas are warm.'

There was a pause while Dr Muldoon tried to work out what to make of that last remark, then she soldiered on.

'Well, then, you understand. I don't have the resources to do what you're asking. Even if I wanted to – I couldn't promise anything on behalf of either of our planets.'

'We have thought of that,' said Sklat-kli-Slkak.

One of the other Krakkiluk crew – a smaller lobster-person decorated with modest black polka dots – did something at a workstation, and the deck filled with the most unsettlingly familiar, human, ordinary noise. A phone ringing.

And then, even stranger, someone answered it:

'Hello?' said a friendly female American voice, impossible trillions of miles away. 'Darla's Dog-Grooming Dream Palace, how can I help you?'

'I am Lady Sklat-kli-Sklak of the Grand Expanse and I carry demands from the Emperor and Empress of the Krakkiluk nations!' barked our captor.

I had an instant to think what a wonderful place Darla's Dog-Grooming Dream Palace undoubtedly was and how much I wished I was there, before Darla sensibly hung up the phone.

The Krakkiluk officer did whatever they'd done before again, except this time it wasn't one phone ringing but two, ten, hundreds – thousands – swelling to a droning purr. And then the alien chamber began to flood with human voices: '*Moshi moshi?*' '*Pronto?*' '*Sí?*' '*Wèi?*' '*All our operators are busy. Please stay on the line,*' until that too became an incomprehensible chaos of sound.

'Are you . . . phoning *everyone on Earth?*' whispered Noel.

Sklat-kli-Sklak ignored him of course. She resumed, in various languages, telling Earth that she was very angry and wanted, on behalf of the Grand Expanse, to talk to someone about the moon of Quattitak.

'That shouldn't be possible,' said Josephine. She was tight-lipped and round-eyed behind her helmet, but there was a pucker between her eyebrows that meant she was curious. 'How are you sending the signal through hyperspace?'

'They're *not going to answer you,*' I said through gritted teeth. It was the first thing I'd said to her since the fight on the *Helen.*

Josephine met my eyes then quickly looked away. 'Rhetorical question,' she said to the floor.

'I'm putting rhetorical questions on the list of prohibited modes of self-expression,' said Lena.

The chorus of increasingly frightened human voices was fading; you could hear distinct voices again as they vanished:

'*What is this? What's happ–?*'

'*Vi prego, non far' mal i bambini.*'

Meanwhile we were all crouched there on the ground, waiting for the next dreadful thing to happen.

'You know what, I gave 'em a fair chance, but I've

decided I don't like these guys,' said Carl, who had started drumming a complicated rhythm on the glossy red floor.

'It's going to be fine, Carl,' said Noel.

Carl looked vaguely affronted. 'Yeah, I *know*,' he said. 'I'm not *worried*.'

'Can you . . . *think* of anything?' Ths*aaa* whispered to Josephine.

Josephine shook her head tersely. I knew she was *trying*, though – her eyes were skimming busily over everything within sight: every surface, every button and panel and weapon and claw.

But I didn't see there was much she could do about the fact we were massively outnumbered and impossibly far from help.

'You want to kick seven million Morrors off the planet and you don't even want to live on it yourselves? What *is* Takwuk, anyway?' Carl demanded recklessly. 'Hey. Hey, hey, I'm down here, spawn with a question.'

Lady Slat-kli-Sklak ignored Carl, of course, but the soldier standing guard over us cracked: 'Spawn should be silent,' he-or-maybe-she said shortly.

'Why?' asked Carl.

'Krakkiluk spawn cannot speak,' said the soldier.

'Really? Well, fine, but we can, so what's Takwuk?'

'Not Takwuk. *Takwuk*,' insisted the soldier unhappily. 'Takwuk is . . . it is a substance derived from a plant.'

'Is it *drugs*?!' said Carl. 'OK, if you need an entire planet to grow your drugs on, that's a sign you have a problem.'

'Maybe it's lifesaving drugs,' suggested Noel charitably. 'Medicine.'

'*Is* it medicine?' pressed Carl.

'*Tsshk-lu-krrt-prruck*,' Sklat-kli-Sklak quacked, which went untranslated but doubtless meant 'Tell the spawn to shut up,' so we did.

We could hear Morror voices on the speaker system now. 'It's the Council of Lonthaa-Ra-Mo*raa*,' whispered Th*saaa*.

Then a new human voice spoke. It was very familiar; it was on television every day. And I'd been on Mars with its owner's nephew. 'My name is President Chakrabarty of the Emergency Earth Coalition. I believe you wanted to speak to me.'

'Are you widowed or unwed?' said Sklkat-kli-Sklak indignantly.

'Er,' said President Chakrabarty. 'No?'

'Then where is your wife? We will not be insulted! Your wife will enter the discussion at once!'

President Chakrabarty coped pretty well. 'All right. My wife is happy to . . . er, talk. A moment, please.'

Sklat-kli-Sklik relaxed. 'I had begun to worry we would encounter *no* married pairs today,' she said jovially, which the crew seemed to find very amusing.

'Hi!' said the First Lady, her voice shiny with panic, and having started talking, she had some trouble stopping: 'Hi, how are you, I hope you're having a good day.'

'Yes, it is going well so far, thank you,' said Sklat-kli-Sklak courteously.

'We are delighted to make the acquaintance of a fellow spacefaring civilisation,' said President Chakrabarty very carefully. 'But you can't expect us to negotiate while you're threatening the lives of children.'

Again, Sklat-kli-Slkak seemed confused. 'Why would we stop threatening the lives of your spawn before our demands are met? That is the whole point of this conversation.'

'*Au-leee neth ele vilamaaa poru!*' cried a voice from the Council of Lonthaa-Ra-Moraa, which I was pretty sure was: 'Don't you have children of your own?'

'*Eth-hraa vilamaaa au-thraal ruu!*' said Sklat-kli-Slkak through her translator box.

'Th*saaa*,' I whispered. 'Did she say, she has *thousands* of children?'

'Yes,' said Th*saaa*, who was already sickly shades of green and yellow.

'*Aulereth-laa puul lashowuu*,' pleaded one of the Council of Lonthaa-Ra-Moraa. This time I understood: 'You cannot do this . . .!' but not the rest.

'. . . for the sake of a crop!' supplied Th*saaa*, shuddering through translucent greys and reds.

'What is Takwuk?' asked President Chakrabarty.

'Takwuk stimulates the senses, invigorates the body and mind,' said Krnk-ni-Plik. 'Takwuk is the lifeblood of civilisation.'

'It's drugs,' said Carl flatly. 'You guys officially need help.'

I know why he said it. He was scared. So he wanted to act like he wasn't. Especially in front of Noel.

Sklat-kli-Sklak looked at Carl. It was the first time she'd looked at any of us. She said something the boxes didn't translate.

Then Tlag-li-Glig picked up Carl and threw him out of the airlock.

It happened so quickly, and yet I saw every layer of every second of it. The effortlessness with which Tlag-li-Glig plucked Carl into the air. My arms, slow and useless, swinging up to grab at him; Carl's legs kicking as he dangled from Tlag-li-Glig's diamond-crusted arm. Tlag-li-Glig yanked the oxygen tank off his back as easily as pulling the wrapper off a bar of chocolate, slammed Carl down on to the trapdoor and slapped a button on a plinth. The trapdoor opened like a mouth and swallowed him into the chamber below, sealing up again before I could finish shouting his name. Then I was on top of the door, banging against it, but the surface was as seamless as stone, and for an instant he was still there; I could see his eyes, wide and terrified. Then the chamber opened to the void outside, and Carl was gone.

Everyone on the bridge who wasn't a Krakkiluk was screaming.

'Carl!' howled Noel.

'The oxygen tanks – for God's sake, you took his oxygen –' Dr Muldoon babbled.

'Of course. Far kinder,' replied Lady Sklat-kli-Sklak. 'We have thrown one of your spawn, the older male one, out of the airlock,' she announced loudly, though I think President Chakrabarty had already understood what had happened, from all the noise.

'Get him back!' Noel was shouting. And so was I, I realised. 'Get him back – he's still alive, he must be – you have to –'

'We will continue this discussion shortly,' said Sklat-kli-Sklak to President Chakrabarty, while Noel reached up and grabbed desperately at the soldier who'd ejected Carl. Tlag-li-Glig flicked him to the floor and that did something to me, I guess. Though I only realised I was in the process of charging at Tlag-li-Glig with raised fists when someone tackled me to the ground.

'Alice,' Josephine's voice hissed. She was lying across me, gripping my arm with painful force, her helmet pressed against mine. '*Shut up.* You hear me? You *have to shut up.*'

'Carl –' I said, my voice cracking.

'I know. I know. If we have any chance at all, it's *not that*, OK?'

I stared past her at a picture of Krakkiluks fording a mighty river on the wall.

'Say OK,' she said, ruthlessly.

'OK,' said my voice, apparently by itself.

She crawled off me. I sat up. I *could* sit up, after all, and look around and talk. It didn't seem to make sense, that I could do that. 'How long has he got?' I asked, staring at

Carl's oxygen canisters. 'The air in his suit – do you know how long he'll last out there?'

'Yes,' she said, drawing her knees close to her chest, not looking at me. 'I know how long.'

She didn't elaborate and I ran out of things to say.

Noel was still howling. 'Please, he must be alive, you have to get him back!'

'Silence that spawn,' said Sklat-kli-Sklak.

'NO!' I screamed and, 'Au-*laaa!*' wailed Th*saaa*, dragging Noel into their tentacles and clutching him tight.

Noel sobbed into Th*saaa*'s cloaked shoulder, while Th*saaa* flickered dizzyingly through black and violet and fiery orange, but apparently Sklat-kli-Sklak had just meant she literally wanted Noel to be quiet, not that she wanted him to be quiet out in the depths of space.

Yet.

'Christ, all right!' Dr Muldoon was shouting. 'All right, I'll do it, I'll engineer you the best crop of Takwuk ever, if you like – somehow we'll do it – just, stop; get him back, please –'

'You said you could not do it without help,' said Sklat-kli-Sklak.

'Earth *will* help – I'm sure Earth will help. You have to give us time – time for the Morrors to migrate –'

'*Hal ra'thruu ath-shal, vshoor uha-porshelel,*' keened a Morror voice. *Where can we go, we have already travelled so far.*

'Have you really thrown a child out into space?' asked President Chakrabarty, in a winded voice.

'Of course,' said Sklat-kli-Sklak.

'Can . . . can one of the humans you have with you answer?'

'They have,' said Dr Muldoon, 'Mr President. They have. It has to be possible to get him back on board –'

'The scientist says she will restore the moon to its proper state. Does she have the assistance of Earth and the Mo-*raaa* uh-*raaa*?'

'*Aulereth-laa. Ath-thraal shasuu*,' cried one of the Council of Lonthaa-Ra-Mo*raa*. 'Seven million of us,' I heard. 'You can't . . .'

'You do realise,' said President Chakrabarty, softly, 'that this amounts to an act of war?'

Sklat-kli-Skak rattled amusement. 'War would be a far greater misfortune to your peoples than the loss of a handful of spawn. If you meet us in war, it will never be by *your* choice. You will by now have tried to locate the source of our transmission. You will never find it. And if you could, you have nothing that could threaten the Grand Expanse.'

'Perhaps not yet,' said President Chakrabarty.

'Is that a refusal?' asked Sklat-kli-Sklak.

'We need time,' said President Chakrabarty, the steely note in his voice giving out.

'We were under the impression that humans and the Mo-*raaa* uha-*raaa* placed disproportionate value on lives of spawn,' grumbled Sklat-kli-Slkak. 'Were we misinformed?'

There was silence as everyone realised she expected

118

an answer to the question. Her eyes swivelled towards Dr Muldoon, who tried not to writhe.

'I don't have sp– I mean, children, myself,' Dr Muldoon said.

'That is not what I asked.'

Dr Muldoon hesitated. I could see her trying to decide which of the possible answers was the least dangerous. 'No,' she said.

'Well, then,' said Sklat-kli-Sklak.

'*No!*' said Dr Muldoon again, but this time it meant something different.

Krnk-ni-Plik was advancing towards us. And we shouted and clung together and I could only think, No no no no, and which of us – which of us was it going to be this time?

Pincers closed around my arm.

My turn.

Krnk-ni-Plik hoisted me up. I felt hands and tentacles clutching at me, but how do you fight back against someone covered in spikes? My body seemed to have shut down – I couldn't make it do anything. There was no time, anyway.

Krnk-ni-Plik gave me a dizzying little shake to disentangle me from the others. And I'd seen every detail of every moment when this was happening to Carl, but now it was happening to me I couldn't keep up with it; I barely felt the oxygen canisters pulled from my back, or felt myself drop through the trapdoor into the chamber beneath. I heard screaming but I couldn't single out words, and then the airlock snapped closed. I heard the roar of escaping air as the hatch underneath opened.

And then just the rasp of my own breath. All around me silence. It dragged me spinning into its depths and bore me away like a gnat in a torrent of water.

Silence that was going to last for the rest of my life.

PART 2

9

There was a light, where there hadn't been a light before.

I couldn't get a good look at it. My eyes were still plugged with tears, and I was spinning head first through the bright and dark, tasting hot, dried-up emptiness on every breath. Josephine hadn't told me how long the oxygen would last, and every now and then I would come back to myself to notice how I seemed to be blurring out at the edges and to wonder whether that was the spinning or the onset of suffocation. And then I would wonder whether Mum was happily shooting Vshomu at the moment, or whether she'd been on Earth to hear all those ringing phones, and I'd think, Sklat-kli-Sklak must have told President Chakrabarty that they'd thrown one of the human female children out of the airlock. Would my dad know yet that it was me? And then I would start fading away again, and my eyes would drift closed behind the bandaging of tears.

But whenever I opened them, each time my tumbling brought me round to face the ship, the little orange pip of light was there, and each time it was *bigger*, which should have been impossible.

Something was coming.

A pulsing orange light, with two bright blue eyes . . .

The Goldfish was powering through space towards me. And it wasn't alone. Someone was clinging to its tailfin, body extended like a diver's behind it.

I sucked in a big reckless gasp of air, and my head cleared a little. Someone was coming for me, soaring through space in the Goldfish's wake, silhouetted against the stars. Somebody human, and too big to be Noel, and too small to be Lena or Dr Muldoon, and anyway, I *knew* who it was.

Josephine let go of the Goldfish and flew free. I tumbled over again and lost sight of her, but she was there. I no longer felt as if it might be a wishful trick of my oxygen-starved brain; I could *feel* her there.

How did she have the Goldfish with her? Krnk-ni-Plik wouldn't have thrown it into the airlock with her.

But somehow I didn't think the Krakkiluks *had* slammed her through that trapdoor. It was something about the purposeful way she was moving. She came closer still, and I could see she still had her oxygen canisters. She hadn't been thrown out. She had *jumped.*

Of course she had, I thought. It was the sort of lunatic thing she would do.

Josephine crashed into me. She gripped me by both shoulders and at last I wasn't spinning any more. We glided on above the golden planet, still travelling at enormous speed, and yet I was lying still, like a shipwreck victim on a raft, Josephine beside me.

She leaned forwards and put her helmet against mine.

'Hello,' she said, and through the contact between the layers of transparent ceramic, through the air that filled our helmets, I could hear her.

'Josephine,' I croaked. 'What . . .?' I shouldn't be glad, I thought, I shouldn't be hopeful – what could she *do*, out here, even with the Goldfish?

'Be ready to grab Carl,' she said. She took my hand. The Goldfish swooped back towards us and Josephine reached out with her free hand, grabbed its tail again, and we were swimming through the airless sky towards the tiny flailing figure in the starry distance.

I grabbed Carl by one foot. He flipped and twisted, like a fish on a hook – trying to see what was happening. And I pulled him and Josephine pulled me and the Goldfish pulled Josephine, and we skimmed along in one crazy line like that through space, until I could no longer see the Krakkiluk ship behind us.

There was something else here in orbit, I saw. Something shaped like a crown or a throwing star, made of red-painted metal, bristling with barbs and dotted with lights like eyes. A satellite, squatting above the planet like a spider in a web.

Carl managed to arch up to look at us in amazement. His mouth was moving but I couldn't hear what he was saying.

Josephine let go of the Goldfish again. I didn't like her doing that – we were so helpless when not in physical contact with it. She pulled me towards her and we both grabbed at Carl until we were floating in a huddle, our helmets together again.

'The Goldfish wants me to tell you: "Hey, kids,"' said Josephine.

'Oh, God, oh, God, what the hell,' Carl said, which was probably what he'd been saying the whole time.

'What next?' I whispered. 'Where can we go?'

'Only one place,' said Josephine. She pointed. Down towards the planet.

'We'll burn up in the atmosphere,' I said.

'There's probably no *oxygen* down there,' Carl moaned.

'None up here, either!' said Josephine, almost cheerfully.

'I guess . . . it's worth a try,' I said.

It wasn't as if there was a real choice.

The Goldfish ejected a cable from its tail. It wasn't meant for grappling kids floating in space; it was an ordinary, plastic-coated data cable for connecting to other robots or computers.

Josephine grabbed it, twisted it around her arm and passed the end to me. I did the same and passed it on to Carl.

'Hold on as long as you can,' Josephine said.

We didn't have a ship. We didn't have a parachute. We had one fish-shaped teacher robot.

It was too late to think about it – it had been too late ever since Josephine jumped out of the ship. The Goldfish dipped towards the planet, towing us with it. The atmosphere of the planet pummelled us, scraped at us like flying gravel; my ears screamed with pain, pressure battered me all over. I felt my skin scorch – the suit, I was pretty sure, was starting to *melt*. I saw sparks fly from my boots.

Hello, down there, I thought madly, as we ripped through, into freefall above an alien world.

Green-tinted clouds rushed up to meet us, looking as welcomingly soft as sponge. Of course, we plunged straight through, though the wetness swept a little heat from my skin. Miles below us, a green sea glittered like a spill of diodes and emeralds, against a red and gold continent.

The upwinds wrenched at me. I tried to keep hold of the cable but the howling sky tore me loose, away from the others, away from the Goldfish – whirled me out of consciousness.

I don't know how long I fell like that. But then something hit me, and I came to, still hurtling helplessly through the air – but somehow I was moving through a steep *arc*, flying sideways, not plummeting straight down. Then it happened again: a hard, rounded shape knocked me sideways, and this time I clutched on instinct and found myself clinging to the Goldfish's back. The Goldfish strained upwards, against the current of my fall.

'Gosh, Alice,' said the Goldfish conversationally, its voice tinny in my abused ears, through the roaring wind. 'This sure is hard work!'

I couldn't answer. I couldn't see Carl or Josephine; they'd been torn away, just as I had, and the cable lashed loose in the air. I tried to grab for it, felt it whip against my arm, but then I slipped from the Goldfish's back, into the fury of the air.

The sea and the land below spun into a whirlpool of

colour. This time I glimpsed the others scattered through the air around me – but we were plunging so fast that I couldn't tell who was who. And there was the Goldfish, swooping to meet another falling body, slamming it sideways, darting onwards to the other, then speeding back towards me. The Goldfish was more or less *juggling* us, bouncing us sideways, never stopping our fall but *slowing* us, soaking speed from us with each bruising strike.

It won't be enough, though, I thought. The planet was rising to meet us like the open mouth of a hungry animal.

I could see separate crests of foam on separate waves now. On the land I saw glossy, vase-like structures of many sizes that might have been buildings or plants or volcanic vents for all I knew, and purple-red moving specks that might have been – what? Vehicles? Animals?

The Goldfish batted me sideways again. The sea was so huge and close that the massive expanse of ground had dwindled to a narrow golden band of shore. Then even that vanished. I thought I heard the Goldfish say my name again, but there wasn't anything else it could do to help me. I brought up my arms to protect my face on useless instinct.

And then the surface of the water hit me like a brick wall, or at least that's what it felt like for the split second I had to think about it. Because I'm pretty sure I passed out again.

That only lasted for a second or two, I think. But it meant I had to go through the unpleasant business of *waking up*, which I guess was better than the alternative, but didn't feel it. Ow? What? Why? Help? I thought, if you could call it thinking rather than just an unspoken accompaniment to all the muted screaming into my helmet I was doing.

And then my brain began filling in what had happened, in a series of questions and 'oh yeses', none of which were at all reassuring.

1) Alive, which is surprising, because . . . ? Oh. Yes.

2) Everything green? Underwater! Help! Why underwater . . .?
Oh. Yes.

3) Everything hurts because . . .? Oh. Yes.

I broke the surface and glimpsed the green sky, uttered a strangled yelp of general protest at it, then sank again. I don't know if you've ever tried to swim in a pressure suit but if you ever have to do it, try not to have just plunged from outer space first. You will be confused and upset and will have a limited grasp of what your arms and legs are even for. Also make sure the water you're swimming in isn't teeming with little pink wriggling things; it's off-putting.

My helmet had miraculously survived, though it didn't feel as if there was more than a puff of oxygen in it now. But at least it meant none of the pink things got inside, because I think that might have sent me right over the edge. The pink things were various sizes – mostly the size of a newborn kitten, I suppose, but some as big as a large dog, and they were six-legged and bristling with fluttering little rosy cilia and sometimes emitting little yellow puffs of I didn't like to think what.

I'm not sure it was rational or fair to find them so disgusting when they squiggled past my face (I'm sure Noel wouldn't have done), but I would refer you back to the recently-kidnapped-and-nearly-murdered-and-then-fell-seven-miles-from-outer-space thing. Fortunately the creatures were at least as alarmed by me as I was by them and were wriggling away for all they were worth, and soon I was left in a clearing of empty water.

'Hello!' I croaked into the green waves. The first human word to sound in the air of that strange world.

The next words were not any more impressive, although they were extremely welcome:

'Hey, Alice!' The Goldfish was hovering above me. It looked a little melted around the edges.

I flipped open my helmet. There wasn't any good reason not to; the air outside would either kill me or it wouldn't. It's not as if waiting a few minutes would help matters.

I did not instantly die. In fact there was a kind of heady rush from that air that made me feel . . . not *better* exactly, but a little more alert. It also smelled funny. I decided the details would have to wait.

'You're OK!' the Goldfish exulted. 'Boy, that was a close one, huh?'

'Yes,' I said. 'Where's . . .? Where's . . .?' I wondered if I was in fact badly brain damaged, because I couldn't seem to manage things like my friends' names.

'JOSEPHINE!' called a voice, most of the boom stripped out, but with a desperate quaver in it that made me feel cold.

'Carl?' I tried to shout back. 'Goldfish, what's wrong?'

'Grab on, Alice,' it suggested, spitting out the cable from its mouth.

The Goldfish towed me through the water – it *was* water, I established, when some got in my mouth. It tasted awful, but at least it wasn't sulphuric acid. And it was relatively warm. The strange blue sun was bright overhead, so hypothermia wasn't going to be one of my immediate problems. I kicked as best I could, but you couldn't really call it swimming and the Goldfish had to do most of the work.

Something colourful was bobbing gently on the water – a puffy cluster of squashy-looking spheres each perhaps the size of a beach ball, gathered like grapes into heaped bunches as big as a car. The puffballs ranged from orange to white to violent blue, and a sickly sweet scent drifted off them across the waves and made me cough. I thought they might be something like fruit or maybe fungus, but if they turned out to be eggs on the point of hatching into something nasty, it would hardly be surprising after the kind of day we'd had. And enormous round, scarlet leaf-like things spread around the clusters like lily pads on the surface of the sea.

Carl was clinging to the edge of a leaf, gasping as if he'd just surfaced from the water. *'Josephine!'* he shouted again, then took a breath and forced himself back down.

'Carl?' I called, splashing towards him.

Carl's face was pale when he surfaced. 'She was here – she hit the water here – but she was tangled up in something – Alice, she *didn't come up.*'

'She had oxygen,' I said. 'She still had her oxygen.'

But Carl shook his head. 'Something was *wrong*, the oxygen tanks – it's like they were pulling her *down* and I think they were broken; there were all these bubbles coming up. I couldn't stay down, I couldn't – and when I went back I couldn't see her.'

I flipped my helmet down again and ducked underwater. The great leaves had many thick, ropy stems under the water, all coated in a gooey golden fuzz, on which all kinds of creatures were happily feeding. Blue blobby things with lots of eyes and orange things with lots of mouths. And yet more of the pink wriggly things.

The water was murky. I couldn't see any sign of Josephine. No bubbles, even.

I couldn't dive very well – not only was every inch of my body vigorously protesting my doing anything at all, but the air in my helmet kept pulling me up. I grabbed one of the stems and tried to pull my way down, hand over hand, but the fuzzy stuff glued my palm to a stem. I tore it free only to trap a foot in a gummy loop. I wrenched back in panic and lost a mouthful of air in a burst of gold-green bubbles. Someone yanked at my arm – Carl, pulling me free of the glue.

I came up again. I'd barely made it down a few feet. I pulled my helmet off completely and tried diving without it, but the water stung my eyes so much I couldn't keep them open.

It had been too long. It had already been too long. It takes people about four minutes to drown. We'd hit the water much longer ago than that.

And it's an awful way to die; lots of people don't realise that. But I'd had medical training.

I clutched at the edge of the leaf, gasping, and I glimpsed Carl's face. It looked horribly *young*, younger than I'd ever seen him look before, and after that I couldn't look at him at all, we just both kept swallowing down air that might be lethal and ducking underwater and coming up and going down again –

'Guys,' said the Goldfish quietly. 'I think you should get out of the water.'

'No,' I said, to the rubbery surface of the leaf. Then: 'Wait, *yes* . . .' I scrambled up on to the leaf, scanning the water and the red islands of leaves from this new height. 'Maybe she came up somewhere else – maybe there are currents. Maybe she couldn't hear us calling . . .' I filled my lungs again: '*Josephine!*' I screamed.

My voice sounded so awful: desolate and wrecked. It shredded away into the air and nothing came back but the sigh of the greenish waves. It didn't *sound* like someone calling to a friend out of sight. It sounded like someone screaming in anguish at what they'd just lost.

Carl heaved himself up and lay there on the leaf, his fists clenched beside his face.

'She jumped out,' I said to the Goldfish. 'Didn't she? After the Krakkiluks threw me – she grabbed you and she must have hit that button and – she jumped out.'

'Yes,' said the Goldfish, and for once in its life didn't say anything else. It just kept staring at the waves.

'She *jumped out of a spaceship*,' I repeated, a little louder. She'd saved my life. She hadn't even been talking to me. And she'd saved my life. And she'd *died* doing it. 'The *stupid idiot*,' I added. 'How could she do that?'

A soft wind was keening across the water.

'She was my best friend,' I said very quietly.

There was a splashing sound. Something heaved itself half out of the water on to a neighbouring leaf pad, and lay there, panting.

'Guys, *look!*' cried the Goldfish.

'Oof,' said Josephine. 'Hi.'

Carl claimed later that he did not jump a foot in the air and scream, but I was there – I heard him.

'It wasn't stupid,' Josephine remarked, pulling the rest of her body out of the water. 'It was pretty clever in the circumstances. It worked, didn't it?'

I sort of folded up on the lily pad and sat there, staring at her.

'Josephine, good to see ya!' cheered the Goldfish.

'Jo,' Carl quavered. 'What the hell. You were down there way too long.'

'Oh,' said Josephine. 'Well, yes. About that.' Looking slightly sheepish, she pulled down the neck of her tunic, and it occurred to me vaguely that she'd been wearing high-necked clothing the whole time we'd been on the *Helen*.

There were rows of fine, horizontal slits on the skin of her neck below each ear. Sort of like scars, but somehow *not*, at the same time.

'Gills? You got gills?' asked Carl.

'*Why have you got gills?*' I demanded in a high-pitched voice I didn't recognise.

'Well, you know Dr Muldoon wanted to get gills on to humans after photosynthetic skin went so well, and I wanted them, and we were working together, so . . . I volunteered . . .'

All of a sudden, I had never been so indignant about anything in my life.

'WHAT?' I roared. 'That is . . . APPALLING!'

'Um, why? I think it's pretty cool,' said Carl.

'BREACHES OF MEDICAL ETHICS ARE NOT COOL,' I howled. I pointed a quivering finger at Josephine. 'She is *thirteen years old*! Dr Muldoon performed . . . *medical experiments* on a *child*.'

'It's just gills. She wouldn't give me any kind of cortical implants,' said Josephine soothingly.

'OH, WELL, THAT'S FINE, THEN.'

'So I'm thirteen, so what – I *wanted* them. Like you wanted to go to space!'

I made a noise like an injured bison and aimed a reckless kick at one of the puffballs. 'What about the *risks?!*' The puffball burst into a cloud of blue dust and a swarm of flying creatures rose into the air, making a warbling sound.

'Alice . . .' Josephine looked baffled by now. 'Are you sure this is a good time to get upset about this?'

'Jo, just guessing here, but that's not actually what she's upset about,' said Carl.

'YES, IT IS!' I bellowed, all the more annoyed. I wanted to write extremely angry letters to everyone on Earth right then and there. 'This is a *disgrace*. Dr Muldoon should be *struck off.*'

'That's for medical doctors,' said Josephine. 'They don't strike off biochemists.'

'WELL THEY SHOULD,' I said. I was so upset by this failure of the scientific establishment I was on the point of tears. 'They should,' I repeated, sniffing.

'OK, Alice,' said Carl, gently. 'We'll take it up when we get home.'

'I'm sorry you don't like my gills, but they work very well, and I *would* currently be dead without them,' pointed out Josephine. 'Also, you know, you could say *thank you.*'

'AAARGH!' I said instead, and hurled myself at her. I wasn't absolutely sure if it was affection or murderous rage when I was doing it, and it knocked her over. But it turned into a hug on the way down and, also, I kind of burst into tears.

'You can't do that!' I sobbed. 'You can't just *jump out into space*! You can't get gills without telling me! And you can't rescue me and then *die*!'

Josephine lay there looking shocked, and then patted me. 'I haven't died,' she said gently. 'And nor have you. It's OK.'

But of course, that wasn't really true.

'Look, normally I'm all for girls wrestling or hugging or whatever you're doing there,' said Carl. 'But you're rocking the lily pad. And we've gotta figure out what we're going to *do*.'

Josephine detached herself from me. She looked around at the alien seascape, the floating orange leaves, the blue and yellow puffballs and the occasional splash of the pink wriggly things in the water and pursed her lips. 'Well,' she said, 'for starters, have we got any duct tape?'

'No,' I said. 'We definitely haven't.'

'Oh my God,' said Josephine.

10

〰️ Please. Turn that thing off. I know you're really into history and culture and things, Th*saaa*, but I don't *want* to document my experiences for future generations right now.

Can't we just play I Spy?

⬛ *Noel, If Weeseru-Uu had chosen to play I Spy rather than to record the third battle of Swaleeshashalafay Athmaral-haaa-Thay we would know nothing about the fall of the Aluufa-vem-ral-Faa and the memory of their civilisation would have been lost with our planet.*

If we survive this, a record will be useful to the Council of Lonthaa-Ra-Moraa, and if we do not, it may be found by some explorer, some scholar, years from now.

〰️ Please can you stop talking about us not surviving and about doomed civilisations and stuff?

⬛ *I think it is reassuring to think our story might at least be remembered.*

〰️ Well I . . . don't?

⬛ *And besides, I am required to write an account of my experiences on this trip for school. And, should we return home after all this, I would like to get an exceptional graaaaade.*

╟┅┅╢ If you get a bad grade for anything after all this, like, *ever*, I think your parents should complain.

I think Carl's alive. Don't you? I think all the others are OK. Josephine wouldn't have done what she did if she didn't have a plan, and she's smart, and Lena didn't look worried. Well, not that she really ever looks worried . . . she doesn't really *do* facial expressions . . .

 Aaaaaaah. She appears blank, even to other humans?

╟┅┅╢ Sometimes. And she did look a bit worried. But I still think she wasn't THAT worried, and so she must think Josephine knew what she was doing. So . . . I think they're OK. Like, maybe they're on the planet we saw, because it doesn't seem like they came back to the ship. So that's probably where they are and I think they're OK. Don't you?

 We know nothing about the atmosphere of the planet or whether it is capable of supporting human life. I mean, yes. I am sure they are quite well.

╟┅┅╢ Are you?

 Yes.

▐▌▌▐▌ Then why are you orange?

⬛ *I'm not. I aaaam . . . aaaaaah . . . amber. The implications are quite different.*

▐▌▌▐▌ I think you look really orange, though.

⬛ *I am not. Look, I am quite green in places. The light in here is not good. Perhaps you cannot see how green I am.*

▐▌▌▐▌ So you think they're fine.

⬛ *Yes.*

What is happening with your face? What colour would you be if you were normal?

Are you crying?

Please do not cry, Noel – I will play I Spyyyyy with you.

▐▌▌▐▌ O-OK. Do you need me to teach it to you?

⬛ *Of course not, I have been learning all about human children and their games – I have been assisting the reconciliation process, it is important. I am very good at Cat's Cradle although I do not understand its purpose. I could also play Oranges and Lemons or Huckle Buckle Beanstalk.*

⊢∙⊪⊪⊢ I don't know what those are.

 How strange. I will begin. I spy with my little eeeeeye, something beginning with U.

⊢∙⊪⊪⊢ U? I can't see anything in here starting with U. Ugly . . . wall paintings? Underfoot . . . floor?

 No.

⊢∙⊪⊪⊢ Then I don't know.

 I was spying 'Uncertainty'. I win.

⊢∙⊪⊪⊢ You can't . . . look, no. You can't see uncertainty.

 Of course you can. Look.

⊢∙⊪⊪⊢ Is that the colour you are? Look, never mind. Fine, let's do historical documentation. Turn the recording thing on again.

 I didn't turn it off.

⊢∙⊪⊪⊢ OK. So look, we're on a ship, we're hiding in a kind of cupboard, we're waiting for –

 No, no, that won't do, you cannot start with our

141

situation now. You should explain how we came to be here. You must begin with how we were travelling to Aushalawa-Moraa when we were kidnapped by the Kuraaa-Kalaaaa.

┣╾┿╢╌ That's not how they say their name. They say it more like 'Krakkiluks', I think.

⬤ *That is about as accurate as 'Morrors', I suppose, which is to say minimally.*

┣╾┿╢╌ All right, so like you said, we were travelling on the *Helen of Troy* to Aushalawa-Mo*raa* and we got kidnapped by the Kuraaa-Kalaaaa or the Krakkiluks or whatever you want to call them. There, OK? They said they'd throw us out of the airlock if the humans and Morrors didn't terraform Aushalawa-Mo*raa* back to how it was. But all those Morrors *live* there. And they – they –

⬤ *I have documented that part already. They ejected first Caaaaaaarl and then Aleece from the ship.*

┣╾┿╢╌ But then Josephine grabbed the Goldfish and hit that button and jumped out. She *jumped out*. She didn't say anything to either of us first, she didn't even *look*, she just got up and hit the button and jumped on the round hatch and it, like, spat her out, before anyone could do anything.

Everyone was freaked out by that.

● *I was indeed freeeeeeaked.*

┡╫┦ Lena sort of clenched her fists but didn't say anything. Dr Muldoon shouted and nearly toppled over again, and Lena and Mr Trommler had to hold her up.

But it wasn't just the humans who were freaked out: the Krakkiluks were too. Lady Slat-thingy was making noises a bit like hermit crabs make when they're distressed, and everything . . . stopped for a while. They'd been telling President Chakrabarty everything about what they were doing – they told him about Carl and about Alice. But they didn't say anything about Josephine.

● *It iiiis in their interests to appear in complete control of the situation. Josephine's actions disrupted that.*

┡╫┦ Dr Muldoon had already said she'd do what they wanted. And anyway they were kind of running out of kids to throw – I mean, what are they going to say to Earth or Aushalawa-Mo*raa*, 'Oops, all the kids are already dead, but you should do what we want anyway'?

So Lady Slat-thingy said she'd continue talking with President Chakrabarty later and then she pointed at Dr Muldoon and said, 'You will be privileged to enter the heart of the Grand Expanse.'

And Dr Muldoon's all: 'Uh . . .'

Then Lady Slat-thingy said, 'You will demonstrate your ability to shape a planet to your will, so that our colonists can learn.'

143

'Oh, God,' Dr Muldoon said. 'Do you need me for that? I mean, surely . . . the science of the Grand Expanse far surpasses that of Earth.'

'No,' Lady Slat-thingy said, and then stopped, and waggled her eyes like she was annoyed. 'That is to say YES,' she corrected herself loudly. 'You and your accelerated terraforming are an aberration. By some accident of the universe you have happened upon what should have been Krakkiluk knowledge.'

'You are an exceptional scientist, Valerie,' said Lena, with a little smile.

Dr Muldoon squared her shoulders. 'Look, I said yes to Aushalawa-Mo*raa*, to undoing what I did – but I can't help you conquer other planets. I'm not one for grand gestures, but well, there it is. Can't do it, so I suppose you'll have to kill me too.'

'No, Dr Muldoon!' I said.

'We're not going to kill you,' said Lady Slat-thingy, clanking some golden panels on her exoskeleton a bit like how parrots puff out their feathers. Like she was maybe offended. 'At least not without the proper procedures. What do you take us for?'

'People who just threw children into space without oxygen?' said Dr Muldoon, her voice getting kind of squawky now.

'But those were *spawn*,' said Lady Slat-thingy, confused, clanking some more. 'And we will of course throw the remainder if you give us cause.'

Dr Muldoon rubbed her face with her hands, and then she was sort of looking around like she was trying to think of some way to not have this happen. She said to us, 'I'm so sorry.'

I said, 'It's not your fault.'

And Dr Muldoon was going to insist that it was her fault, I think, but then Lady Slatty-slat poked Lena with a golden pincer and said, 'Do you need this person to assist your science?'

Poor Dr Muldoon was on the spot again, trying to decide whether she should say no, so Lena wouldn't be taken even further away from Earth than she already was, or yes, so at least the Krakkiluks would have a good reason to keep her alive.

'We work in completely different disciplines,' said Lena firmly, looking hard at Dr Muldoon.

'That's right,' said Dr Muldoon, looking a bit less upset. 'No need at all, absolutely fine without her. Goodbye, everyone.'

The Krakkiluks let Dr Muldoon *walk* off the bridge rather than carrying her. But there was a Krakkiluk soldier with a pincer on each of her shoulders.

Then Lady Slatty-thing said, 'Take this one and question him,' and pointed at Mr Trommler, who looked as if he was about to be sick.

'Papa?' whimpered Christa.

'You're making a *mistake*,' insisted Mr Trommler. But Tlag-li-Glig, the one covered in diamonds, scooped him up, and he and Krnk-ni-Plik, the one covered in spikes, went with them, and Lena *did* look worried after that.

A few minutes later I saw a tiny ship whisking past the window before it vanished into hyperspace and I guess Dr Muldoon was on it. I don't know where she is now.

I hope she's OK. And Lena. And Mr Trommler. And Christa – even she doesn't deserve all this. And Ormerod – I hope maybe *Helen* can feed her. And I hope *Helen*'s OK.

I hope everyone's OK.

There was this one thing. This thing I noticed before they took Lena away. And I think Dr Muldoon saw it too and that's why she looked a bit less unhappy. Lena was wearing these big, fancy gold earrings inside her helmet. And she isn't a fancy jewellery kind of person, and I didn't think she'd been wearing them before we'd been captured.

So anyway after that the one with the battle painted on his chest – at least, I think he was a he – picked me up and carried me off the bridge and into a long red corridor lined with doors. I could see you, Th*saaa*, dangling over one of the others' shoulders. But I got thrown into a cell by myself. The guy with the battle on his chest pulled my helmet off – really easily, too. And he walked out and shut the door, and there was a hissing noise and a funny smell. If I'd never been gassed unconscious before I guess I'd have been really scared, so it's a good thing I have.

⬤ *I too was rendered unconscious, and I believe at least one day, and perhaps more, must have passed before I awoke.*

⊢⊪⊩⊢ Waking up on the floor of the cell and remembering why I was there and what had happened to Carl was really bad. I kind of figured the Krakkiluks must be going to take

146

us back to the bridge and throw us out if they didn't get something else they wanted. But it was ages before anything happened, and I had nothing to do but look around. There wasn't anything in the cell, no windows, and nothing to lie down or sit on. I'm not sure if that was them being cruel to prisoners or if they just don't do furniture? The floor was kind of rubbery, though, so lying on it wasn't that uncomfortable. And there were lots of paintings.

⬛ *Their paintings are impressive but extremely sensationalist in style.*

In my chamber, the walls displayed what I think was a hero Kuraaa-Kalaaaa couple being praised and adored by members of other species.

⊢╫╫╫┈ In mine, there were lots of Krakkiluks playing musical instruments and then this big picture of a Krakkiluk who was dead and another Krakkiluk was like bending over the dead one and waving their arms.

And there was a sort of fountainy thing and a drain in the floor so you could have a drink or go to the loo, though it would be embarrassing and weird. After a while I tried to get interested in the paintings because, well, it is interesting, so I thought, Ooh, look, I'd have thought their blood would be blue, like lobsters', but it's yellow, which is more like beetles. But, I couldn't get all that into it. I mean, *Carl*. And Mum and Dad . . .

Oh, I was there such a long time all by myself. It was so bad. Do I have to keep talking about it?

● *No, I will use a Paralashath here to convey your feelings.*

⊢⊪⊢ Huh. OK. So I was there for ages and I tried to go back to sleep on the floor because everything was so awful and even the dead Krakkiluk in the picture was making me upset.

Then I heard all this noise outside: the Krakkiluks tramping up and down and clattering at each other. And then the door opened and two came in – I think they were another married couple, they all seem to go around like that together. One of them was painted shiny black like an oil slick, and the other was painted with different skies in different weathers, like sunsets and moons and clouds.

They brought me some food, human food from the *Helen*; I guess that was easier than giving us whatever they eat and finding it was poisonous for us. Anyway instead of taking me back to the bridge they *talked* to me, which was weird because they don't normally talk to spawn. They seemed to think it was weird too; they kept looking at each other and clacking their armour and sometimes they held pincers or patted each other, like: 'I know it's weird talking to this spawn, but hang in there, we can get through this.'

But they didn't say that, at least not in English. They asked me lots of questions about Earth and was it true that the seas were warm. And I said they were a lot colder than they used to be because of the Morrors coming and freezing the planet, because I got the feeling it wasn't a good idea to say yes.

But mostly, whatever they asked, I said, 'I'm sorry, I'm just a spawn, I don't know anything.'

And then they started asking about Morrors and what makes them disappear.

'I'm just a spawn,' I said. 'I'm only nine. Nine-year-old spawn are total idiots.'

And they said, 'But you are capable of speech. Human spawn mature improperly quickly. You must have acquired some information along with language.'

'Well, Morrors *can* disappear,' I said. 'I know that. Everyone knows that. But I don't know how they do it because I'm just spawn. No one tells spawn anything.'

And you know what, they clearly found talking to me so unpleasant they actually believed me. And then they went and I was by myself again.

Then there's this voice right by my ear going: '*Nooooooooel*, I am here.'

⬤ *I don't sound like that.*

┣╫╫╫┤ Oh, sorry.

⬤ *You made a very peculiar noise, certainly.*

┣╫╫╫┤ I can't see that shimmer in the air Alice talks about being able to see, but I could feel the cold of your invisibility gown. You didn't take it off.

You said, '*Nooooeel*, be quick, come closer!' And then you

149

threw the invisibility gown over my head.

⬤ *I had folded my amlaa-vel-esh very small, under my kilt. I'd had no opportunity to put it on when the Kuraaa-Kalaaaa seized me, and could not tell anyone I had it. In my cell I was made unconscious before I could use it. But when at last I awakened, I had my chance. I was not sure if I was being watched, but I hoped I was, and I retreated into a corner and threw on the amlaa-vel-esh as swiftly as possible, so it would appear as if I had ceased to be in the room at all. If they had invisibility technology at a standard matching ours, of course my plan would fail, but they had confessed that in the matter of terraforming they were behind humans, so I was hopeful.*

It was a greeeeeeeeeeeeeeeeee-ehhh-eeeeeaaaat relief to be inside the amlaa-vel-esh. This ship is so hot and moist. Even wrapped in a light cooling cloak, it had been scarcely bearable. The air in the cell had been cooled a little for Morror needs – survivable, but not comfortable. I spread my limbs within the amlaa-vel-esh and tried to soak in its cool.

I had not loooong to wait. In due course the Kuraaa-Kalaaa did come, and opened the door to investigate how their prisoner had vanished.

While the door stood open, I gathered the amlaa-vel-esh as tight around me as I could, and slipped through it. Here, it was an advantage that they are soooooooo much larger than we are. Outside the cell, I ventured down the red passageway. The Kuraaa-Kalaaaa were, of course, not using their translator boxes to speak among themselves and they neither change colour like Morrors nor move their faces, so their intentions were not easy to understand – however, they do gesture somewhat like humans.

 Th*saaa*, they are *nothing like* humans. They are like lobsters and *parrots*. I wouldn't say that about *your* species.

 Very well, I apologise.
However, they do express agitation like humans, with waving of the arms. They were alarmed by my disappearance and anxious to learn where I had gone. Some of them came and went, and spoke into their devices. But two – the shiny black one and the one painted with clouds – approached Noel's cell; I knew because I had seen them place him inside the room when we were brought to the prison.
So when they entered Noel's cell, I followed them.

 I'd never been under an invisibility gown before. You can see through it from the inside, but everything looks – I don't know how to put it – almost *more* bright and detailed than normal, but sort of as if it's floating and not real. And maybe slightly purple?

 No.

├┤├╫┼├ And of course I could also see you –

⬤ **Not 'you'. You are not talking to me. You are talking to the historians of the future.**

├┤├╫┼├ All right, fine. I could see Th*saaa* – at least, their tentacles, wrapped around my shoulders, flickering all light green and pink, but we were squashed so close together I couldn't see their face. It was also *very* uncomfortable under there, because the gown was really, really cold on my face and Th*saaa* was burning hot against my back.

It didn't *feel* like we were invisible, it felt like we were having a weird hug in a freezing cold bag in the middle of the room for no reason.

'We must wait,' Th*saaa* said.

It felt like we were sitting there for ages, all hot and cold and tangled up. The fountainy thing kept trickling away and I wished I'd used it earlier. Obviously it was too late now.

Then the Krakkiluks did come back and discovered I'd disappeared too. And yeah, to be fair, they did wave their arms around a bit.

'Crunch, clak, crunch!' went the one with the clouds.

'Crackle, splat, clop!' went the one in shiny black. I mean, not really, it just sounded a bit like that. I guess I'm being kinda rude. But they did *kidnap* us, so . . .

The door was still open. We shuffled and tripped towards it and nearly fell over each other inside the cloak and it felt like we were the most obvious thing on a ship full of people covered in spikes and diamonds, but the Krakkiluks didn't see us even as we waddled right past their legs and out into the corridor.

And for a moment I was all like, 'Yay we've escaped!' and then I was like, 'Oh, no we haven't.' Because we were still on that prison-corridor, and still on an alien ship in the middle of nowhere. We couldn't even get out of the corridor because it was filled with Krakkiluks and the door was shut.

Then, I guess giving up on finding us, one of the soldiers laid a claw on a panel beside the door, which slid open, and all the Krakkiluks started filing out.

And we went after them.

As the last Krakkiluk skittered through, the door slid down and there was, like, not even a foot of space left when Th*saaa* hurled themself through, dragging me in a tangle of tentacles, and the door shut and there we were on the floor on the other side, almost under the feet of the departing Krakkiluks.

We were in . . . well, a wider corridor. But this one had some windows, at least. I could see the golden planet. I wanted to go and look at it, like I'd maybe be able to see Carl and Alice and Josephine down there, somehow OK.

'OK,' I said. 'Well. Here we are. Now what are we going to do?'

'We must try to seize the *Helen* and escape,' said Th*saaa*.

11

So, we had no duct tape, though arguably that was not as bad as the fact we had no first aid kit and definitely not as bad as the fact we had no spaceship. The Goldfish had said we were about three miles from land, and we were absolutely in no condition to swim that far.

What we *did* have, once we managed to break Carl's helmet into shards, was a kind of knife.

'We need to cut this leaf away from the stem,' I said. 'Then we'll have a raft.' Although by 'we' I really meant 'Josephine'.

'I don't think it's my *turn* to go back in the water,' Josephine said.

'You signed up for all the underwater jobs when you got gills,' said Carl.

'I didn't sign up for wriggling pink things,' complained Josephine. But she slid into the water with her ceramic-shard knife, and ducked under the leaf. Carl and I lay back to soak up the possibly carcinogenic sunshine and felt the leaf bobbing as she worked. The sky above me was pale jade, the water deep emerald. The sun was light blue. I lay on the leaf, wondering if I might have broken a bone or two in my foot when I hit the sea. It sort of definitely felt like it. Apart from the whisper of the waves and the occasional splash of the wriggly pink things, it was utterly silent. It was kind of peaceful. In fact, it was *very* peaceful, except for how we had to keep an eye out in case any enormous sea monsters showed up to eat us, or, alternatively, in case someone whooshed along in a boat or a spaceship in order to rescue us.

Neither of those things happened.

At last Josephine pulled herself back on to the leaf. 'There,' she gasped, and she coughed a little, then leaned over and, rather disgustingly, ejected all the water she'd just breathed from her gills. I managed to limit myself to yelping quietly and adding a paragraph to the Outraged Letter about Dr Muldoon's behaviour I was writing in my head.

'My *hair*,' she moaned, plucking a few strands of wet goo from it. She gave up, pulled her hair out of the soaked and mangled braids, and tied it back with a torn-off length of lining from the collar of her spacesuit.

I found this oddly encouraging. She looked like a revolutionary or a pirate queen or, that is to say, like my friend.

'There,' she said. 'A raft.'

Carl and I cheered raggedly.

'Let's go, kids!' chirruped the Goldfish. I don't think there was any way we were up to making a sail or oars, even if there was a way to do it from the materials available. In the end we had to just hold on to the Goldfish's cable while the Goldfish towed us towards land.

'At least we got stuck on a warm planet this time,' said

Carl drowsily, spreadeagled and dripping in the sunlight.

'And there's oxygen!' said Josephine.

I kept quiet. There was something worrying me about that, but there wasn't anything we could do about it – or if there was, at the very least we'd have to get out of the sea first, so there wasn't any point worrying anyone else. In any case, I might be wrong.

We weren't the only living creatures out on that floating leafscape. There were the buzzing blue things, and little gold creatures about two feet long, which went hopping from leaf to leaf on three pairs of flippers to nibble with sharp green beaks at the puffballs, while others lay basking in heaps in the sun, their slick fur or feathers (or maybe something in between) drying to a soft amber fuzz. They didn't seem at all afraid of us.

'Maybe we can eat them,' Carl said.

I wished he hadn't, because I hadn't noticed being hungry before that. I'd been thinking how cute the golden creatures were, but now they did look temptingly edible.

'Probably poisonous,' said Josephine.

The land rose slowly on to the horizon. The puffball plants grew thicker and thicker in the water, until the Goldfish couldn't tow us any further. So we had to leave our leaf-raft behind and make our way from lily pad to lily pad on foot for the last half-mile.

The gravity was a little lower than on Earth, I thought, but not as low as on Mars. I wished it had been; we'd have been on dry land in a few effortless leaps. As it was, we were panting and sweating by the time we stepped off the last lily pad on to the shore.

At once, I felt ten times as exposed as I had on our peaceful little leaf on the water. We had no way of knowing who, if anyone, lived on this land, but we were *trespassing*. We were uninvited and almost helpless and maybe we were going to get in terrible trouble.

For the moment though, no one came charging over the hill to either kill us or ask to see our identity papers.

'So, those lobster guys,' said Carl. 'This is their planet, right?'

'They talked about an "Expanse", but I think they meant an empire,' said Josephine. 'They'd claimed Aushalawa-Mo*raa*. They've got lots of planets.'

But if it wasn't *the* Krakkiluk planet that still meant it was probably *a* Krakkiluk planet.

'It's better than asphyxiating in space!' exclaimed Josephine, as if she'd been accused of something.

'No one's saying it's not, Jo,' Carl said.

'Earth will find us,' said Josephine. 'Or Aushalawa-Mo*raa*; the Morrors have more experience with hyperspace. If it's possible to send a transmission through, it *must* be possible to pinpoint where it's coming from. They'll be working on that now. And Lena. We just have to stay alive.'

I thought again about the thing that was worrying me about the air, and didn't say anything.

We trudged up the beach. The sand and pebbles were just ordinary, like you might get on Earth, and the beach rose like any other up to a shallow scarp. But a thick carpet of red and orange egg-shaped blobs was growing on the scarp, and that wasn't Earth-like at all. We climbed up on to it and the blobs squished a bit underfoot, like rubber, but didn't burst. Further back from the water some of them had little holes at the top, and some of them opened out into funnels like tiny vases. And ahead there were much bigger funnels, of deep red and bright gold, as tall as trees.

We flopped down in the shade of one of those funnels and lay there in a heap for a while.

Our spacesuits were far too hot by now. Josephine was the first person who could summon the energy to move; she began hacking the sleeves of her suit off with the ceramic shard from the helmet and cut her neckline a bit lower. She passed me the blade when she was done and I did the same and then passed it on to Carl.

'Oh, dear,' I said, looking at the array of scorches and bruises we'd just revealed.

'Duct tape,' mourned Josephine.

'I'm so thirsty,' said Carl.

'The seawater isn't salt,' I said. 'But I don't think we should go ahead and drink it,' I added, thinking of how nasty it tasted and also how much yellow stuff the wriggly pink things were spraying into it.

'We have to filter and boil it,' said Josephine.

Carl and I groaned, because that was plainly going to be a real pain in the neck.

'OK, helmet-as-cooking-pot, that part's obvious,' said Carl.

We used his helmet, seeing as we'd already smashed the ceramic visor out of it. We stripped out the lining and the micro-circuitry as best we could and filled it with water. Then we looked for firewood, which was difficult because none of the plants we found seemed to produce anything as basic as a *stick*. But some of the funnel things were dead and dried out and broke into flakes when we poked them.

Which left the matter of how to actually set them on fire.

'If I had my warning and defence unit . . .' mused the Goldfish, darkly.

'Well you *don't*,' said Carl, irritated.

'It's OK,' said Josephine. 'We can use the sun.'

We made a little hearth of stones on the beach and piled the dried-out flakes inside. Josephine angled one of the helmets that was still intact until a bright speck of focused sunlight appeared on the kindling.

I didn't think this would work. But the next second there was a flash and a huge plume of fire burst out of nowhere and if we hadn't been on the beach I think we'd have started an ecosystem-wrecking inferno right there. As it was, the only really flammable stuff about was *us*, so we screamed and fell over and threw ourselves into the waves.

'Eyebrows?' Carl was saying urgently. 'Have I still got eyebrows?'

We established that no, no one had quite as much hair

as they used to, we grieved for its loss, and we went back to look at the blackened wreckage.

'Right,' said Josephine. 'So, there's a *lot* of oxygen on this planet.'

'Better than the other way round,' said Carl.

'Actually . . .' I said, and stopped. The others looked at me.

'What?' said Carl.

'Too much oxygen is . . . kind of . . . bad,' I said.

There was another pause.

'How bad,' said Josephine, her voice flat.

I twisted my hands together. In other circumstances getting the chance to tell Josephine something scientific that she didn't know might have been kind of fun, but in this case I wished she'd looked up 'oxygen toxicity' the last time she'd happened to be bored. But she wasn't the one who wanted to be a doctor.

'Well . . . it's just that sometimes when people have hypothermia and frostbite, you can treat them with high levels of oxygen,' I began. 'But you have to be careful, and give them breaks with normal air, because things can happen. Though it depends on how high the oxygen levels *are*, and the air pressure . . .'

'How *bad*,' repeated Josephine.

Somewhat ironically in the circumstances, I took a deep breath. 'Disorientation . . . breathing difficulties leading to pneumonia . . .'

'Spasmodic vomiting, drowsiness,' chimed in the Goldfish, helpfully.

'Neurological damage affecting vision and balance, and with prolonged exposure, eventually . . .'

'*Death*. God, we get it. Eventually: death!' exploded Josephine. She sat down on the ground, and stared straight ahead. 'How soon?' she asked quietly.

'Oh, I think we should be fine! For at least . . . four days?' I said, as positively as I could.

'Gosh, Alice, you've been studying hard,' said the Goldfish after another pause, and scattered a spray of holographic golden sparkles over me.

'Well, I try,' I said dolefully.

'OK, so we've got to get off this planet,' said Carl.

Josephine nodded jerkily, not looking at either of us. 'We've got to find help,' she said in a small voice.

The Goldfish towed us on our leaf-raft up into the depths of the vase-forest.

We'd limped along the shoreline until we'd come to the slow, nameless river, uncrossably huge and electric green under the crimson forest. On the far bank, the funnels spread as far as the eye could see, with a complete lack of encouraging things like houses and multistorey car parks to disturb their peace.

'There *must* be settlements on the river,' Josephine said, as we floated along. 'Civilisations always build close to water.'

'What if we landed on a desert island?' said Carl idly.

'Oh shut up!' I moaned. 'And anyway, it's a continent, I could see that much when we were falling.'

Carl nodded, but he didn't have to point out that that might take care of the 'island' but didn't address the 'deserted' part of the issue.

At least we weren't thirsty any more. There were tiny pools of freshwater in the funnels – at first we only dared to lick drops from our fingertips, and it tasted a little odd, kind of rubbery, but not obviously lethal. So we plucked tea-cup-sized funnels – warily, in case this caused the plant to come to vengeful life and attack us. It didn't, so we drank, first in cautious little sips with pauses to see if anyone died, and then with desperate abandon.

'I think maybe these are just one underground plant?' Josephine said, looking a little bit more like her old self. 'Or maybe more than one, but I think all the funnels are sucking water and sunlight down to one big root system . . .' she trailed off. 'This planet belongs to a culture with spaceships,' she announced abruptly. 'It *has* to be unlikely that there's no way off it.'

'I know,' I said. 'We'll find the spaceships. There was a satellite, at least; I saw it, up there.'

Carl was trying to angle away the dubious expression he was making so Josephine wouldn't see it, but she did anyway, or maybe she sensed it.

'Yes, the spaceships may belong to the same species of people that threw us out of a spaceship in the first place,' she said with exaggerated patience. 'But we have only met a handful of Krakkiluks. It would be illogical to assume we know what all of them are like.'

162

'Yes. Illogical,' agreed Carl, this time trying to go for no expression at all.

'And there might be *other* people. If the Krakkiluks aren't using this planet to live on and they aren't using it to grow Takwuk, maybe they're using it for *labour*. In which case the locals are our natural allies! The enemy of my enemy is my friend!'

But so far there was no visible sign of anyone else using it for anything, unless you counted the flippery gold creatures basking on the floating leaves. They were having a great time.

The forest was not silent: the funnels sang in the wind like a choir of ghosts, and the creatures nestling in their ledges or gliding on double wings across the river chittered and hooted. On the banks the funnels spread wide and low, casting crimson shade over the water. The landscape changed as we floated on. Hills heaped high on either flank of the river, and then grey arches emerged from the ground amid the spreading funnels.

'*Architecture?*' muttered Josephine eagerly.

But it was soon obvious the arches hadn't been made by people. They supported no roofs or roads or waterways. They were of all sizes, some dried-out silver, some tinged with living red, though as we floated on they grew larger and larger, serpent-like lengths piling up on each other in crazy loops and spirals before burrowing into the earth again. And as the river narrowed and turned they cascaded down a bank and reared in tangles over its course.

'Roots!' I realised. 'Like you said,' because there were red and gold buds on the arches' sides, opening here and there into more funnels, some spreading out towards the sky like those that rose from the earth, some hanging down like bells. And creatures scampered and swung and dangled from the loops and warbled within the funnels.

'If you're stuck in a jungle,' said Carl, 'you can tell what's safe to eat by watching what the monkeys eat. If you're in a jungle *with* monkeys.'

'We'd better not eat *anything*,' I said gloomily. 'Poisoning can kill you a lot faster than starvation.'

'Hey, kids,' said the Goldfish suddenly, in an unusually hushed voice, stopping in its flight. 'Looks like we found somebody!'

A huge, furry face, plum-coloured and as large as the wheel of a car, was watching us from above a loop of silver-grey root. It was round and flat as a dish, except for a snub snout right between its two pairs of round black eyes. Apart from the number of eyes, and the colour, and the long, snake-like neck – OK, apart from lots of things – it reminded me of a sloth's face; it had the same sleepily placid look.

'I think you should say hi,' suggested the Goldfish brightly.

'I guess,' said Josephine faintly, and the Goldfish towed us towards the bank.

Two more mulberry-purple faces suddenly appeared among the tangle of vegetation and blinked at us. *Probably*

164

two different creatures, not one with three heads, I told myself, biting the inside of my cheek.

Josephine set her jaw and stepped from the leaf to the bank. Carl and I went after her, not liking to seem wimpy.

'Hi,' I said, hoping that didn't sound like, 'Your mother is ugly and I would enjoy being slaughtered now,' in their language.

We stood there feeling scared and silly. First contact is incredibly socially awkward.

'Wuuuurgh,' responded the first creature affably, in a deep, rumbling bass.

'Wuuuurrgh!' agreed its companions, in unison.

'WURRRGH!!!!' volunteered Carl, gamely, and at enormous volume.

Here the conversation ground to a halt. The aliens looked mildly startled, and snaked their necks around, and continued staring at us while we stared back.

'So, uh, yeah, someone else say something,' said Carl.

'We were hoping you might have a hyperspace-capable ship,' said Josephine helplessly.

One of the aliens (though, of course, really we were the aliens), waddled down the bank to get a closer look at us, revealing a large, shaggy, egg-shaped body the size of an elephant's. Oddly, it moved on four short but slender legs. Everything else I'd seen here had six. We flinched together on instinct – it was *very* large, and coming *very* close. When it reached us it put its face close to my chest and sniffed, started back in surprise, then sniffed the others.

'I think these are maybe . . . animals, not people?' Carl said, as the creature ran its face curiously over his chest.

'How are we going to know?' I asked.

'People don't *sniff* you,' said Carl. 'That's just basic.'

'They might. For all we know that's *polite* around here,' I said.

But the alien appeared to lose interest in us. It bent its neck to lap at the river, then turned and galloped up the bank to join its friends and disappeared among the loops of root.

'Come on!' said Josephine, charging after it. So we followed, because at least the creatures hadn't tried to hurt us and they were the first things that had interacted with us in any way. We scrambled up the bank and through the coils of the roots, until the tangles of grey stem got so thick we had to start climbing, from loop to loop, then walk along the spine of a root that rose as high as a cathedral, like a bridge to nowhere in the air.

From up here, we could see the land beyond. The towering arches of wild root thinned out into lower, more sporadic loops, and between them spread a moorland carpeted with living gold velvet, something like moss and dotted with blue, bead-like flowers. And there were hundreds of the huge purple creatures roaming, bending their necks to eat the blue flowers. They were oddly graceless– lumbering on stalk-like legs, so disproportionate to their bulk.

'They're animals,' said Carl, sighing. 'Bison. That kind of thing.'

I felt this was probably true, but what if it wasn't? Maybe the people here were perfectly capable of going to work or fighting wars or watching cat videos, but just happened to like standing around in a field and eating flowers more. And if so, maybe they had a point. Or then again, maybe the golden flipper things that lived on the giant leaf pads were the people, or the blue buzzing things. Maybe the *funnels* were people, communicating with each other by the wind ringing through their chambers, though I hoped they weren't, given that we'd picked and *drunk* a few of the little ones.

I wondered if the Morrors had had any hilarious misunderstandings where they turned up on Earth and tried to explain to sheep or cars that they were colonising the planet, but they'd been scanning our communications for a long time before they actually landed, so probably not.

'We have to be sure,' said Josephine.

Getting down to the ground was even more difficult than climbing up into the roots in the first place, but the purple creatures didn't seem to be going anywhere in a hurry, so we clambered around until we came to a tall funnel sprouting those ledges. These didn't bear our weight as well as we'd hoped, but we at least hit the ground more gently than we might have done and the golden moss turned out to be thick and soft.

The nearest creatures raised their heads and looked at us. We picked ourselves up, wincing, and wandered about saying hello and feeling embarrassed.

'This is useless,' said Carl. 'We're trying to make friends with, like, wildebeest.'

'Maybe there aren't people. Maybe the Krakkiluks just use this place for tourism,' I said, before I could stop myself. Josephine grimaced.

I pretended I hadn't said anything. 'Alice,' I said to the nearest alien, pointing at myself. '*Human.* You?'

'Wurrrh,' the alien replied.

'US – FROM – UP THERE!' bellowed Carl, pantomiming appropriately, on the off-chance the creatures would stop grazing and say, 'Oh, sorry, in that case come this way to our conveniently located government headquarters/space port.'

But they didn't do that. Instead, whether because Carl had startled them or because they'd been going to do it anyway, they all began to move. They broke into a simultaneous charge which shook the earth. And wherever they'd decided they were going, we were in their way.

So, as you would, we screamed and threw ourselves out of the way, which would have been fine if it was only one enormous charging creature instead of hundreds. The nearest creature did make an effort not to step on us but the one *behind* it didn't seem to notice us at all. We dived out of its path only to stumble into a collision course with another, and the faster we had to dodge the harder it was to look where we were going and I tripped over a tussock of the golden moss and fell right under the feet of another charging beast –

There was a sound like a million sheets being shaken open in the wind and a down-draft of air blasted over me. I'd curled my arms over my head on instinct; I lowered them to see the creature skimming into an impossible leap from which it *wasn't coming down.* All around us, purple wings dappled with amber were unfolding from the creatures' sides. Their funny little legs tucked under their bodies and they rose as one, as elegant in flight as they'd been clumsy on the ground, their long, silly necks swanlike, their wings beating powerfully at first then slowing as they caught the winds and were free to glide.

'*Wurrrrgh!*' they cried, all that huge herd, but it sounded like singing now. They rose in deep, droning harmony, and the sky rang.

For a moment we forgot that we were stranded and breathing poisonous air and that we'd nearly been trampled to death. We just sat on the golden moss and watched them. They circled in lazy loops over the meadows, chanting their enormous song, and soared away beyond the golden hills. I wished, suddenly, that I'd touched one, that I knew whether the mulberry pelts were as soft as they looked.

'Oh, Noel would love it here,' said Carl, and then flinched and lowered his eyes from the sky and the moment was emphatically over.

'We'll find a way off this planet,' I said. 'We'll find him. And Th*saaa.*'

'Yeah, that's nice,' said Carl bleakly. 'Except odds are

good they've thrown him out the ship by now.'

'Dr Muldoon said she'd do what the Krakkiluks wanted,' I said.

'Did she?' asked Carl. Because of course, he hadn't been around for that. 'But, uh, I'm noticing *you're not on that spaceship*, Alice, so I guess they didn't listen too hard.'

'They have no leverage at all if they dispense with all their hostages,' said Josephine. 'And they have only two human children left.'

Carl shook his head and pulled clumps of the golden moss out of the ground and I hoped that it wasn't either a) people or b) poisonous.

'The river curves that way, kids,' said the Goldfish, pointing with its nose towards the hills the purple creatures had vanished over.

So we headed on instead of climbing back through the roots. The slopes of the hills were gentle and the moss was pleasant to walk on at first, but after a while it got kind of exhausting, like trudging through snow; it soaked up the energy you put into each step and didn't bounce any of it back, and the blue sunlight got hotter and hotter and my burns and bruises began to ache and sting again.

'*Why* didn't they make you strong enough to *carry* people?' I moaned to the Goldfish, which was a mistake, because of course it *told* me.

'. . . So can you work out *how much* it would have cost to build a higher load-bearing capacity into my manufacturing process?' it was still chattering, a good fifteen minutes later.

At last, we reached the crest of the hill. 'Oh!' said Josephine.

The hills broke away before us into steep cliffs over the river. Standing astride the gorge, carved from russet stone, was an immense statue of something – no, *somebody* – a bit like a fruit bat and a bit like a gibbon, wings expanded and teeth bared. And though whatever it had once held in two of its four hands had fallen away with time, the other two still grasped what were very clearly swords.

It stood guard over a city of arches and towers.

'There *are* people!' breathed Josephine.

12

⬛ *Eeeee. Be quiet. I can hear them coming.*

〜 I don't hear anything.

⬛ *There! Aaah . . . No. You are right – I am sorry. I thought – I am so hooooooottt.*

〜 Th*saaa*? Th*saaa*, are you all right? OK, I'm going to take this thing off.

⬛ *No, no. It is not safe. I am well.*

〜 I'm heating the gown up too much. I don't like your colours. It's fine, they don't know to look here. I don't like your colours. There, you can have it. Oh, it's weird how now I can't see you.

Does that feel better?

⬛ *Yeeeees. A little. This amlaa-vel-esh has been overtaxed.*

〜 It's going to be OK. We're going to make it off this ship real soon.

■ *Keep going. You must finish your account.*

⊢╫┼ Are you sure? Maybe you should rest for a bit.

■ *I'll feel better – if I can think of something other than how hot I am.*

⊢╫┼ OK. If it helps. So where was I?

■ *After . . . after we escaped the prison. We found we were in a wider passage – red, with windows to the stars. I said, we must seize the* Helen *. . .*

⊢╫┼ Yeah. That's right.

'We can't *just* seize the *Helen*,' I said, like that was so easy. 'We've got to rescue the others too.'

Th*saaa* said, 'I do not think the disappearing trick will work again.'

And yeah, they weren't going to keep tramping into prisoners' cells if that always ended up with the prisoners vanishing.

'We've got to try,' I said.

But we didn't know where the others were. And we had only the vaguest idea of where the *Helen* was: down lots of floors and shut in the hangar.

The corridor we were in was kind of a tube . . . I mean, the floor was curved, a bit like the tunnels of an ants' nest. So that would have been cool, except everything was so red and humid it was also a bit like being inside something's guts or veins, which was kind of gross. Anyway, I guess if you've got that many feet and they're all pointy, you don't need the floor to be flat, and everything was kind of nubbly, like car tyres, I guess so the Krakkiluks didn't slip. Except there was a flat disc set into the floor by the door we'd come through, and there was a hole the same size in the ceiling above it, so I reckoned that was another lift.

'Lena *can't* be that far away,' I said. 'You'd put all your prison cells together, wouldn't you? Unless you had loads and loads of prisoners – but it doesn't seem like they do? I don't think there's anyone else back in *that* bit.' And I pointed at the door we'd slipped through.

Th*saaa* looked at the lift. 'They *maaaaaaay* be above or below, perhaps.'

Then two Krakkiluks came back and we had to shut up and concentrate on not getting stepped on. They were holding gadgets – like maybe they were scanning for clues of something. And then another two Krakkiluks came along and they all clanked around and made crunching noises that maybe meant, 'Where have those spawn prisoners gone?' and, 'I don't know, do you think we'll get in trouble? Let's kill them very hard when we find them.'

Or maybe they were saying, 'Who cares, they're just spawn, it doesn't matter where they are,' and, 'You're right, I was overreacting, let's go and relax.'

That's what I hoped they meant.

So whether they were going to relax or not, the Krakkiluks

did go away. The cloudy one and the shiny black one touched a panel on the wall and stood on the lift and rose up into the ceiling. The others went clomping away along the passage, and we pressed as close against the round wall as we could. The way they each had *four* feet, stamping past us, kept making me feel as though there were twice as many Krakkiluks as there actually were, which was not a great feeling.

We couldn't hang out against the wall forever, so we went and looked at the lift, and at the panel that Shiny had touched, and we were worried about even trying because maybe it would tell the ship where we were. But eventually Th*saaa* reached up a tentacle and touched it.

Nothing happened.

'Maybe it recognises Krakkiluk DNA,' I said. 'Or, you know, what they have instead of DNA because maybe it's something different.'

So that was bad, because it looked like we were stuck on that floor. We couldn't go back or up or down or sideways, so we had to go forwards. And so we were back to shuffling along together and I fell over Th*saaa*'s skirts and Th*saaa* fell over me and basically we were like the world's worst pantomime horse. The amlaa-vel-esh is very stretchy and clingy, so one Morror can move in it easily. But one Morror and one human: not so much.

So we kept on picking ourselves up and falling over again and bumped and tripped and got annoyed with each other all along the corridor until we caught up with the Krakkiluks who were finishing up a crunchy conversation in an open doorway.

175

And even though we didn't want to be close to them it was just as well, or we wouldn't have been able to duck through under their legs and we wouldn't have got out of that corridor at all.

The Krakkiluks finished talking and clumped ahead on to another lift-disc. The doors we'd come through slid shut, leaving us alone in a kind of lobby with no windows.

'So, I guess we'll try to find the *Helen* first,' I said. Because we couldn't go back now.

We also couldn't use the lift, but there was an open door into another passage. And that led to this huge semicircular room – like, three times as big as my parents' whole cinema – with lots of pipes and big tanks in it. And it was all steamy and red like everywhere else and it absolutely *stank*. Like, *wow*, I thought I was going to throw up. It was kind of like rotting fish and filthy feet but a whole lot *worse*. And down below, an open vat of grey-black sludge was bubbling and pipes coiled up and led down to a big round tank of water on the other side of the space that was nearly clean but not quite, yet.

'*Uuuuuuchhh*,' went Th*saaa*.

'What *is* this?' I said.

'Suuuurely the sewage works,' Th*saaa* moaned. 'But what are they *eating* to *account* for this?'

I felt a bit offended that the Krakkiluks kept their prisoners next to their poo. I know when people are throwing people out of airlocks already, nothing they do that's *less* bad than that should really matter. But I don't know, it still seemed really rude.

But there were a couple of good things about the sewage

works. One was that I guess the Krakkiluks didn't like it there much either. So it was nearly empty, just a couple of workers all the way down at the bottom, one cleaning out an empty tank while the other was mending a bit of piping. They were the only Krakkiluks I'd seen so far wearing actual clothes, sort of plastic-looking capes to protect their shells from anything icky. Also, it was noisy, because of the pipes and the horrible squelching and plopping noises from the tanks, so we could talk quietly to each other and not be heard.

And another good thing about the sewage place was that it was so big; it was like four floors deep (we were on the highest level) with a walkway at each level running around the space. So we could maybe get somewhere else and not just go round and round the same floor forever after all.

I couldn't see *how* you could get from one level to another at first. Then one of the Krakkiluk workers went over to this long strip of heavy diamond mesh that ran vertically from floor to floor, and scuttled up it in no time at all. It stood there in mid-air, hanging on with four legs with both upper arms free to work on another bit of piping. And then I realised that there were lots of these strips and of course they were *ladders.*

But, ladders that were not built for people who only have two arms and two legs and are four foot three and a half and jammed under an invisibility gown with their Morror friend. The gaps between the joints were as big as me.

'*Weeela splaflak!*' said Th*saaa*.

'Yeah, I know,' I sighed.

We watched the two Krakkiluks working. The one on the

177

ladder swung off on to the second level and clattered around to check a panel on one of the walls that maybe said, 'The sewage plant is working fine, time for a break,' or, 'You are not mending those pipes fast enough, work faster,' but hopefully not, 'Haven't you noticed those alien spawn watching you from over there?'

'We can't climb down if we're both in this,' I whispered, plucking at the freezing folds of the invisibility gown.

'No,' said Th*saaa*. 'You must wear it,' they added bravely, after a pause.

'That's really nice of you,' I said. 'But you're used to wearing it – I'd get all tangled up in it and fall off. And anyway, what if you go bright yellow or something? You'd show up too much.'

'I have more control than *thaaat*,' said Th*saaa*, huffily, but didn't press it. So we bump-tripped round to the furthest ladder from either of the Krakkiluks and I slipped out of the gown and stood there completely visible to anyone who happened to look over, although at least there were these big coils of piping in the way.

I stepped out on to the ladder. That was OK. Getting down to the next diamond shape was not so good. I had to sort of like sidle down, hanging on to the sides of the diamond, until I'm like crouching with my bum hanging out into space right over the horrible vats of sludge, and then I had to sort of slide my feet diagonally down one side of the next diamond, and then do it all over again.

A flutter of cold air told me Th*saaa* was still climbing beside me, otherwise it felt as if I was completely alone. I was sure they were climbing slowly on purpose to stay next to me, because it had to be easier for them with all those long tentacles. Carl would be better at this than me, I thought. He's taller, which would help, but he also likes climbing things more than I do and he is better at just *doing* things rather than thinking about all the ways they can go wrong.

We'd just cleared the third level, when one of those round doors opened up and Krnk-ni-Plik and Tlag-li-Glig clanked through on to the second level. As in, right below us and right opposite us.

'Aaaah!' cried Th*saaa*, very softly, and there was a chilly whoosh as they lunged sideways and sort of hugged me in their tentacles, wrapping me up in folds of amlaa-vel-esh as best they could, and we both froze. I almost *literally* froze, actually – I couldn't feel the warmth of Th*saaa*'s body through the amlaa-vel-esh from the outside, just the cold, cold, invisible fabric.

'Clunk! Crack! Splunk!' said Krnk-ni-Plik and the two worker Krakkiluks came to attention, bowed, and then hugged each other.

'Splack, clap, slop,' they said apologetically. I buried my face into Th*saaa*'s freezing invisible shoulder and clenched my teeth to stop them chattering.

I knew that I was only *part* invisible and if the Krakkiluks looked they'd see my head and maybe one hand and half a leg floating together by the ladder.

Tlag-li-Glig and Krnk-ni-Plik started patrolling round the walkway. I mean, *maybe* this was just something they did every day, but they were ninety-nine per cent definitely *looking* for us, and then Tlag-li-Glig came round to *our ladder.* If he started climbing up, if he even *looked* up . . .

He started climbing downwards, which was good, except my fingers were going numb and I started to worry about falling on his head, and meanwhile Krnk-ni-Plik swung on to a ladder across on the other side of the semicircle, and she *was* climbing up.

Krnk-ni-Plik investigated the third and fourth level and Tlag-li-Glig tramped around on the ground, and the sewage-worker Krakkiluks waggled their eyes anxiously, and I tried not to move my head and got colder and colder and colder.

And then they went. The sewage-worker Krakkiluks seemed almost as relieved as we were.

Then I couldn't hold on to the ladder any more and fell off.

It felt like I had a very, very long time to watch the vat of sludge coming closer and think about drowning in alien poo, and then Th*saaa* whipped an invisible tentacle around my wrist and caught me.

Hanging on to something invisible is really, really weird.

Also, I guess I kind of screamed a bit, when I fell. I didn't mean to. But I didn't want to die in the vat of poo. Because of the angle and the loops of pipe, I don't think the sewage-worker Krakkiluks could *see* me dangling in mid-air. But they definitely *heard* something. And I heard them clattering and rustling in their capes as they came to take a look.

Th*saaa threw* me on to the second level with a flick of their tentacles and then launched themselves sideways like an invisible flying squirrel. I only knew about that when they landed on top of me like a heap of invisible snow, completely hiding me.

The Krakkiluk sewage workers scuttled around and crunched at each other, like maybe: 'Did you hear that?' and, hopefully: 'Yes, but it was probably just a pipe creaking or some steam escaping or something, oh my adorable darling.'

I think, if they'd been soldiers, they'd have been more thorough at looking around, but they were poor overworked sewage workers who Krnk-ni-Plik and Tlag-li-Glig hadn't been very polite to, and they were probably tired and they'd never seen invisible things before.

Well. Not seen. But you know.

But anyway, they *did* look, and one of them went over to the panel again and crunched into it, maybe asking for help or instructions. Meanwhile I managed to scramble down the next length of ladder in a much more reckless, Carl-like way, or maybe it wasn't exactly reckless, just *committed* – anyway it was *faster* and then when we got to the first level from the floor Th*saaa* picked me off the ladder, lowered me down as far as they could with their tentacles, and dropped me the rest of the way.

And then we were on the ground. I was so cold I had to sit by a hot pipe behind one of the horrible vats for a little while, to warm up. While I was doing that a loud bonging noise sounded, and the two Krakkiluk workers pulled off their capes and made for the big set of doors on the lowest level. Th*saaa* threw the invisibility gown over me again and we trip-shuffled off to catch them up and sneak through with them. And at last we were on our way again.

Which, I remembered a bit late, wasn't necessarily a *good* thing. We were maybe a bit closer to the *Helen* now, but also probably a lot further away from the others. But we couldn't go back if we wanted to, because the doors had shut behind us and there was no way to open them.

After that, there weren't quite so many locked doors. We passed through a cargo bay, I think – there were lots of bundles hanging like honeypot ants in a nest or flies in a spiderweb from more diamond meshwork on the domed ceiling. Also there were these large *balls*, stacked on the ground in big crates like eggs in egg boxes. They were kind of irregular, a bit like what a dung beetle makes, but made of this kind of flaky-looking whitish-grey stuff. One ball had been taken out to rest on the floor, sawn in half. I could see long fibres bristling on the inside, and the scrape marks where some of it of had been gouged away. It gave off a strong sharp smell which made the back of my throat feel all burny, but it wasn't exactly bad . . . At least not the way the sewage was. Kind of resiny, but way too strong.

'Is *that* what they eat?' I wondered.

'I think,' said Th*saaa*, 'that perhaps that is Takwuk.'

I got upset, then, because I thought that if Carl was there he'd want to try licking some of the Takwuk to see what would happen. Or he would make a joke about 'gigantic balls'. And he wasn't here and I *knew* he was on the planet and fine, but still I couldn't help thinking what if he wasn't, what if he was never around again, acting like a maniac just because he could.

After that we weren't so lucky at finding places with hardly any Krakkiluks about; in fact, the next place we bump-shuffled into was a huge bath area and there were at least seventy of them all splashily enjoying the hot water. They weren't any more naked than they normally were; all their decorations seemed to be waterproof. The two Krakkiluk workers were there, gratefully sinking into a hot tank in the floor where a few other Krakkiluks were already bathing, crunching at each other in a friendly way or wallowing blissfully under the water. They were all much more pinkish than normal and I couldn't help thinking weird thoughts about my aunty Marikit boiling shrimp with chilli for *sinigang na hipon* back home, and getting kind of hungry.

The steam was full of the smell of Takwuk, and I guessed this was how they used that stuff – I suppose if you don't have clothes to take off and put back on you can have a bath break for your nice Takwuk as easily as humans have a tea break.

We couldn't exactly help breathing the steam, and I wondered nervously what it was going to do to us. We waddled past the pools trying not to slip, and I seemed to be OK, but Th*saaa*'s tentacles flashed reds and pinks so bright they were nearly fluorescent, and they started going '*eeeeeee*' and '*mmmmmmm*' under their breath.

'Shh!' I begged them.

'You *wooorry* too much,' said Th*saaa*, flailing invisible tentacles.

'No I *don't*,' I groaned.

183

'All will be well, Noeeeell,' Th*saaa* said grandly. 'We can find the *Helen*. We can rescuuuuuuuee the others. We can do it. We can dooooooooo *anything*.'

'That's the Takwuk talking,' I said.

'Noooooo. liiiiiiissssn't,' Th*saaa* insisted, their words getting particularly long and slow. 'Y'aaaaaaaaaare wrooooooooong, 'bout maaaaaaany things. But still I consider you . . . v'ryyyy *fiiiiiiiiine* human.'

'Aww, thanks,' I said, rather pleased even though I knew Th*saaa* wasn't quite themself.

They were still wheezing and mumbling away when we shuffle-bumped into the first of several workshops where Krakkiluks were mending or recycling their scary zappers and other stuff. There were a lot of open doors here, so we picked one at random and after doing this a few times we found another lift shaft. But the lift itself wasn't there – there was just an empty hole, and the shaft was lined with the diamond mesh for climbing.

'We'd better go down,' I said, though I wondered if maybe we should wait for Th*saaa* to sober up first. But it seemed quieter on the floor below, and going down would take us closer to *Helen*.

I slipped out of the amlaa-vel-esh and quickly lowered myself into the shaft.

'*Caaaaare*,' said Th*saaa* anxiously. 'Caaaaareful. You are very bad at climbing – you have tooooooooo few aaaaaaaarms. And you are not invisible.'

Maybe I had been a teeny bit affected by the Takwuk after

all, because I thought I was getting loads better at climbing, personally. In fact it was getting to be sort of fun – so fun that I couldn't help giggling as I slithered down extra fast, both to show how good at it I was and so I'd be safely invisible again sooner.

I landed in another steamy room. And there was a big Krakkiluk standing there, staring right at me.

13

'I know you've always wanted to do Space Archaeology, Jo,' Carl said. 'But, maybe like some time when we're *not* being slowly poisoned?'

High above the worrying depths of the gorge, Josephine was crouched on the peak of a stone arch, scraping enthusiastically at the red coils of root that entangled it. 'They've got wings!' she said. 'They've got wings! They don't need *streets*. Look at these struts. They're as comfortable hanging upside down as standing upright!'

'You'll bring that whole thing *down*,' I moaned, though it wasn't the first time I'd said something along those lines and she hadn't listened.

'But this is useful!' she said.

'I don't see anything here that's going to fly us home,' Carl said, sitting in a coil of root and swinging his legs, while a troop of little scarlet-and-tangerine things swooped down from the cliff tops and perched irreverently on the statue's head, chittering.

The city was in ruins. Golden moss grew from the cracks between blocks of stone, and overflowed into foamy hanging masses. The towers bristled with arms like candelabras: many of them were smashed, the arches were broken backed, whatever had dangled from those broad struts had long since fallen away. It was all sinking into the forest as if the land had dreamt the city and was gradually forgetting it. There was nobody here.

'But if we know something about the people before we meet them,' Josephine said. 'Don't you realise humans have never had that before, with an alien species? The Morrors, the Krakkiluks – they both turned up knowing our languages, knowing who we are – and we didn't know anything. And that's gone *badly* for us. But this time the balance of information will be in *our* favour. We'll be less *helpless*.' She peered down at the stonework she'd cleared. 'There's writing here,' she said happily. 'Goldfish, can you scan this?'

'Oh good, let's Google the translation,' said Carl.

'Well, when we meet them –' began Josephine.

'Maybe they're all dead,' Carl said. 'Maybe the Krakkiluks exterminated them.'

'Carl,' I said, starting to get a bit exasperated.

He shrugged. 'I'm just saying. These fruit-bat guys aren't *here*, are they?''

I looked around nervously, in case a lot of annoyed bat-people emerged from the undergrowth.

'The Krakkiluks could have killed everyone on Aushalawa-Mo*raa* and taken it back that way, but they didn't,' said Josephine. 'I don't think mass exterminations is how they operate.'

'What they *did* do was pretty bad,' called Carl, as Josephine scampered recklessly over the arch to the far side of the gorge.

'I'm not *defending* them!' she yelled back.

'You've got to stop running around and *breathing*,' I moaned.

But Josephine had found what looked at first like a length of root stretching out along one of the struts. Inside it was bristling with wires – wires so corroded and rusted they were scarcely recognisable.

'This is copper. Like we used to use on Earth. Electricity cables,' said Josephine, delighted now. 'They weren't just . . . stonecutters, they were . . . *advanced*. Light, and computing, probably – they might have had space travel already.

'Time didn't do this,' Josephine went on, looking at the broken masonry. 'They didn't just leave. Someone invaded.'

'Well, we know who,' I said.

'I want to know *when*,' said Josephine. And she began muttering to herself under her breath: 'Copper would oxidise faster in this atmosphere . . . but estimating a rate of two picometres per year . . . Goldfish, can you help me with a measurement, here!'

I amused myself by picking blue bead-flowers and flicking them at Carl.

'Two hundred years,' Josephine announced at last. 'The Krakkiluks have been here two hundred years. At least.'

I shivered a bit, because it made me think of the war with the Morrors and how it could have turned out. The Morrors had planned to cram us all on to Mars and have the Earth to themselves, and after two hundred years of

188

that, who knows whether we'd even have known where we came from?

'The people here won't remember anything different,' I said.

Josephine looked at the huge statue of the warrior bestriding the gorge, brandishing its sword. 'I don't think the people who made that would forget,' she said. 'And I don't think they'd give up. Not completely.'

'If they're alive at all,' insisted Carl. 'This is a *ruin*. There's no one here *now*.'

'*Look!*' I all but screamed.

The blue sun was sinking into streaks of turquoise, and three moons shone palely in the sky. And far away, beyond the warrior's raised sword, was the trail of vapour from a distant flying machine.

After that Carl wanted us to hurry off towards the plane – or whatever it had been – as fast as possible, and maybe find the place it had taken off from. But it was getting dark awfully quickly.

'I think we should spend the night here,' I said. 'We can't just walk through the dark. There's nothing but this mossy stuff for miles, and those big purple flying things maybe coming and landing on us in the middle of the night. At least it seems safe here.'

'I agree,' said Josephine.

'You just want to stay because it's an ancient alien city and you think it's cool,' said Carl.

We did stay. We found some intact buildings – like great stone wasps' nests bulging out over the gorge. Their oval doors and windows opened to the air above the depths and there was no way in, unless you could fly. But we climbed down a tangle of roots on to a round platform where Josephine thought some kind of structure had once stood, and we padded it as best we could with lumps of the golden moss stuff.

I wished we could build a campfire, but we didn't want to cause any more explosions. And if we had it would have just drawn attention to how we had no food to cook over it. All we could do was drink water and huddle and watch the stars come out as the night creatures trilled and the little blue hovering things buzzed relentlessly around the Goldfish's glow until the poor thing darted into one of the wasps'-nest houses to hide.

But soon it wasn't the only light in the ancient city. Specks of bright red and blue began to glimmer around us and we started up, wondering if we'd found people after all. But the lights – small as candle flames – rose from tussocks of golden moss dangling from ledges within the gorge, and drifted into the air like so many tiny Chinese lanterns, blue and indigo and scarlet, humming softly.

'Like glow-worms,' said Carl, and he smiled for the first time in a while.

'I wish I had my tablet. No, I wish I had my *harmonica*,' said Josephine, lying back and trailing her hand through a glowing cloud of the little creatures, leaving an eddy of swirling light behind.

'When we get home, you'll write a song about them,' I said. But Josephine's expression darkened at that and I wished I hadn't said anything at all.

It wasn't easy to sleep out there with all the light and humming and the hunger and the fear. Still, the next day started OK, kind of. We had a breakfast of water, and Josephine danced across an archway and called, 'Come on then, this way!' from the other side of the gorge. 'Well, do you see a better way over the river?' she demanded when we didn't instantly follow.

Carl grumbled, but we picked our way over the arch and struggled on through the root forest, until it thinned to golden mosslands again, and the sea glittered ahead under the grassy sky.

But we got so, so hungry and there was nothing we could do about it. Inevitably Carl tried eating one of the bead-flowers to see what would happen. It didn't kill him but it did give him stomach cramps. Josephine grew quieter now she didn't have a ruined alien city to play with: first she stopped talking and then her mouth went all tight and gradually she stopped looking at people. And Carl, well – Carl *moaned.*

'Stupid, poisonous planet with nothing we can even *eat* on it,' he said, to no one in particular, as we trudged on. 'And we don't even know that wasn't a Krakkiluk plane.

191

Oh, good, gigantic roots everywhere again – climbing through those'll be fun.'

Josephine sighed heavily and didn't say anything.

'It could have been a lot *more* poisonous,' I somehow felt obliged to point out.

'Well, that's great isn't it,' Carl growled.

'We're not doing *that* badly. We're not dead, it's not raining, I think my foot's only slightly broken and, like Josephine says, there might be fruit-bat-people *rebels*.'

Josephine did glance at me then, and smiled with one corner of her mouth, but she looked back down at her feet again almost at once.

We made it across the peninsular and back down to the sea, by which point the sky was getting unreasonably dark again and we still hadn't found any people.

'It *can't* be night already,' said Josephine. She squinted at the sky. 'Is that . . . So how long a day has this planet got?' she asked the Goldfish, too tired to try to work it out for herself.

'I make it seventeen hours and thirty-four minutes,' said the Goldfish. 'We've been here twenty-five hours, gang, and look at all the amazing things we've seen and learned already.'

'Yeah, whatever,' said Carl heavily, not even bothering to actually complain.

So that was only twenty-six hours we'd been without food and overdosing on oxygen, and not thirty-two.

My legs were getting kind of shaky anyway, though.

We collapsed on the beach and drank from the little funnels growing there, and that made us feel a little better, but not much.

'You guys need to rest,' said the Goldfish, hovering above our panting bodies, annoyingly immune to needing to rest at all. 'When you're tired and stressed a rest is –'

It broke off.

'Best?' I supplied, because the unfinished rhyme left me feeling all itchy.

'Well, yeah, Alice! That's right! But I guess I was thinking, maybe you don't need a song right now.'

'Oh,' I said, unnerved. The song *had* been annoying, but I couldn't remember the Goldfish ever being the least bit concerned about that before.

'You *can* sing, if you want,' I said, sort of furtively because I wasn't sure how well that would go down with the others.

'We can't stop here,' Josephine said, gulping down another funnel's worth of water. 'The oxygen . . . we have to keep heading towards where we saw that plane.'

'Who says *she's* in charge?' Carl muttered.

'I'm not in charge,' objected Josephine. 'I find leadership roles restrictive.'

'We're doing what you say,' argued Carl.

'That's not me *leading*, that's you being intelligent enough to recognise the most logical course of action,' Josephine said acidly.

'Which always comes from you.'

Josephine looked at him. 'So far.'

'Gosh, being tired and hungry sure makes people grouchy!' said the Goldfish valiantly. 'But hey, at least from here on you can rest and keep going at the same time.' I felt a weird moment of solidarity with it, like apparently we both had the job of uselessly trying to raise morale.

We cut another leaf-boat and this time tried really hard to attach the Goldfish's cable to it ('Duct tape,' said Josephine mournfully) and we couldn't, so we looped a coil around Carl's arm and we pushed the leaf out into the water and lay down, and the Goldfish pulled us onwards as the sun vanished into the malachite sea.

A leaf-pad floating across the sea is a lovely place to *rest*, but not so good a place to actually *sleep*. It rocks all the time, and not always in a nice, lullaby-ish way, and sometimes we got stuck in a tangle of puffball plants and had to get up and drag our raft over the leaves to clear water again. It got cold in the night, under those clear, pine-green skies. Still, I did sleep a bit, off and on, and I woke up to find an inky blue dawn was spreading over the sky.

The dawn wasn't what woke me, though. I woke up because Carl was coughing.

I looked at him, but he just shrugged and made a face, so we didn't say anything about it. At least it eased off once he'd been sitting up for a while.

Then Josephine, who had been curled into a tight ball on the leaf beside me, started awake as if on instinct.

'Look,' she whispered, pointing.

The sky ahead was full of lights. Green and white like the puffballs on the water, they illuminated a city like a three-dimensional spiderweb, metal arches piled upon arches into a tangled pyramid that rose through the dawn sky to pierce the clouds – twice, three times as high as any tower I'd seen on Earth. Homes dangled like fruit or rose like flowers from its curling heights. Little flying machines buzzed around its distant upper heights like fruit flies.

And people – *people* – were emerging from their homes into the damp dawn air; *people* were spreading their wings and flapping off in great flocks like starlings (and yet also they were like crowds of humans at rush hour); people were riding sky-buses; people were gathering in little airborne clusters to chat, and hooting like airborne howler monkeys to greet a new day. You could see they were people instantly, even at this distance. You would have known even if you saw one alone, without the city they'd built. I can't explain it. You can just tell.

14

⬛ *You screamed, and I hastened down the ladder, afraid for your life.*

⊢┤╫├┤ I didn't *scream*. You were still spaced out on Takwuk; you probably heard it way screamier than it was. But OK, yes, I did make a bit of a sound as I jumped backwards, and I heard the Krakkiluk make a low *grrrrrkrr* sort of noise.

But – it was coming from *behind* the Krakkiluk. And down a bit.

I felt Th*saaa* land beside me in a rush of cold.

The Krakkiluk didn't move. It was *facing* me, but it wasn't looking at me after all. It didn't have *eyes*. And it didn't have internal organs: it had a long split down its abdomen, and inside it was empty, like something soft and squishy had pulled itself out.

'It's *moulted* its *shell*!' I said, suddenly very excited.

'Eeeeeeeee,' said Th*saaa*. 'That is *disgusting*.'

'It's not disgusting,' I said. 'It's *interesting*. Don't any Morror animals shed their skins? Aww, I wish we could have seen it do it. And now it'll have to wait for its new shell to harden, and I guess it'll have to have all its decorations done again, and –'

There was a splash from behind the shell.

The shell was standing on, like, a special, round, shedding-your-shell platform, and a ramp led back from this into a bubbling Takwuk bath. The actual Krakkiluk was lying in the water, all pink and raw and floppy-looking. Its eyes swivelled towards me and it moaned and tried to sit up. It managed to lift a weak, rubbery arm, but it sank back into the water. I came a little closer, and it shrank back and curled up behind all its legs.

It was *scared*, I thought. It could hardly move and with its new shell still growing it was as soft as a poached egg and weak as a kitten. I wondered if it felt naked, and embarrassed, so pink without any paintings or decorations. There weren't any other Krakkiluks about, so I think maybe moulting was very private. Even though it was twice my size, it couldn't hurt me, but I could hurt it, I realised. I could probably even kill it. I mean, of course I wasn't going to, but it – I mean, he or she or they – didn't *know* that.

I wondered if it was also a nice person, in a Krakkiluk kind of way, and whether there were any Krakkiluks anywhere who didn't agree with the kind of thing the ones we'd met had been doing. Not that it was very helpful right now if there were, but it was still sort of nice to think about.

'It's OK,' I said to it. 'We're just passing through. No one's going to hurt you.'

But there was no translator box, so it couldn't understand me.

'Quick!' breathed Th*saaa*. 'Before it recovers its senses and calls for help!'

I looked around. The only obvious way out of the room was back up the lift shaft – there was a door too, but we'd seen the only way to open them was by DNA recognition or whatever.

'Oh, *wait*,' I said.

And I went back to the shell and took hold of the claw piece and snapped it off. The Krakkiluk managed to sit up a bit and groan some more when it saw what I was doing, but it soon flopped back again.

'Sorry,' I said. The Krakkiluk's eyes stared up at me despairingly from above the surface the water. 'I expect taking bits of other people's exoskeletons is rude. But you know, so is kidnapping and trying to kill people, so you have got it coming a bit. You should get a different job.'

It won't work, I thought as I approached the door. There's no way it's going to actually work.

I couldn't reach the panel, even when I jumped. 'Th*saaa*, come over here,' I called.

I held out the claw and apparently empty air took it, causing another round of alarmed groans from the pool. 'Ohhh, I seeee . . .' Th*saaa* said, and they reached up and laid the claw against the panel.

The door opened.

'Yes!' I said, and Th*saaa* went, '*Wooooooo!*' and flung their tentacles wide. I know, because one nearly knocked me over. I don't think I'd ever known them get so enthusiastic about anything, except maybe tomato ketchup. 'Did I not say, Noooooell,' Th*saaa* cried, 'we can do *aaaaanything*!'

'Bye-bye!' I called to the raw Krakkiluk in the bath, as Th*saaa* threw the invisibility gown over me again. It was silly, but maybe I *was* a bit hopped up on Takwuk.

We waddled down another corridor, past a mess room where Krakkiluks were eating things that all seemed to have been rolled up into balls – surprisingly tidily, you expected them to be maybe slobbering like jackals or something. The fresher air in the corridor cooled Th*saaa*'s head a bit.

'I think we should go back to the cells,' they said. 'Now we have that claw we can free the others, perhaps. We know where to look for them, at least. But if we go onwards – this ship is so large, even if we find the *Helen*, we might never find our way back.'

I hesitated because we might be really close to the *Helen* and if we found her we could maybe go and rescue Carl and Alice and Josephine straight away. But Th*saaa* was right. And Lena was so clever, she could probably help. 'Yeah,' I said, 'OK.'

So we doubled back, past the poor, naked Krakkiluk and back through the Takwuk baths, trying not to get all giggly and full of ourselves, and through the cargo bay, and the sewage room – but we didn't have to climb up the ladders this time, we used the *lifts*, and finally we were back on the same corridor that led to our cells. And there was the lift that should take us to where the others were being held.

Th*saaa* touched the claw to the panel and the lift carried us upwards. And yes, there was another row of cells like ours. Th*saaa* opened the nearest one.

'It would have been polite to knock,' said a voice.

Lena Jerome was sitting against the back of the cell, her hands folded in her lap, calmly doing nothing at all. And she was wearing not only big fancy earrings but also big fancy bracelets and a big fancy choker necklace that I hadn't seen before; they must have been inside her suit.

She was a very unsurprisable person, but one eyebrow did go up a little bit when she saw the door open and didn't see *us*.

'Ah,' she said. 'Well, that puts a different complexion on it. Hello, Th*saaa*.' She snapped her fingers. 'Resume,' she said.

Her jewellery poured off her, like it had melted, and split into hundreds of tiny spider robots. They spread into a pool around her, before reorganising themselves into a little gold device which projected a virtual screen on which Lena was soon entering commands, her fingers a blur.

'Wow, that's awesome,' I said. 'What are you working on?'

She was again surprised enough to raise one eyebrow. '*Noel?*' she said.

I stepped out of the amlaa-vel-esh. 'It's both of us.'

Lena nodded. 'I imagine that must be very uncomfortable.'

'Yeah, it is,' I said. 'Can I have a drink of water? Anyway, we're rescuing you. You've gotta come with us.'

'Hmm,' Lena said, getting to her feet. She is *very* tall. 'I congratulate you on your escape. But how do you plan on rescuing me?'

There was a pause. Th*saaa* took off the amlaa-vel-esh, gave it an awkward little shake, and threw it over Lena's head.

Lena's calves and feet stood there looking strange and large and completely visible. 'Well, there we are, that won't work,' said Lena. She pulled off the invisibility gown and gravely handed it back Th*saaa.*

'Perhaps, we can go down to the *Helen* and get a couple more invisibility gowns?' I said.

Lena, already back at work, shook her head once. 'It would give them too many opportunities to intercept you.'

The door had slid shut behind us, but a column of gold spider robots crawled in under it and joined the others.

'What are they doing?' Th*saaa* enquired.

'Spying. Infiltrating,' said Lena. 'Building on the data from the *Helen*'s scans. I'm developing a virtual model of the ship, and at the same time, analysing its computers.'

'You're *hacking* the ship?' I asked.

'Of course. Why do you think I wanted to delay our capture even when it was inevitable?'

'How can that be *possible*?' breathed Th*saaa.*

'I am a genius aided by thousands of robots that experiment endlessly until they find something that works,' said Lena. 'But yes –' she frowned at her virtual screen, '– I did not expect to be successful. This is going remarkably well.'

'Can you open the main doors and let the *Helen* out?' I asked.

'It's going to take more than that,' Lena said. 'But if this algorithm completes successfully, then yes, perhaps, and I may be able to put out the lights on most of the ship and tamper with the ship's life support systems.'

'What, you mean like, *kill* the Krakkiluks?' I asked, alarmed.

'Probably not, but I have some other ideas,' said Lena,

staring at her virtual screens. One showed strange shapes and dots that I think must have been Krakkiluk writing and the other was in Häxeri, like it was the translation.

'That should allow you to rescue Mr Trommler and his daughter and escort them to the *Helen*.'

'What do you mean, *we* can rescue them?' I said. 'You're coming too, right? You can turn all the lights out and then you won't need an invisibility cloak and it'll be fine.'

'The lift shaft that leads to the hangar is here,' Lena went on, ignoring what I'd said and bringing up another screen. It showed a map of the inside of the Krakkiluk ship – it wasn't quite complete, there were big blank patches, but a lot of it was there. 'I'm labelling this deck 571b for convenience. You'll need to be able to override the systems.' She looked up. 'You'll be going without me,' she added. 'When we have concluded this conversation I will stay in this cell for perhaps another twenty minutes. Then I will head here.' She pointed to a detail of her map. 'There appears to be a cavity between floors where I can continue to work without being detected.' She reached for the Krakkiluk claw and snapped off a joint. 'Do you mind? I could use the robots to get through the doors, but this will save time.'

'What?' I said, feeling all of a sudden very tired and helpless and a bit like crying. 'Why would you want to stay on the ship?'

'If they lose their hostages they lose their power to blackmail either of our species,' Lena said.

'But you toooooo are a hostage,' Ths*aaa* said.

'Only one,' said Lena grimly. 'Not very much leverage in

only one.' And for a moment she looked down, and her mouth went tight. And I didn't like it.

'President Chakrabarty told Lady Sklat-kli-Sklak her actions amounted to an act of war,' Lena went on. 'But right now, Earth and Aushalawa-Mo*raa* have no idea where the enemy is, or where *we* are. We reached the Alpha Centauri system and then vanished. And our captors have succeeded both in sending communications through hyperspace, and in disguising the source of the signal so that it is impossible to trace it back to our present location.' She looked at us patiently. 'Are you following me so far?' she asked.

'Yes,' I said, feeling a bit patronised.

'They also have Rasmus Trommler, who has supplied ships and weapons to the military for years,' Lena went on relentlessly. 'And he is familiar with Morror technology too; he copied it to build the *Helen*. He knows more about the military hardware of both our species than anyone. Certainly more than I do. The Krakkiluks already have the advantage. If they learn what he knows then any attempt to correct that imbalance will be useless if it comes to war. And suppose they torture him. Do you understand that?'

'*Yes*,' I said again. 'I'm not stupid. I wouldn't want to leave Mr Trommler even without all that. But I don't see why this means you've got to stay on this stupid ship and probably get killed. I know you've got to open the doors and stuff, but why can't you do that from the *Helen*?'

'I might be able to open the doors of the hangar from on board the *Helen*, said Lena. 'I might be able to disable the tractor beam which brought us on board in the first place. But I could not *keep it* disabled. Before we were a mile from the ship I would lose any control over it, and the Krakkiluks would drag us back.'

'Oh,' I said.

'But you could, maybe, leave these robots behind to do your wooooork,' suggested Th*saaa*.

'They'll need my supervision once the Krakkiluks realise they're being hacked and start trying to fight back,' said Lena. 'But there is another reason. I think I can hack the communication systems the Krakkiluks used to telephone Earth. I can contact Earth and Aushalawa-Mo*raa* through hyperspace, *without* the disguise on the signal. I will have to stay on the ship to keep the channel open for as long as possible so that Earth can trace it. I can transmit everything I have learned about this ship and the species that produced it, and all the data I have not been able to analyse. I can show them where we are. Information about the enemy is critical in a time of war.'

'But there can't be an actual *war* – we've just had one,' I groaned. 'If we all get away, then the Krakkiluks can't make Earth or the Morrors *do* anything, and then –'

I stopped.

'We can't expect this to be the end of the Krakkiluks' claim to Aushalawa-Mo*raa*,' Lena said. 'And they have Valerie. If they return, knowing her methods, I don't know what will happen. But I can give our side a chance to respond to what has happened *now*, before the enemy makes their next move.

Earth may be able to send ships to rescue Josephine and the other children.' She paused. 'And just possibly, me.'

'But *we* can do that!' I said. 'That's, like, the whole plan! If we can get the *Helen* out of the ship, we can fly down to the planet and pick them up and then we'll –'

'*No*,' said Lena, with the most amount of expression I've ever seen. 'Listen to me, Noel. If you make it as far as the *Helen*, you must *not* waste time and squander my work on a fool's mission to that planet. Your sentiments are understandable, but you do *not* have time to indulge them. You *must* get yourselves and Rasmus Trommler as far out of Krakkiluk hands as fast as possible. You must get back to Aushalawa-Mo*raa*. The *Helen* should be capable of retracing her steps through hyperspace. The EEC and the Council of Lonthaa-Ra-Mo*raa* will take it from there.'

'But my brother's down there! I know he is, he must be.' Because I was working really hard at knowing that all the time. 'And your *sister*, and Alice – we can't fly off and *leave* them. Don't you *care*?' I said. I didn't mean to. I suddenly felt very angry about everything, Lena included. 'Don't you *care* whether you make it or not? Aren't you bothered about Josephine? You talk like maybe someone else can rescue her as, like, an *afterthought.* Anything could happen by then! Maybe Earth won't be able to send anyone back! But we're right here *now*. And Th*saaa* and I care about her, and Carl, and Alice, even if you don't.'

Lena looked up from her work and stared at me in silence so hard that I squirmed a bit. 'I don't wish to discuss this,' she said, not angrily, not like she was upset. She just said it. She turned back to her device and did something to it, and it separated again into thousands of robots. One part of the swarm broke off from the rest and remodelled itself into, like, a little gold rod, about the size of a chocolate bar, with a button on one end.

'You'd better leave now. Take this,' she said. 'Press the button and you will have a virtual screen that operates much like a tablet. You should find it easy to operate. Use it to receive my instructions. Find a suitable hiding place close to Trommler's location, and await them.'

'You knooow where he is?' Th*saaa* asked.

'Yes. There is a map of the ship already loaded on the device you're holding. But perhaps this would be easier still.'

She held out her hand. A single spider robot scurried in excited loops around her palm.

'Put it on the ground and follow it,' she said. 'It will take you to Trommler. I will contact you when it's time. Once you are safe on the *Helen* with Trommler and Christa, you will *not* attempt to rescue the others. Do you understand why not?'

'Because it won't work,' I said crossly.

'Because it will wreck the chances of escape for *any* of us,' said Lena, looking a little desperate. 'Please. I have to be able to trust you.'

I scuffed at the rubbery floor with my boot. 'All right,' I said in a messed-up little voice.

'Good. Then follow the spider.'

I reached for Th*saaa* and felt the amlaa-vel-esh sweep

over me. I was glad. I wanted to get out of the cell. I'd thought that finding another human would make me feel a lot better than it had.

'Noel,' Lena said, as Th*saaa* opened the door. 'Are you still there?'

'Yeah,' I said. I looked back. She was trying to look at where she thought we were but she hadn't got it quite right.

'I saw what appeared to be a forest fire on the planet,' she said. 'And when I was left alone in here, the first thing I did was instruct the robots to assemble themselves into a spectrometer. Examining the sunlight through the planet's atmosphere, I observed clear A and B bands in the Fraunhofer lines.'

'So what,' I said sulkily. I didn't know what any of that meant, obviously.

'It indicates oxygen on the surface,' said Lena. She sighed. She looked kind of younger. I mean, she acts like she's about a million but when you think about it, she's only like two years older than Christa.

'I wish –' she said, and broke off.

'What?' I asked.

'I wish I had some duct tape.'

The tiny gold spider got its bearings immediately, and ran away down the corridor.

It led us right out of the prison block, which was surprising – unless Lena was wrong or the spider wasn't working, Mr Trommler was being held in a completely different part of the ship. We followed it to one of the lifts and when Th*saaa* touched the claw to the panel the spider crawled up their tentacle and flashed rapidly, which I think made us whoosh past a lot of floors without stopping so the Krakkiluks couldn't get on or stop us. We heard angry crunching sounds and clatters as we zoomed past – the Krakkiluks knew by now that someone invisible was running around their ship, and they wanted to catch us. But they couldn't: the lift stopped and the spider jumped out so fast we barely had time to follow it off before the lift rocketed on down and then almost immediately zoomed back up again. We watched it for a few seconds, bouncing up and down the shaft like a crazy ball and then stopping somewhere above us. So I think that made it hard for the Krakkiluks to know where we'd gone. I hoped so, anyway.

And the spider led us on, past exercise grounds, and through a really *tall* room which I think was like the energy reactor, and then up again and into another prongy bit, where there were lots of meeting rooms, I guess. They were big and covered in gold and paintings. The spider stopped outside a door. There was a window too; neither of us was tall enough to look through it into the room, but we could *hear*.

Mr Trommler was in there talking in Swedish – and so were the Krakkiluks, through their translator boxes. So all I could understand was Mr Trommler saying 'nay' a lot, which must mean 'no', and he sounded very scared and very miserable. But we couldn't do anything – we *can't* do anything, until Lena calls to tell us what to do, or she makes the lights go out or *something*.

So we went and found this cupboard place in a meeting room a few doors down from Trommler and we're here now. We're hiding and waiting for something to happen. And it's true, the screen does work pretty much like a tablet, so we've been using it to record all this. But I don't know how to transmit stuff through hyperspace, so unless we do manage to get to the *Helen* and fly home somehow, I don't see how anyone's going to get to listen to it except us.

⏺ *If Lena is right – if my people and yours send their ships . . .*

⩜ I just . . . I don't know if I think they'll do that, Th*saaa*. Even if they know where we are, it's such a long way. And we don't *have* many ships that can do hyperspace, have we?

I hope Lena does something soon. Because I've been in this cupboard a long time. And now I really, really need to pee.

⏺ *Oh, Nooooooooell. Why did you not use the convenience in Lena's cell?*

⩜ Because you and Lena were both *there*.

⏺ *We would have looked away.*

⩜ Yeah, but you could've *heard*, and I just *couldn't*, not in front of you, and definitely not in front of Lena.

● *Your scruples . . . are . . . absurd.*

⊢╫⊣ Well, I don't care, I'm going to wait until we're on the *Helen* and there's a proper toilet.

You OK, Th*saaa*? How are you holding up?

● *Hot. Veeeeeerry . . . hot.*

⊢╫⊣ It's going to be OK.

It can't be much longer now.

PART 3

15

'So, are we just going to roll up and say hi?' I asked, my voice getting slightly squeaky at the thought. None of the fruit-bat people had noticed us yet.

'I think we should get closer and watch for a while first,' said Josephine. 'We don't want to say hi to the wrong people.'

'Yes!' I said. 'Just . . . ease into it. That sounds fine.'

'Goldfish, dim down!' Josephine said. The Goldfish did, until it was just a blue pair of lights in the shadows. We waded ashore, and picked our way through the tangle of roots and funnels, towards the very edge of the city. Here and there between the arches we could see white columns of water descending from upper tiers and the fruit-bat people flying in and out of the spray, drinking and *washing*, like birds at a waterfall. Some of them swung upside down from arches to preen themselves; others filled pots and swooped off to lower levels. They had no more need for clothes than the Krakkiluks; they were covered in fur of a colour that was hard to make out in the electric light. But when we were closer still we could see that they wore jewellery – flashes of gold at their throats and wrists and feet.

Except some of them did wear a little more than that. 'Look at those guys,' said Carl.

'What?' I said.

'In the flying car thing.'

The flying car things were a bit like Roman litters: platforms mostly open to the air with the passengers reclining inside, but borne up on four rotary blades at each corner. I'd noticed several making leisurely circuits of the lower reaches of the city before soaring away.

'Which one?'

'There – oh, they've gone. They were wearing, like, armour,' said Carl. 'Breastplates and things on their arms and that.'

'OK, so?'

'*Painted* armour. And covered with beads and stuff. Don't you get it? *Trying to look like Krakkiluks.*'

I thought about the social and cultural implications of this.

'Oh, dear,' I said.

'Well, we're not going to talk to those ones,' Josephine said.

'How much say do you think we'll *have*,' said Carl, and I remembered the cough and the imperilled little brother and managed to stop myself snapping at him. I was starting to have trouble remembering the last time he'd said *anything* that wasn't about how everything was going to go even wrong-er than it already was.

Carl glanced at me and maybe sensed what I was thinking, because his expression softened a bit. 'What is that smell?' he asked, after a pause.

The smell was not nice. Climbing up on to a higher loop of root, we could see that while the city was like a tower of lace glittering in the morning dew and hung with houses like coloured lanterns, it also had a giant rubbish tip heaped beneath it.

There were far fewer lights down there amont the lowest arches, just occasional strands of bright filament strung between them. But some people obviously *lived* there. We could see them emerging and flapping up to join the throng above, from hundreds of basket-like structures that looked as flimsy as paper lamps, dangling just above the mess.

And there were people living even lower down than that. People perched atop arches choked in rubbish or dangling from webs of rope with nothing but homemade canopies of lily-pad leaves to shield them from wind and rain.

We crept closer through the heaped coils of the roots, the Goldfish hovering low, to where the grey cables twisted around a massive strut right at the city's base. We crouched at the bottom of a red funnel that spread into a wide trumpet-shape above us and as the daylight grew stronger, we could see people fluttering about over the tip, picking at things, among a flock of little flying scarlet animals, scavenging like seagulls back at home. The people were all kinds of deep red and warm purple, from bright burgundy to deep magenta to violet, and some were a pale, silvery lilac. Every now and then one would fly up and tie their pickings to a growing store of booty dangling from a crown of an arch; sometimes there were tussles in mid-air, sometimes one would find some kind of prize amid the rubbish and soar up, whooping, while the others gathered around to see or share or try to snatch it.

They were small, these rubbish-tip people. At first it was hard to get the perspective right because nothing in sight was familiar, but then a group of larger fruit-bat people swooped up and perched on an arch, and the little ones gathered round with the bundles of things they'd collected, and something changed hands – food, or money, maybe – and then the bigger fruit-bat people gestured and flew off and the little ones got back to work.

'They're *kids*,' I said. 'Kids living on a rubbish tip.'

At this point we very nearly got discovered. A trio of fruit-bat-people adults came swooping from some of those lower basket-houses and out a little into the forest, and hung together from a loop of root barely thirty feet from us, chatting and eating breakfast. We froze. There was no other way to hide. Their voices were high and musical and very loud; they *sang*, almost, like birds. One fruit-bat person was a deep, garnet red and two were plum purple; they wore sensible belts with pouches at their waists and the bare skin of their wings was painted with swirls and spirals of yellow and blue. They shared out a package of something like fruit and something crumbly that looked a bit like cheese but almost certainly wasn't, and my stomach growled. Thirty-four hours since we'd eaten, now.

The fruit-bat people finished their meal, sighed gustily, dropped their litter into the forest, and flipped themselves round so they were standing upright atop the arc of a root.

I noticed that none of them were wearing colourful jewellery or Krakkiluk decorations – but they all had plain, tight-fitting black collars round their necks. One of them tapped their collar and cocked their head meaningfully at the others, before all three flew away. When I thought about it, the ones in the flying cars had been wearing the collars too.

'We should maybe have said something to them,' I said. Our instinct had been to stay still and hope they didn't see us, but they hadn't been particularly scary-looking. How *were* we going to pick the perfect person to reveal ourselves to?

'I think rush hour's over,' said Josephine. And it was true that the city's heights were growing quieter. A great flock of flying vehicles and fruit-bat people flapping along under their own power were heading out across the sea.

'Maybe they have a very active fishing industry?' I wondered.

'Look, this is not going to *work*,' said Carl. 'If anyone has a spaceship here it's going to be the ones who are *literally on top*, and those guys? Are *dressed up like Krakkiluks*.'

Josephine scrubbed her hands over her face. 'OK,' she said. 'So, what do you *want*, Carl? If I ever was at all in charge I abdicate and anoint you leader, so: you decide.'

'I want to not *be here* to begin with,' said Carl, and there was a dangerous flash of something between him and

Josephine, something he didn't quite say but got much too close to.

'Well, let us know when you've got a plan to make that happen,' grated Josephine.

'Carl, she *saved our lives*,' I said.

'*Did she?*' said Carl.

'You're alive, aren't you?' said Josephine.

'Hey, kids,' chirped the Goldfish, desperately. 'How about we all – well, maybe no singing what with the oxygen situation – how about a, no, guess it's not a group hug moment – how about a time out? Five minutes, everyone cool down, breathe, but not too deeply . . .'

It was actually a good idea. But it was also too late.

'Jo,' Carl said roughly, 'to me it looks like Alice and I are going to die slow instead of quick, and you're going to die for no reason at all.'

Josephine's skin went ashy. Without another word she turned and stalked away among the roots.

'Hey, wait, Josephine!' said the Goldfish, bustling after her.

I dithered, not sure whether to go after her or stay and yell at Carl. I thought I'd decided to follow Josephine, but somehow I found I had too much yelling to do and swung back to make a start on it.

'For God's sake! Why did you have to say that?'

'She might have been OK,' said Carl emptily. 'If she'd stayed on the damn ship. Dr Muldoon was going to do what they wanted. You said that, Alice. She'd have been OK.'

'Or she might have been thrown out without the Goldfish and without oxygen! God, Carl. None of us want to be here. None of us wanted to get kidnapped by Krakkiluks! But we're not dead *yet*. Can you just . . . just be a bit more positive for five seconds? You did it on Mars, and we got through that, and this is not *that much worse*.'

'Yeah it *is*, and I can do the whole bright-side thing for *Noel* and he's not *here*,' said Carl, and to my horror his eyes were glistening and his voice cracked.

'Well, what about me?' I said, and bad things were happening to my voice too. 'What, you could keep it together if Noel was here? Then why can't you damn well try and do it for me? I've been doing it for *you*.'

Carl blinked rapidly and opened his mouth to say something, but ended up coughing instead.

'Yalu! LuWEEma!' interrupted a new voice.

And suddenly, hanging between us, was an upside-down, pointed lilac face. It turned from Carl to me and back. Four round black eyes considered us. Carl and I stared back at it.

'Hello,' I said weakly.

The dangling lilac person extended a small three-fingered hand and poked Carl hard in the forehead.

'Ow,' said Carl, and 'HEY yalu!' the lilac person exclaimed.

'OOO ma HIN-NIN!' yodelled another voice, and something hit me on the shoulder. It was a hunk of a broken pot.

The kids from the rubbish tip had us surrounded. A group of them were holding Josephine, her hands already tied behind her back. Many were holding lengths of metal pipe, and stones. The Goldfish was nowhere to be seen.

'Um. We come in peace,' said Carl.

16

'So, well, this happened,' said Josephine heavily.

Now the rubbish-tip kids were close up I could see that some wore necklaces and bracelets of coloured plastic. Others had shaved strips into the fur of their chests, and they all had patterns painted on the insides of their wings. But none of them wore the collars we'd seen on the adults. Lilac-fur had pierced ears, though ribbons of bright plastic were threaded through the holes instead of earrings.

Lilac-fur fluttered down in front of us to grab a handful of my hair, exclaiming in intrigue. Then she/he/they seized Carl's arm and waggled it up and down, apparently fascinated by the absence of either wings or additional legs.

'HIN-NIN ulanae lalOONha, Uwaelee,' pleaded another of the kids, a tall, plum-coloured one, who maybe thought Lilac was a bit too happy to get their hands all over the alien invaders. I'd never heard anything like the way their voices leaped from a solid chest voice to ringing soprano within a single syllable, as effortlessly aerial as their bodies in flight. It was dizzying to listen to.

Carl was trying to communicate through improvised sign language: he pointed at the sky, mimed a rapid descent that ended with a splat and then walked his fingers across his palm and finished up with his hands spread in a 'so now here we are' gesture.

Lilac tipped their head this way and that, interested, but it was hard to tell what they'd understood. And then decided to grab my hair again.

'Ow,' I said, as Lilac yanked rather hard, and I tried to twist away. This alarmed the onlookers, and a small indigo kid with a green plastic pouch-belt round their waist threw another lump of rubbish and hit Carl on the head.

Fortunately it was something squashy and smelly and Carl was not seriously damaged. But Lilac flapped over to Small Indigo – using me as a jumping-off post on the way – and, as far as we could tell, delivered a good telling-off.

'BULin-NIN aelOONya,' complained Plum, who I was going to assume was either Lilac's second in command or joint leader, and then Lilac and Plum flew up a few yards among the tangle of roots to hold an animated discussion in mid-air. They somersaulted and hovered, sometimes gesturing at us or at the group – several of whom, in the meantime, indulged themselves in experimentally poking us.

And then all of a sudden, Plum and Lilac reached some kind of agreement. 'HIN-nalay!' called Plum, and the whole gang closed in on us. Four small hands seized each limb, and with some difficulty, they hauled us into the air.

'Yalu, EEN naweeta,' grumbled the one straining with my right arm.

Flying is, in theory, a wonderful thing to do. But dangling face down between grabby bat-people was horribly uncomfortable, and hurtling through the forest with no way to even shield our faces from arcing roots was terrifying. They didn't fly us far, though. In barely a minute we were under the city and above the dump, where they dropped us. Unsurprisingly it smelled even worse close-up. Plum swiftly tied my hands and then Carl's with a length of twine – which had the effect of removing what little ability we had to even *try* to talk to them, as we weren't going to get very far by speaking English loudly and slowly.

And then, before we'd had a chance to adapt to our new surroundings, four more of the kids flew in carrying a large funnel they'd cut from the forest, which they dropped over all three of us like a glass over a spider.

We were trapped and helpless.

The inside of the funnel was humid, and it trapped the smell of the dump in there with us. At first the darkness seemed total. But gradually our eyes adjusted and I realised a little light did filter through the funnel's glossy flanks; I could see the others, silhouetted in a blood-red glow. But for a long time, no one spoke.

'We could probably push this thing over,' I said, eventually.

'And do what?' said Josephine listlessly. 'They outnumber us. We can't even move our arms.'

'I know,' I said. 'I'm just, you know. Brainstorming.'

But the brainstorming session didn't get any further.

'It's kind of up to them,' said Carl dully. 'What happens next. Sometimes you just can't do anything.'

And it was true. I'd always been able to at least *keep*

going, before, but right now we couldn't even do that.

Josephine whispered: 'I keep messing everything up.'

'What?' I said.

'I don't mean to. I didn't used to. I used to get things right. But now . . . first the exams and then everything with the . . . with the *book*, and with Dad and now this. I didn't even know about oxygen toxicity.'

'Josephine,' I said, alarmed. 'What are you talking about?'

'We should have kept walking, the first night. Carl was right. We shouldn't have slept in the other city.'

'We'd still have ended up here,' said Carl.

'But we'd have more *time*,' said Josephine. 'I should have . . . Like you said, I shouldn't have brought us down here. I mean, I couldn't just *leave* you out there – I had to do *something*. But maybe I could have got us back on to the ship. The hull doors were shut, but maybe there was another way. Maybe we could have got to the *Helen*. For *months* I've made one mistake after another.'

'Jo,' groaned Carl. 'Don't do this.'

'What do you mean, *for months*?' I said.

Josephine sighed. 'It doesn't really matter now,' she said. 'But. You know I was retaking the Baccalaureate?'

'Yeah.'

'You don't have to retake things you get right the first time.'

'Well . . . that just means you had a bad day,' I said, confused. The world of exams felt a very long way away. 'That's all.'

'I wanted to go to university.'

'You're *thirteen*,' I said.

'I know that,' said Josephine, with a bleak trace of amusement in her voice. 'But I thought I could do it anyway.'

I thought about it. 'Yeah, you probably could. But everyone would be older than you. It'd be lonely.'

'Oh, well, I can deal with that,' said Josephine blankly.

'*Why* did you want to go?' I asked, but Josephine didn't answer that.

'Dr Muldoon thought I could do it, too. But she was wrong. When I took the exams, I made all these stupid mistakes. I've never *done* that before. I thought, if I could discover something new on this trip then I'd be sure to get in this time –'

'Jo, no offence,' said Carl, slumped against the wall of the funnel, 'but that's got nothing to do with why we're stuck on this stinking planet.'

'It doesn't matter about university now, I know,' agreed Josephine. 'Except that there's a pattern of things going badly because I keep . . . *thinking I know how to do things* when obviously I *don't*.'

'No. Look. I'm sorry I said all that, OK?' Carl sighed. 'Can you stop sitting there believing stuff I said when I was in full-on drongo mode? I mean, you want to talk mistakes, how about being the bloke who thought mouthing off to the guys with the airlock was a good idea?' I couldn't see his expression, but he nudged me and I thought he was trying to smile. 'Remember, we're not dead, it's not raining, and Alice's foot is only slightly broken.'

I was glad he was trying. But there was no sign that it was doing Josephine any good. And I wanted to think of something else to say but it smelled so bad under there and I was feeling so woozy from not eating. I thought if anyone had a history of doing incredibly stupid things it was the girl who'd run away to space against parental advice in the first place.

'It's the Krakkiluks,' I said. 'It's all the Krakkiluks' fault.'

'*Ul-nik-prrk-klidikehk!*' bellowed a loud Krakkiluk voice and I nearly jumped out of my skin. And something flew hard at the upturned funnel and knocked it over, and we blinked in the restored sunshine.

'Kzet pli kleng!' said the Krakkiluk, as the rubbish-tip kids screeched in shock.

Only it wasn't a Krakkiluk. It was the Goldfish.

'Yaeeee!' wailed Lilac, leaping into the air and hurling a lump of broken plastic at the Goldfish, which it dodged.

'If you kids'd just *listen*,' said the Goldfish in its normal voice, exasperated.

'Goldfish,' I whispered. 'You . . . you learned Krakkiluk?'

'Well, some of it, Alice, sure!' said the Goldfish merrily. 'Boy, all this new processing power is super-useful. They were speaking and translating it right there in front of me on the ship, and those big bullies had plenty to say about spawn being silent, remember? So that's what I said to these feisty little guys. And: "You would be wise to listen,"

– the guy with the diamonds said that too . . . KIHL-YIH TLUL TAKT-TLITOP!' it thundered at the rubbish-tip kids, several of whom decided this was all too much and scampered away.

'YOOLwa,' retorted Lilac-fur who was made of sterner stuff, putting one pair of hands on their hips and throwing their wings wide.

'So – can we talk to them in Krakkiluk?' I said doubtfully.

'Klhel-ol-zlik tlak,' the Goldfish crunched.

I didn't know what it was saying, but Plum and Lilac looked at each other. Then Lilac held up one pair of hands, the fingers close together. 'Trrnk-skuk,' they said, hesitantly. A *bit*. I didn't need the Goldfish's translation to know they meant they spoke the Krakkiluk language 'a bit'.

'Well, why don't you guys take a look at this and say what you see,' said the Goldfish, and projected an image of a Krakkiluk – Tlag-li-Glig, from the look of it.

'Oooh,' breathed Plum. If I'd known the Goldfish was going to do that, I'd have worried the alien kids would be scared; they'd been understandably freaked out by the Goldfish's Krakkiluk voice. But they weren't. They knew the projection wasn't real. They circled the image cautiously: impressed, but not astonished.

'Krakkiluk,' said the Goldfish, and left a meaningful pause. 'Krakkiluk.'

'KraKLOO!' said Lilac, understanding, pointing at the image.

'Krakloo – in your language, Krakloo?' repeated

227

Josephine. Lilac stared at her and swivelled their head about. Josephine tried again, this time pitching her voice up on the second syllable as high as she could: 'KraKLOO!'

Lilac burst into a series of deafeningly high-pitched chirps that had to be laughter and somersaulted over backwards. 'Heewa. KraKLOO!'

Josephine couldn't move her hands – she had to point from Carl to me with one foot, then nodded down at her own body. 'Humans,' she said.

'YUUma!' hooted Lilac.

'*Humans*,' repeated the Goldfish sternly, not one to let slapdash pronunciation go.

Plum tried: 'H'yoo. Humans.'

'GOOD JOB, BUDDY,' crowed the Goldfish, delighted. It showered Plum with a cascade of golden stars, which nearly caused a riot. Even the kids who had run away in a panic came fluttering back.

'Eyma OOOhula!' they chorused, which I was willing to bet meant: 'Do it again.'

'Goldfish, tell them you'll give them sparkles all day long if they untie us,' said Josephine.

The Goldfish was rather flummoxed, as the Krakkiluks hadn't said anything like that in front of it. Eventually it pointed a beam of light at our bindings and told the kids to *restore us to our proper state*. I'm not sure the kids understood, but we writhed and grimaced and wriggled our hands until they got the message.

Though that didn't mean they were sure about it.

'HIN-NIN aelOONya,' worried Plum.

'OONyel lal-ne,' volunteered Small Indigo.

'Whssh!' Lilac scoffed.

'Oh come on, we're not going to hurt you,' said Carl, and then went off in a fit of coughing. Which was worrying, but also quite well-timed, because the kids looked at him and their postures softened a little.

'Ool NYEE bul-lul,' said Plum and, fluttering closer, patted Carl on the head.

Lilac said something to the Goldfish in the Krakkiluk language: 'Ul-nik kzet?'

'Do you know what that means?' I asked.

'They want to know if you're kids,' said the Goldfish. 'Well, "spawn" – you know.'

'Heewa,' said Josephine. '"Heewa" mean yes in their language, right? KraKLOO,' she continued. She looked pointedly up at the sky.

'Ahh, KraKLOO!' said Lilac, and mimicked the little sign-language story Carl had performed before.

'Heewa, heewa!' we said.

'Pssh,' Lilac decided suddenly, and in a second swooped over to us and bit through our bindings. The feeling of small, alien teeth nuzzling against my wrists was very odd, but the Goldfish, obligingly, provided another round of sparkles.

'Waaay!' cheered the rubbish-tip kids.

'Well, I guess we can kind of communicate,' Josephine said.

'Oh, boy!' said the Goldfish happily. 'Kids, you know what this means? You know how we're going to learn and grow and make new friends?'

'Oh, no,' said Carl.

'That's right. It's SCHOOL TIME!' whooped the Goldfish, barrel-rolling in the air in glee.

To begin with, the Goldfish didn't have to do anything. The kids did most of the teaching themselves.

'Eemala,' volunteered Lilac eagerly, encompassing all the kids in a sweeping gesture. Pointing at us again: 'H'yumans.' Then back at the kids, and the city. 'Eemala.' And then pointing to their chest: 'Uwaelee.'

'Uwaelee? Your name is Uwaelee?' I said.

'Heewa AY! Uwaelee,' agreed Lilac, then she told us Plum's name: 'Naonwai!'

'HIN-NIN, Uwaelee!' complained Naonwai, who hadn't agreed to this.

'Ael-ay, ael-ay?' Uwaelee asked us.

'Josephine. Alice. Carl,' Josephine answered, guessing that Uwaelee wanted our names in return.

They'd said 'ael-ay' before while pointing at us, so that probably meant 'you', I thought.

'Shosfeen. Ally. Cal,' said Naonwai.

'EEPla-lae-YEE?' demanded Uwaelee, bouncing into the air and rapping a small fist on the Goldfish's back.

'That's the Goldfish,' I said.

'GoltFEESH,' exulted Uwaelee. 'H'yumans, Shosfeen, Ally, Cal, Goltfeesh.'

So, they had all of that, and we had:

Eemala – Fruit-bat people.

Heewa – Yes.

KraKLOO – Krakkiluk.

Ael-ay – You.

It was a start.

'Do we have *no*, yet, Goldfish?' asked Josephine.

We hadn't. 'I know!' I said. I picked up a warped plastic pot from the heap and pushed it into Carl's hands. 'Give that to me,' I said. Carl did. 'Heewa!' I said, happily taking it from him. 'Now do it again.' I handed it back.

Carl did, and this time I made a great show of refusing to take the pot; of course the head-shaking didn't mean anything to the Eemala kids, but they understood when I held up my hands, then crossed them and turned my back.

'OON,' they said. *No.*

The bad thing about the language was that it took a lot of lungpower to get it right. After singing 'OON' somewhere around high C a few times we got faint and woozy and needed to sit down. But the Goldfish didn't, and it didn't forget anything, or need anything to be repeated. At least lessons were voluntary, for once. When some of the rubbish-tip kids started looking anxiously at the heights of the city and drifting off to pick through the litter again, the Goldfish let them go and just kept teaching the ones that were left. And when we got so tired and wobbly we couldn't think straight, the Goldfish let us crawl to the edge of the tip and fall asleep on a mat of dried lily-pad leaves. I was starting to get used to the smell.

When I looked up I saw the Goldfish leading a pack of tiny Eemala children in an aerial dance around the rubbish tip, singing.

'NOOla yaon-wi LA, ael-ya linoolay NA,
Ael-YALA leyu EE, OOhoola NEEN-a YEE.'

It must be nice for it, I thought, to have pupils who could follow it into the air.

'Did they teach you that song?' Carl asked woozily, when the Goldfish jigged close.

'Not that one! They taught me oh . . . five others, but can you believe that they didn't have any songs about *math*.'

'You're teaching the alien kids maths,' said Carl. 'You're *making up new maths songs* for *aliens*.'

'Well, gosh, Carl, someone has to!' said the Goldfish, its eyes tingeing ominous red. 'Do you know you don't get to go to school up there in the city without one of those things round your neck? Or to go see a doctor? Or pretty much anything? Most of them down here don't even have parents. Why, if I had my warning and defence unit. Why, I could just say –' it paused, glowing with frustrated feeling, '– *heck*.'

Uwaelee and Naonwai came swooping over. 'Yey, LEE-laas-yala?' said Uwaelee, flicking a lilac ear so that the strips of coloured plastic threaded through it shook.

'She's asking if you guys are sick,' explained the Goldfish.

'She?'

'Sure! And Naonwai there's a boy. But it looks like little Tweel hasn't decided yet.'

Tweel was the one I'd been calling Small Indigo. I didn't know how 'not decided yet' worked among the Eemala but it didn't seem the most important thing at present. I thought I could tell that the girls were slightly bigger and had a tufty ridge of fur from the middle of their foreheads to the centre of their backs, and the boys had darker fur on their ears and around their eyes. But Tweel didn't seem to have either of those traits.

'We're OK,' I said to Uwaelee.

'No OK,' said Naonwai, unexpectedly. 'Ael-ay HEENla.' And he dropped a package of red plastic in front of us. Inside was some of the white crumbly stuff, and brownish sheets of something papery that didn't look like food but presumably was, and a heap of scarily purple capsules that might be fruit.

They'd brought us lunch. I could have almost cried from the kindness. Especially as it wasn't as if they had food to spare. I'd begun to notice how thin they were.

'Ael-ay NEEla,' I said. *Thank you.*

But it could still be poisonous to us.

'Oh, God, can we at least try it?' moaned Carl.

We nibbled very, very tentatively at the food. The fruit and the crumbly stuff were so bitter we hastily put them

233

down, but the papery stuff tasted of almost nothing and between being so hungry and desperate and wanting to be polite we ate most of it. It made us feel slightly less hungry and weak, but slightly more sick. So at least that was a change.

There was a sudden scream of 'YALU!' from above.

A flying car swept down from the city's heights and powered under the lower arches. 'EEena lill naley!' shouted Naonwai at us. He made shooing gestures with one pair of plum-coloured hands and pointed warningly at the upper reaches of the city with another.

'Hide, kids!' said the Goldfish.

We had to dive into the fallen red funnel to take cover, as the kids scattered into the air, shrieking. Lying motionless, watching from the funnel's mouth, we saw the car surge above the mounds of the dump. And for the first time I saw what Carl had meant about Krakkiluk armour: a tall Eemala male, standing upright in the vehicle, wore panels of some glossy, acid-green substance strapped to his body. He didn't actually look like a Krakkiluk, of course, but the influence was clear. There was another Eemala, this one armoured in electric-blue patterned with black, crouching beside him, steering the car.

Acid Green yodelled something and then leaped from the car into the air, reaching long, slender arms for the fleeing kids.

'They're *cops*,' said Carl.

The kids whirled in the air like autumn leaves on a

234

flurry of wind. Uwaelee, who had almost cleared the edge of the city, doubled back to snatch a mauve toddler from Acid Green's fingertips. She dragged it down to the surface of the rubbish mound and burrowed right inside it. Acid Green hesitated for a second, but evidently decided that following was too disgusting.

'Being caught must be pretty bad,' Carl said. 'Because, ew.'

'Why are they trying to catch them? The kids weren't doing anything wrong,' I said.

Most of the other kids had broken past the outer arches of the city and were making for the shelter of the root forest. Acid Green focused on one straggler in particular, a wine-coloured kid of maybe Noel's size – some distance away but with one injured wing, so that she flew in short, clumsy bursts, often bouncing awkwardly off the surface of the rubbish tip. Naonwai came speeding back to help. He grabbed Wine Red by the scruff of the neck and flew with her, wings pumping desperately.

'No, no,' I found myself moaning. Because the weight was slowing him down too much, and they were flying over a patch littered with spars of rusted metal and something like broken glass – nowhere soft enough to burrow down.

'Naonwai!' screamed Josephine, rising on to her knees at the funnel's mouth. 'Here!'

Acid Green looked around at the strange cry, but couldn't, thank God, place where it had come from. But Naonwai understood. He swept towards us and hurled the wine-red child in through the mouth of the funnel and we caught her, a shaking bundle of bones and fur. And Acid Green didn't follow – but only because he was after Naonwai now.

Naonwai zigzagged desperately beneath the lowest arches, sometimes catching hold of buttresses as he banked, sometimes skimming close to the surface of the tip, trying to throw Acid Green off long enough to make it to the forest.

'Go on, *please*,' Josephine urged.

But Acid Green was too fast, and too long-limbed. He pounced like a falcon on a sparrow, grabbed Naonwai out of the air and dragged him screaming and flapping to dangle from the nearest arch until Acid Green's electric-blue colleague came flying back to pick them up. Acid Green manhandled Naonwai into the car, which soared out from under the arches and away, but we could hear poor Naonwai still shrieking and struggling for a long time.

It seemed a long, long while before anyone stirred. The little red child Naonwai had rescued whimpered in Carl's arms.

Uwaelee emerged from the tip, a long, sad whoop already on her lips. She stood upright, her wings wrapped tight around herself like a blanket, her four eyes huge and unblinking.

A sad chorus of cries rose from the forest as the kids returned to the dump in desolate dribs and drabs.

'Naonwai,' moaned Tweel.

Uwaelee shook out her wings and began brushing rubbish from her fur. 'YOOLwa nunoon in!' she called briskly. 'Yanael-ul tia LEE.' Which probably meant something like, 'Stop crying and get back to work,' because the kids began wearily picking rubbish again, though many of them clustered around the Goldfish for comfort. The Goldfish did what it could, with songs and sparkles and bubbles, which did seem to help a little.

Uwaelee let them play, and within a few minutes she was as lively and boisterous as ever. But she was acting like that for the others, like Carl did for Noel. And if I could see that, all but the youngest of the Eemala kids must have done too.

'This happens often,' said Josephine flatly, watching. And it had to be true. There was no shock. The kids' ears drooped sadly against their heads, but they carried on working or playing, resigned.

'What will happen to Naonwai?' I asked.

The Goldfish asked, or did its best. But Uwaelee only gave an impatient shake of her wings and said shortly, 'Yia-OON eetala.'

'"Not dead", I think she's saying,' the Goldfish reported soberly.

'But I bet the cops are going to put one of those collars on him,' said Carl.

'Can you ask her if there's any organised resistance to the government,' Josephine said.

'Whoa,' said the Goldfish. 'Those are some complicated ideas . . .'

'No,' said Josephine, getting to her feet. 'They're simple.' And she pointed at her neck, then put both hands around it like a collar.

The Goldfish already knew the word for collar: 'Nangael,' it said.

'Heewa, Shosfeen! Nangael! *Znng*,' Uwaelee volunteered. But I didn't think the last sound was a word; from the way Uwaelee grimaced and splayed out her hands, it was what the collar *did*. It hurt. Uwaelee launched into a vigorous series of mimes; she was scooping something imaginary off the ground, but then she looked around stealthily and straightened up with a theatrical sigh of relief. '*Znng!*' she cried, flailing and grabbing at her neck. 'Eep-alye, wee, KraKLOO!' And she raised her fists, and began fighting an invisible enemy apparently much larger than she was. 'ZNNG!' she shouted again. And acted out falling over dead.

'The collar shocks you if you goof off your work? And if you try to fight the Krakkiluks it *kills* you?' Carl interpreted.

'Nangael,' said Tweel and pointed to the sky.

I wasn't sure what the sky had to do with it, but Josephine's eyes flashed with understanding. She held up one fist and spun a fingertip round it, then pointed up.

'Heewa,' Tweel agreed.

'The satellite,' I said, understanding. That ugly thing I'd seen in orbit before we fell; that controlled the collars.

'KraKLOO nangael Eemala?' asked Josephine. *Krakkiluks collar Eemala?*

It was the first proper sentence any of us had attempted and it was not at all grammatically correct. But Uwaelee understood.'Heewa!' she confirmed. 'Nul-ul LEEL ta-ha.'

'Yes. Many years ago,' translated the Goldfish.

'Ugh, KraKLOO,' Uwaelee finished.

'No kidding, UGH,' echoed Carl.

'Eemala OON nangael?' said Josephine, putting her hands around her neck again then taking them away as if the collar was disappearing.

Eemala with no collars?

Free Eemala?

Uwaelee tilted her head in confusion. 'Heewa,' she said, pointing to herself. *Yes, us.*

'What about grown-up Eemala? More Eemala?' asked Josephine, miming appropriately. 'Do you know the word for "fight"?' she asked the Goldfish.

'Yes – well, I don't have all the cases yet, but: LaeWA.'

'Eemala OON nangael laeWA KraKLOO?' asked Josephine.

Are there Eemala with no collars who fight Krakkiluks?

There was a pause.

At first I thought they hadn't understood. But then Tweel hissed something urgent to Uwaelee and I knew that they had.

They weren't sure whether to tell us the answer. They weren't sure, and that had to mean . . .

Uwaelee put one pair of hands round her own neck, and then, with the other pair, wrenched them away. A collar breaking.

'Heewa AY!' she admitted.

Yes, she was saying. *Yes.*

17

The planet was called Yaela. The city was called Laeteelae. The language was WOya.

But the Goldfish knew far more words than that. It was cheerfully but palpably disappointed with my progress in grammar.

But Uwaelee had produced something rather like an old-fashioned mobile phone, and was circling above the root forest, talking into it. The kids had mostly returned to rubbish-picking, hurried and anxious-looking, trying to make up for lost time. Every now and then, new showers of rubbish would fall like rain into the dump, catching in the intersections of arches and pattering on to the mounds, and the gang would swoop to search for useful things to sell to the tinkers and scrap merchants who sometimes flew down to trade while we hid under our funnel.

Uwaelee dived down to us again. 'NaeYAEna,' she said.

'They come,' translated Tweel soberly, and the Goldfish showered them with stars again.

'Now you see that, kids? That's what happens if you apply yourself. You remember the verb "naeYAE"? Who's going to use that in a sentence?'

No one mentioned Naonwai again.

*

The rebels flew in at dusk.

Two Eemala adults swept through the net of arches and dangled above the dump, and the tip kids came clustering round eagerly. A tall, cherry-red adult closed their wings around Uwaelee, enveloping her. Then rising on their wings again both adults placed one pair of hands around their necks and with the other pair pulled them away.

It hadn't just been a mime. It was the rebellion's salute.

Immediately they noticed what was wrong: 'Naonwai baeYAE-lia?' said the tall cherry one.

'Heewa,' said Uwaelee shortly, and changed the subject, though both adults' ears drooped at once. 'Yalu, EEPla-la-ya "h'yumans",' she said.

The pair stared at us sombrely. The stockier, grape-furred one tilted his head and flicked his ears and the red one exclaimed softly – interested but not amazed. They'd seen aliens before.

Uwaelee introduced us: 'This Hoolinyae, this Eenyo.'

'I think that's a gal and a guy, kids, just so you know,' the Goldfish said.

Hoolinyae, the red one, wore no collar, but there was a bare, furless scar on her neck where one had been – however she'd managed to free herself, it hadn't been easy.

Eenyo, the other one, still *did* wear a collar, resting amid dark mauve fur.

'Amaeleyae WOya?' said Eenyo to Uwaelee. *They speak WOya?*

A bit, I said, or tried to say. The Goldfish said something complicated in WOya and then something in Krakkiluk.

Hoolinyae and Eenyo muttered to each other in WOya; I heard the word 'KraKLOO'.

'OON!' protested Uwaelee.

'They think we might be Krakkiluk spies,' Josephine concluded.

'We're kids,' I said. 'Spawn. The Krakkiluks would never use kids; they don't think kids are even people.'

The Goldfish translated that, and Eenyo took a wand-like device from his pouch belt and waved it over us. It beeped, and this seemed to satisfy him for the time being.

'Goldfish,' I said. 'You sang a song for me on Mars, once – you shone the lyrics into the air . . . like subtitles. Do you know enough now?'

'I'll do my best, Alice,' said the Goldfish.

The rebel adults were conferring: *What can we do, Hoolinyae? Ah – look!*

They turned, and examined the floating letters the Goldfish was projecting into the air. Hoolinyae ran a hand though them, fascinated.

You can understand, through this? Eenyo said in WOya, pointing at the English words that appeared even as he spoke.

'We think so,' said Josephine. The subtitles didn't work both ways – the Goldfish didn't know WOya writing, so it translated aloud. Its WOya voice was changing. It was becoming more natural; less like a human American imitating an Eemala.

Then we will try to have a conversation, said Hoolinyae, with a faint chirrup of laughter in her voice.

Sometimes it took more than one attempt, but from then on we could more or less work out what they were saying:

You are aliens, Hoolinyae went on. *I have seen many pictures of many species, but nothing like you before. Are you subjects of the Grand Expanse?*

'No,' said Josephine. 'Not yet, at any rate. We were abducted.'

'We have to go home,' I said. 'We can't stay much longer on this planet without dying.'

And so we told them everything. I wasn't sure they understood all the details, but they understood enough.

'The Krakkiluks are our enemies too. If you can help us get home, then if there's anything we can do to help you, or anything our planet could do . . .' Josephine pleaded.

Eenyo looked even sadder. *You are lost children*, he said, *and you are sick. We are not yet so cynical that you would need to buy our help. But you would need a very advanced ship to take you home. Only the Krakkiluks and their lackeys have such ships – we Free Eemala have no ships at all.*

And yet, said Hoolinyae, *the ships exist. If all the people of Yaela were free – then we could take those ships, could we not?*

Hoolinyae. That day is very far away, said Eenyo.

I wonder, said Hoolinyae. She was studying the Goldfish closely.

I'm a very powerful computer, ma'am, said the Goldfish

sunnily. *And boy if I can help these kids here by helping you,* *then I will.*

Well, said Eenyo, *you cannot stay here on the dump, and* *even if we cannot send you home, perhaps we can help you* *a little.*

Uwaelee turned a sudden backwards somersault. 'MUNAlae-EEY-yae!' she was saying: *I want to come too! I* *want to see where you go. I found the aliens – I should be the one* *to show them to Ningleenill!*

'Show us to who?' Carl asked, but the Eemala were too busy arguing to tell us.

You never take us! I want to fight the Krakkiluks too. I can *help!* Uwaelee cried.

Sweet one, no, said Hoolinyae. *If the Nangaelyeva find us,* *you must not be with us. Think what could happen to you.*

I don't care, said Uwaelee, and her voice wobbled. Hoolinyae stroked the fur between her ears and Eenyo spread a wing around her shoulders. Like the parents she evidently hadn't got.

Come, then! said Hoolinyae, starting into the air. And she then turned back and looked at us, perplexed. She had forgotten we couldn't fly.

Like Krakkiluks, said Uwaelee. *But so few limbs.*

They are like living rocks, Tweel volunteered. I gave them a betrayed look. It is a bit much to find out the people you've been hanging out with all afternoon think you're like living rocks. Though I suppose we'd been thinking of them as like fruit bats, but surely that's nicer.

We'll help you carry them, said Uwaelee staunchly. *They are amazingly heavy, but we managed it before.*

After this assault on our self-esteem, the team of kids crowded in and hoisted us up again without so much as a by-your-leave, and flew us off over the roots. They held us a little more carefully than before but it was still far from comfortable.

'Erm, please tell me we're not going far like this?!' I squawked.

Only to the clearing, I glimpsed Eenyo saying, though I thought that was more to the Eemala kids than to me.

They set us down on a bare stretch of golden moss between whorls of root.

'So what's here?' said Carl, looking around. It didn't seem like a particularly special clearing.

Now you must go back, Hoolinyae was telling Uwaelee and the others.

Uwaelee sighed noisily. She seemed resigned to being left behind now.

'WURRRRGH!' boomed an enormous voice from above, and a great shadow passed over the clearing. We looked up.

It was one – no, *two* – of the huge purple winged beasts from the mosslands. For all their bulk they lowered themselves to earth as delicately as dandelion seeds. One bent its long shaggy neck and rubbed its face against Hoolinyae and then Eenyo like a friendly cat.

At second glance, they weren't *quite* like the wild

creatures we'd seen before. They were a little smaller, and their fur was brindled with orange. Whether because they were a different subspecies or just because they were domesticated, I couldn't know – but there was a simple harness around each one's shoulders, to which Hoolinyae and Eenyo were now fixing a set of reins.

'We're riding those things?!' said Carl, goggling.

Yes. I am sorry, said Eenyo unexpectedly.

'About what?'

That we have to take you by Wurrhuya. It is difficult to keep any kind of vehicle without attracting the attention of the Nangaelyeva.

'We get to ride *a flying furry brontosaurus* and you're *apologising?*' said Carl, catapulting himself on to the nearest Wurrhuya's back.

A flying what? I don't understand, said Eenyo.

Well, the rich people of Laeteelae had flying cars; I guess I'd have felt awkward if I'd had to take an alien visitor somewhere on a donkey, even if the alien thought the donkey was incredibly cool.

Josephine and I climbed up on to the second Wurrhuya and the creature rumbled agreeably underneath us. I stroked its fur: somehow very soft and coarse both at once.

'NweelaLUya, Shosfeen, Ally, Cal!' shouted Tweel in farewell.

But the rest of the kids weren't so upbeat. 'Goltfeesh,' they mourned.

The Goldfish chirped back to them in WOya without

translating itself for our benefit, and produced the biggest torrent of sparkles yet.

'Waaay!' cheered the kids.

'Huh,' said Carl, which made me feel a tiny bit better about the fact that for an absurd second I'd been slightly jealous. I hadn't known the Goldfish could even *do* that many sparkles.

Then the two Wurrhuya took to the air and we waved as the kids made the collar-breaking salute in farewell. The ground fell away, and tired and ill as we were it was exhilarating, the warm air of Yaela whipping our hair and gliding over our skin, our hands buried in the Wurrhuya's fur, and its song booming into the green evening sky.

'So hey, you guys are like the responsible adults in those kids' lives!' said the Goldfish to Hoolinyae, flying backwards alongside us and projecting subtitles as it went. 'That sure is nice.' And then its eyes went red and its voice dropped three octaves. 'WHY AREN'T YOU TEACHING THEM MATH?'

Hoolinyae had seemed like the more cheerful of the two rebels, but now she growled low in her throat and her expression grew worryingly close to that of the stone warrior we'd seen at the ruined city. *Assume less, robot*, she said.

We do what we can for them, but we are already stretched so thin. And there are so many such children, said Eenyo sadly.

'They do things for you, too,' said Carl, sounding not quite as disapproving as the Goldfish, but still not happy.

We have people in the city – Free Eemala in spirit – who still wear nangael. Everywhere they go they are monitored, every communication is listened to. But the children of the tip are not. They can pass messages from our allies, sometimes hide things for us. We hate to use them, yes. But without them . . . Eenyo sighed again. *Our defeats would have been still greater.*

Eenyo, said Hoolinyae. *Please. We have made such advances.* I figured she was the one who did all the jollying along when things got bad. I could relate.

'You say "people who still wear the nangael",' said Josephine, hesitantly, in case this was rude. 'But . . . you still have one.'

Eenyo ran a hand over the tight-fitting black ring. 'So many have died trying to remove the nangael. A few are lucky, like Hoolinyae – but no one has found a safe way to do it. So instead Ningleenill invented this.' He touched a little device about the size of a matchbox, clamped to the side of the collar. 'It interferes with the data sent to the satellite. Now it cannot tell I am going anywhere or doing anything I should not. But when there are group punishments, I still . . .'

He shuddered and trailed off.

'Group punishments?' said Carl, sickly.

'The device is so simple, but we will never be able to make enough to free everyone,' said Hoolinyae.

We soared past the heights of the city. We could see pendant homes as beautiful as jewels, and a few Eemala in decorated armour enjoying a party under filigree arches.

And close to the top: a pair of Krakkiluks, on a flower-shaped platform, watching the sun set over the ocean with their arms entwined. From the very peak of the city, the Krakkiluk flag flew: huge and golden and bearing a black sun.

'Wurrgh,' rumbled Carl's Wurrhuya suddenly, in a vaguely surprised-sounding way. We looked at it but couldn't see anything wrong. And then we were out over the sea, the puffballs and lily pads tiny gleams of colour below, and the clouds turning Klein Blue ahead of us, and the Wurrhuya intoned again. Josephine spread her arms wide as a flock of little orange flying things swept by, and turned her head to grin at me. For a while flying through that strange sky was all that mattered.

'Wurrgh,' complained Carl's Wurrhuya again. Hoolinyae made soothing noises.

'You said . . . the Nangaelyeva?' I asked. 'Are they the people who took Naonwai?'

Yes, said Hoolinyae. *Eemala in the pay of the Krakkiluks, who force the laws of the Grand Expanse upon their own kind.*

'You don't worry the Nangaelyeva or the Krakkiluks will find out about you? Even though the children know about you and the Nangaelyeva catch them sometimes?'

It is fortunate that they have learned to think so little of children. They are concerned that they should not grow up to be Free Eemala without collars. That is all, said Hoolinyae.

Besides, said Eenyo grimly, *there are always more of us. There are far more of us than they dream.*

'So . . . what will happen to Naonwai then?'

You will see, said Eenyo.

We could see another golden shore in the distance. Below us, the water was dotted with bobbing rafts, on which Eemala stood in ones and twos, scattering something from barrels into the sea. The water splashed and fizzed with activity beneath the surface. The Eemala were feeding something.

Beyond there were great round netted pens in the water, like fish farms, and the Eemala were tending to those too.

'Oh,' said Josephine, in her I-have-just-deduced-something-important voice.

'Yes?' I said warily.

'The pink things in the water. They're Krakkiluk spawn, aren't they?'

I remembered the wriggly things, their six legs, and the pinkness of the Krakkiluks under all their decorations.

'Ohhh,' I said.

'So that's what the Krakkiluks use this planet for,' said Carl.

Naonwai will be fitted with a nangael first, said Eenyo. And he will be set to work here, or somewhere like it, tending to the Krakkiluk spawn. The regime and its servants will say it will be a better life. There is even some choice – perhaps he can grow food for the spawn, or drive a sky-bus for the workers. The spawn spend the first five, six years in the water. Many of them die there, and far more would do so if we did not tend and feed them. When they begin to leave the water, we care for them. Teach them to speak.

We flew over a clutch of little islands. The beaches looked pink at first, until you realised they were heaped with Krakkiluk babies. They were keening softly, perhaps with hunger or perhaps with the recent shock of the transition from water to land.

Flocks of Eemala were busy on the beaches and in the air above; I could see some wading, helping the Krakkiluks out of the water. A lavender-furred Eemala flew in soothing circles above the island, holding a young Krakkiluk, almost as big as she was, rocking it in four thin arms with strange tenderness.

Big and cumbersome as it was, the baby Krakkiluk looked pathetically vulnerable.

'So they conquer your planet and then have their babies in your seas and then *make you look after them?*' I said.

Yes. At the expense of our own children. They are not all orphans, the children of the rubbish tip.

'That's awful,' I said.

'Huh,' snorted Carl. 'It actually sounds really familiar.'

I thought about some things from Earth history that yeah maybe weren't all that different and decided perhaps I'd better shut up.

They have so many worlds like this, said Eenyo. *All subject to the Grand Expanse.*

'Warm seas,' said Josephine, her eyes very wide. 'They can grow Takwuk on a cold world. But you've got warm seas.'

'What?' said Carl.

'Do you remember what Lady Sklat-kli-Sklak said was

252

the main thing they knew about Earth? *It has warm seas.*'

There was a silence, but not because any of us needed to think through what she meant.

'Oh, God,' I said.

The Grand Expanse is always . . . expanding, said Eenyo.

'We have to get home. We have to *warn* everyone,' I said, or tried to say.

Except a fit of coughing mangled the last part.

18

We plunged into a forest of root arches so high and tangled that you couldn't make out the ground below. Flights of four-winged blue creatures drifted up from its coils and the funnels rang like a great wind organ.

'Everything's very tense and all, but I think we should still yell WOO, now,' announced Carl, as a huge loop studded with ruby funnels reared up ahead.

No one objected, so as we soared straight through, Carl and I yelled out all the joy of flying, and the Wurrhuya cried and the sound melted into all the songs of the wilderness itself.

But Josephine stayed silent and Carl and I both ended up coughing again.

Then there were cliffs of grey stone furred with golden moss before us, and we were flying into a cave as immense as a cathedral. The roots burst through the inner rock walls and coiled through the cave, strung with cables and electric lights. Here and there shelves had been built among them, some filled with crates of food, others with strange devices, and others with scrolls that must have been books.

Hoolinyae and Eenyo, rather worryingly, leaped off their steeds in mid-air, leaving us on the backs of flying wild creatures we had no idea how to control. But the Wurrhuya didn't seem to need controlling; they alighted as gracefully as we'd seen them do before, and one lowered its head to a stream winding through the bottom of the cave. We had reached the rebels' hideout.

I was pretty much done with coughing, but Josephine slid off the Wurrhuya and seized my arm in an almost painful grip. I tried to smile at her. 'I'm OK,' I said.

'You're not,' Josephine said wretchedly.

'Tlrrk-ehk plit-li-klep,' crunched a Krakkiluk voice, and once again we all jumped and looked around for the enemy.

This time it wasn't the Goldfish. There was a real Krakkiluk, scuttling close – it hadn't seen us yet, but it was going to – and it carried a huge bucket of feed for the Wurrhuya. And now it was stroking the furry neck of the Wurrhuya and making a low contented grinding sound in its throat that was almost *purring* . . .

It saw us. It hadn't expected there to be anyone still on the Wurrhuya, let alone aliens.

'Aakk. Krrk-tal ni skekh!' it exclaimed, dropping the bucket.

Another Krakkiluk appeared – of course, where there was one Krakkiluk there was almost bound to be another – hurrying towards its mate.

'Okh-rlk akli-trk,' said the second Krakkiluk. This time the Goldfish caught up with the subtitles:

What is it, o rebel jewel?

I'm sorry. We should have warned you, said Hoolinyae, descending. *All of you. Humans, this is Kat-li-Yaka and this is Qualt-zu-Quo.*

'They're on your side?' I said, incredulous.

'Ugh, KraKLOO!' squawked a horrified voice, before introductions could get any further, and Uwaelee shot up from somewhere under the Wurrhuya's belly and hovered in trembling outrage in the air.

'Wurrgh!' sighed the Wurrhuya Carl had been riding, sounding relieved.

'Were you like, hanging on to its fur the whole way?' said Carl, and would probably have added, 'Cool,' but realised from Hoolinyae's and Eenyo's bristling fur that it wouldn't be tactful.

'Uwaelee!' hooted Hoolinyae, appalled. *You were forbidden to come with us.*

Uwaelee didn't pay any attention. *Why are there Krakkiluks here?*

This is foolish and dangerous, said Hoolinyae.

Everything is dangerous, Uwaelee retorted.

The cause of the Free Eemala is not a game for children, Eenyo said.

Uwaelee grabbed hold of a loop of root with her feet and flipped upside down, facing him.

Do you think I think it is? she asked passionately. *Do you think I thought it was a game for Naonwai today? I had to come. I have to fight them. How old were you when you began? Today is the right time for me.*

Hoolinyae's and Eenyo's fur smoothed and their ears drooped.

Also, these are my aliens, said Uwaelee, flipping right

side up and patting us. *Now why are there these . . . hairy Krakkiluks here?*

Kat-li-Yaka and Qualt-zu-Quo held claws nervously and waggled their eyes at us. They *did* look different from the ones we'd seen before. Their shells were patterned with the kind of green and yellow swirls and geometric shapes the Eemala liked for their wings. And they were also, well . . . hairy *was* the only word for it. Reddish bristles emerged from their exoskeletons and quivered slightly. None of the other Krakkiluks I'd seen had had those.

They help us, said Hoolinyae. She paused. *In their own way.*

These are called humans. Josephine, Carl, and Alice, said Eenyo. *The children at Laeteelae found them.*

I found them, Uwaelee corrected.

Are you victims of the Grand Expanse? asked Kat-li-Yaka. *We do not support the Grand Expanse! We have spurned its lies and flung aside its hateful privileges! We were born on this planet. We are true children of Yaela!*

'Oh, OK,' I said.

We yearn for Yaela's freedom! We gladly share the struggles of the oppressed Eemala! agreed Qualt-zu-Quo. *We almost are Eemala!*

'Ugh, KraKLOO,' Uwaelee growled under her breath, the ridge of lilac fur on her back bristling noticeably.

O brave star of Yaela, intoned Kat-li-Yaka.

O untamed flower, said Qualt-zu-Quo.

O defiant heart, said Kat-li-Yaka.

'Oh, they do that, too,' said Carl.

Kat-li-Yaka and Qualt-zu-Quo were well on their way into a romantic trance when a new voice hooted, 'OeLUYA ul-ing SUplae yee?' which the Goldfish gamely subtitled as: *What is all this fuss?*

An Eemala descended from the coils above. Male, I thought from the ears, and he was a lot shaggier all over than any of the others, and fatter than most.

What are those? he demanded, pointing at us.

'Ningleenill!' Uwaelee cried, delighted.

They're aliens, sir, said Eenyo.

I can see they're aliens. Do you take me for an idiot? scoffed the newcomer, and by now I was sure that he was a lot older than Hoolinyae or Eenyo. *What are they doing here?*

They fell from a Krakkiluk ship into my tip! Uwaelee explained eagerly and not quite accurately. *I found them. And look at this!* She gave the Goldfish an enthusiastic thump.

They need help, said Eenyo.

Isn't it enough that we have those two useless Krakkiluks making the place look untidy without you adding more clutter? complained Ningleenill, perching on a root well above the rest of us and yelling down. *Is this a rebel stronghold or a sanctuary for alien strays?*

But aren't they interesting? said Uwaelee, crestfallen, while the two Krakkiluks made a mournful noise. *They cannot even fly. Look how few arms and legs they have.*

Plenty of creatures of the Grand Expanse have that

258

number of legs, or even fewer, huffed Ningleenill.

'Excuse me,' I said, because I was getting tired of being talked over. 'But we're not from the Grand Expanse, and it's *not* just that we need your help. We might be able to help *you*.'

'We've got a very powerful computer,' said Josephine.

Ningleenill flapped into the air and gave the Goldfish an ill-tempered poke. *This is the powerful computer? It looks like a baby's toy.*

'I'm not a toy, sir!' said the Goldfish. 'I'm a *teacher*. Although learning is the best kind of fun!'

Are you up-to-date Krakkiluk technology? demanded Ningleenill, and I did feel sorry for the Goldfish, having to translate the other side of an argument it was having.

'We didn't know the Krakkiluks existed until a few days ago,' I admitted.

'Is Krakkiluk tech that much better than yours?' Josephine asked, cocking her head.

Inevitably, Krakkiluk technology is far the most advanced, said Kat-li-Yaka. *Because the Grand Expanse suppresses everyone else,* she added after a slight pause, when Eenyo and Qualt-zu-Quo looked at her disapprovingly.

'I'm the very latest in human AI technology with Häxeri and neat turbo thrusters!' the Goldfish replied sunnily. 'Josephine here did a super job of upgrading me.'

Josephine grimaced. I suspected mentioning her part in its level of sophistication might be a mistake and I wasn't wrong.

And how old is that one? said Ningleenill.

'I'm forty-seven,' put in Josephine instantly, but it was no good.

'She's just thirteen but so smart she's already taking her Baccalaureate! Boy, I'm proud of her,' said the Goldfish, and Josephine looked surprised, and pleased, and surprised at being pleased all in a moment.

Then why do you imagine you could do better than my own computers? Ningleenill sniffed. *Have you devoted seventy-five years to this one task? I am not having my life's work fiddled with by some alien child's plaything!*

'Well, that's rude,' said the Goldfish.

They're sick. Yaela's atmosphere is toxic to them, said Hoolinyae.

Ningleenill hesitated and his face seemed to soften a little. *Oh, well, help them if you like,* he conceded. *But keep them out of the way. Put them over there with the Krakkiluks.*

He flapped away.

Hoolinyae and Eenyo looked at us rather helplessly. Uwaelee's ears had gone sad and flat.

He's quite kind when you get to know him, said Hoolinyae.

Uwaelee, you may stay for this evening, but then you must go, said Eenyo, and they flapped off after Ningleenill.

There was a horizontal loop of root bulging out of a wall, over which metal beams and plasticky sheets had been laid to make a floor. The two Krakkiluks scuttled up there and, as we didn't have anything else to do, we did as we were told and sat over there with the Krakkiluks. Well, except for Uwaelee, who latched on to a higher twist of root, and dangled there, loftily ignoring them.

He doesn't have to be so unkind, said Kat-li-Yaka, patting the head of one of the Wurrhuya, who were still happily feeding. *It's not as if we're like other Krakkiluks.*

Uwaelee snorted sceptically from inside her wings.

'Who *is* he?' said Josephine.

Ningleenill is a brilliant scientist, said Qualt-zu-Quo. *He was from a wealthy family, and he was so talented he was permitted to study at Krakkiluk schools. When he was young, some of the richest families were not forced to wear the collar.*

But he secretly gave all his money to the Free Eemala and then he told everyone the Grand Expanse was wicked and he went into hiding! Uwaelee burst out, erupting from her wings. Then she caught sight of the Krakkiluks, snorted, and wrapped herself up in them again as if no such thing had happened.

'So, how did you guys end up . . . not being like other Krakkiluks?' Carl asked.

Is it true that you are thirteen years old? Qualt-zu-Quo asked Josephine instead of answering. He eyed Uwaelee uncomfortably. *How long is a year, on your planet? Forgive my asking, but are you . . . adults?*

'No,' said Josephine, bullishly. 'We're still spawn-aged.'

'Akk,' said Kat-li-Yaka, disconcerted, and though neither of them moved away from us it looked as if it took them a conscious effort not to.

We are very glad to sit and talk with you! said Qualt-zu-Quo loudly after a pause.

Yes. We are both very glad to be here. With spawn, said Kat-li-Yaka. They each reached out a multi-jointed arm and gingerly patted us.

'OK, that's fine, please stop touching us now,' said Josephine.

Eenyo came flapping down from a higher level, bringing more of the papery stuff we'd eaten before.

You may be able to digest this. Very simple carbohydrates and sugars. And we are contacting an ally in another city – we think we can bring you gases you can breathe safely. Do you know what you need?

We all cringed a little in anticipation. Of course a question like that was bound to get the Goldfish's attention.

'Well, guys?' demanded the Goldfish. 'Alice, I know you know this; Carl, I want to hear from *you*.'

Carl groaned. 'I dunno, mostly nitrogen?'

The Goldfish paused. 'That's not *wrong*, Carl, but hey, you can be more specific than that.'

Carl stared at it and then had a very heavy fit of coughing that I didn't think was actually natural.

'Seventy-eight per cent nitrogen, twenty-one per cent oxygen, one per cent gases that don't matter right now,' said Josephine wearily.

The Goldfish hadn't learned the words for nitrogen or oxygen yet so Eenyo didn't know what we were talking about, but the Goldfish projected a diagram of their atomic structures into the air and Eenyo said, 'Ahh! Elahiyalaheelon!' and made a note on a little roll of papery stuff from his pouch belt.

'Well, that's something,' said Carl heavily, as we contemplated a future of living in a cave, hooked up to a nitrogen supply, eating simple carbohydrates.

'We'll get scurvy, eventually,' I said, before I could remember to keep that sort of thing to myself.

'If they can get us nitrogen just like that, the Free Eemala must be a very large network,' said Josephine.

Oh yes, said Qualt-zu-Quo eagerly. *Yes, many, many are free in spirit, and they help the cause whenever they can. But there are only a few without collars. And every collared subject of the Expanse has their daily tasks, their path from home to work, and they cannot take a single wrong step without terrible pain. But the Eemala have been fighting to be free for years. Even before Ningleenill defected.*

Long before that, said Uwaelee crossly. *Do you think we waited so long to fight back? Even on the tip we tell the stories. We have been rising since Oohalla fell.*

I wondered if Oohalla was the ruined city where we'd slept.

'How did you end up here?' said Josephine to the Krakkiluks.

We were born here, said Qualt-zu-Quo. *We were raised by Eemala. I can remember swimming in the sea, I think, though perhaps that is just a dream. When I had moulted my tenth shell and was no longer a spawn, I was sent to Quar-ekhluk, in the heart of the Expanse, for training as a grown Citizen. But at once I missed Yaela. I remembered my life before my eleventh shell grew. Others seemed to forget. But I do not know – perhaps everyone remembers and does not speak of it?*

The Eengleeya – the Eemala who took care of me on the beach where I came out of the sea, she told us stories. She told me of the Grand Expanse, as she was supposed to, but also of Yaela, of the days when it was free. I knew I could return to Yaela one day, of course, if I pleased. And I considered that the Eemala could never go back to those days. And I didn't want to cut my tleek-li, and I was of age for it to be done . . .

The Goldfish had left 'tleek-li' untranslated. But Josephine looked at the reddish bristles piercing their shells and said, 'These are your tleek-li?'

Yes.

'What are they?'

Kat-li-Yaka ran a claw over Qualt-zu-Quo's arm, skimming the tleek-li, and Qualt-zu-Quo sighed. *We feel things. More than we can through our shells. Pain, but good things too.*

'And they cut them off?!' I said.

You are not exactly forced to, said Kat-li-Yaka. *But almost no one refuses. For one thing, you see, one cannot wear the most fashionable embellishments when you have tleek-li.*

'Oh my God, that is a terrible reason,' said Carl.

That is not the real reason, said Kat-li-Yaka, who seemed compelled to defend her species' honour. *When they are cut we might not feel so much, but it is also far harder to hurt us. We are stronger, but also less . . . less . . .*

She couldn't seem to find a word. Except in a way she already had. *Less.*

We did not find Love at the Feast of Klulk-ya-Wukuk or at the dances on Drook-lit, said Qualt-zu-Quo. *I was forever mocked and told I was so spawn-like, I never would advance beyond a sewage worker on a trade ship, let alone find my Love. Yet my heart said it was wrong, and though I did not wish to remember being a spawn, somehow I did, and I remembered tales and songs in which things were different. Never could I hope there was another Krakkiluk who felt the same. But then I met Kat-li-Yaka . . .*

And we knew our Love was a wild, free, true love! said Kat-li-Yaka. *All the Expanse would despise us, so we loved each other all the more. And we ran back to Yaela to pursue Freedom!*

'The cutting thing, doesn't that *hurt?*' said Carl, more stuck on that than on Kat-li-Yaka and Qualt-zu-Quo's happy ending.

Yes, said Qualt-zu-Quo. *Everyone says it hurts very much. They call it the Last Pain, because afterwards nothing hurts so much again.*

Uwaelee had shifted a little closer through all this, poking her nose out from between her wings, reluctantly fascinated.

'Ugh, KraKLOO,' she said, though not quite in the same scornful voice she usually said it.

I thought of Lady Sklat-kli-Sklak and Tlag-li-Glig and Krnk-ni-Plik, throwing us out of the ship, and wondered how much easier it must be for them to hurt people, if *they'd* all been so hurt.

'Do they grow back?' I asked.

Never, said Qualt-zu-Quo.

'Why would anyone . . . why would *anyone*?' said Carl.

Josephine said very quietly and tentatively: 'I can . . . see why.'

'What?' said Carl, appalled.

'If you didn't feel things you didn't want to, things might be . . . clearer. It would be easier not to . . . get things wrong,' said Josephine, staring at her hands.

'Er, no it wouldn't,' said Carl. 'You'd already have got something whackingly wrong, because it's a completely screwed-up idea.'

'Yes, but . . .'

I glimpsed the gills through her tangled hair. 'For God's sake, if Dr Muldoon comes up with some kind of not-feeling-things hack for people, you are *not doing it*,' I said.

Please do not do it, said Qualt-zu-Quo earnestly. *I think it is a terrible practice.*

'I was just saying I could *understand*,' said Josephine, getting squirmy under the attention, now. 'You know, *in theory*.'

She started coughing, a little bit. I picked up her hand, not looking at her, as if it had sort of randomly happened, and she didn't take it away.

We had not finished the story of our Love, said Kat-li-Yaka, rather annoyed. *And there is no other Love like it in the whole of the Expanse.*

'In a minute,' said Josephine. 'Now that you're here, what are you trying to do?'

We dedicate our souls to the righteous cause of the Eemala, said Kat-li-Yaka. *I fight for freedom for my beloved's sake, and he for mine.*

'Yes, but *how* do you fight?' Josephine persisted. 'Do you go out and get intelligence from the Krakkiluks, or what?'

There was a slight pause.

We . . . don't have connections in Krakkiluk society on Yaela, said Qualt-zu-Quo.

Mostly we offer our full-hearted companionship and solidarity, said Kat-li-Yaka.

Akk! And we feed the Wurrhuya! said Qualt-zu-Quo, eagerly. *It is . . . more important than perhaps it sounds.*

'OK,' said Josephine. 'But Ningleenill and Hoolinyae and the others – what are they doing?'

Akk, well, said Kat-li-Yaka. *They free other Eemala from their collars when they can. Of course their hope is to bring down the satellite and so free every collared Eemala at once.*

'But I guess you guys don't have, like, missiles or superguns or whatever,' Carl said.

Oh yes, said Qualt-zu-Quo. *We have. Ningleenill has been perfecting the technology for years.*

There was a pause. I tried to clamp down the electric spark of hope that started in my chest – I didn't feel I could take being disappointed. But Uwaelee had no such qualms and burst into airborne somersaults.

Then it can all be over! No more collars. Naonwai – everyone – can be free!

'They have a missile? Why haven't they fired it?' asked Josephine, making an obvious effort to keep her voice very calm.

Qualt-zu-Quo said: *I am not a scientist, but I understand the problem is a matter of setting the missile's course. The planet is moving and so is the satellite. It must be a perfectly precise calculation. If they fired and failed there could be terrible consequences.*

Uwaelee wasn't persuaded. *But we should do it! We should do it now!*

Carl, Josephine and I looked at each other, and at the Goldfish. Josephine was coughing again, but I knew we were all feeling the same quiver of excitement.

If the Goldfish could do the calculations, the Eemala could be free. If the Eemala were free, we could go home.

'Show it to us,' I said.

Qualt-zu-Quo and Kat-li-Yaka waggled their eyes. *We could not show a thing like that to spawn!* Kat-li-Yaka said.

Show *us!* cried Uwaelee.

But at that moment the Wurrhuya lifted their heads and let out a rumbling call. Another Wurrhuya with two more Eemala on its back swept down into the cave, and the new arrivals began unloading canisters that I guessed must hold the gases we'd been promised. Eenyo flapped down from the heights of the cave to greet them.

Eenyo, show us the big gun! Uwaelee begged.

The newcomers hooted in dismay and Eenyo looked very stern.

You told alien children of our most important asset? he accused the Krakkiluks, who clattered and folded themselves up as small and humble as they could. *Ningleenill will be furious if he finds out.*

'Please, it could make all the difference,' Josephine said. 'To us *and* you.'

But Eenyo had nothing else to say about it. *Now help set up this*, he told Kat-li-Yaka and Qualt-zu-Quo, and the Krakkiluks had to vacate their platform so we could sit in a little tent inflated with nitrogen and oxygen to breathe.

You're no different from Krakkiluks, cried Uwaelee, exasperated. *Why don't you listen?*

I think it's time you went home, said Eenyo. *We told you, only this evening. Our friends will carry you back to Laeteelae.*

I'll fly back myself, hooted Uwaelee sulkily. *Goodbye, humans!*

And before we could so much as stop coughing long enough to say goodbye back, she flew off in a huff without a backwards glance.

We felt pretty demoralised by all that, to tell the truth. We let ourselves be ushered into the tent and just lay there breathing.

'We've *got* to get the Goldfish a look at that missile,' I said.

'Well,' said Josephine despondently, 'I suppose if we're here for *years*, we'll manage it eventually.'

'The Krakkiluks'll have conquered Earth by then,' Carl said, and we all stared miserably into space for a bit.

'Goldfish, could you have a look around and see what you can find?' I asked.

The Goldfish tried – which I appreciated, because teacher robots don't really like doing things grown-ups say not to. But being orange and glowing, it was pretty conspicuous. Ningleenill soon noticed it nosing into things and shooed it back down to our tent at the bottom of the cave.

'It'll be no use finding the missile if they won't *listen* to us,' I said.

'I didn't think Uwaelee would just fly off like that,' said Carl.

'She couldn't do anything,' Josephine said.

'Yeah, but still.'

Yaela's rapid night was coming on again. The Krakkiluks were putting the Wurrhuya to bed on mounds of dried moss at the back of the cave. We ate a little more carbohydrate paper and I noticed Carl had gone to sleep. I thought of telling Josephine that we should wake him up so we could go on trying to work out what to do, but it turned out she was asleep as well.

I didn't want to sleep; that would mean another helpless tomorrow to wake up to – but I thought maybe I'd just rest my eyes for a little bit.

When I woke up, it wasn't tomorrow. It was pitch-black except for the soft glow of the Goldfish outside the tent.

The Wurrhuya were rumbling peaceably in their sleep. Everything seemed very quiet.

Except that someone was shaking the tent.

'H'yumans!' sang a voice, as softly as such a voice could. 'I – thing – up! Sky!'

'Uwaelee!' Carl cried, so eagerly that for the first time I wondered if he had just a bit of a crush on the Eemala girl, fur and four eyes notwithstanding. Anyhow, we scrambled out into the poisonous air. Uwaelee greeted us with a triumphant somersault.

'Aww, you came back!' said Carl, happily.

'OON baeYAE-nia!' crowed Uwaelee. 'LIN-yel maYEENwa-nia.'

'What's she saying, Goldfish?' Josephine asked.

I did not leave, I only pretended. And I have found it. I have been creeping and creeping around and I know I have found it. Come on!

She was pointing into the unlit upper reaches of the cave. I'd seen doorways to chambers and passages up there, for which the Eemala had no need of stairs. The Krakkiluks could maybe have climbed the web of roots to get there; we never could.

'Up, up!' urged Uwaelee in English.

'OON awaeya,' I said in what I hoped to be passable WOya – *no fly.*

'Hmm,' conceded Uwaelee, momentarily flummoxed.

'Wurrhuya!' Josephine exclaimed. 'We can use the Wurrhuya!'

'Wurryhuya!' Uwaelee agreed, plunging towards them.

The Wurrhuya were sleeping so cosily, with their necks wrapped around their bodies as cats wrap their tails, that it seemed a shame to wake them. But I climbed the heap of bedding to rub the nearest purple flank, and the creature woke and blinked at us in the Goldfish's glow.

Carl climbed up on to the Wurrhuya's back and it didn't seem to mind. So Josephine and I did the same.

'Now what?' Carl said.

Uwaelee sprang into the air just above the Wurrhuya's head, wheedling and beckoning. The Wurrhuya couldn't take off vertically like a helicopter, but it did seem to understand. It ambled out of the cave and into the starlight on its little legs and then leaped, up into the night air.

Now, you might think that sneaking off with a gigantic flying beast in a cave system full of stressed-out rebels would cause a bit of a ruckus. And you would be right. As soon as the enormous wings swept down, there was a clattering shriek of 'Krrrrrrr!' and another of 'Aaaakkk!' behind us. The Krakkiluks had woken up. Lights blazed and an alarm wailed. The Wurrhuya let out a worried 'WURRRGH!'

'Oh, they're so angry with us,' I moaned.

But there wasn't anything to do but keep going. 'Heewa,' said Josephine encouragingly. 'It's all right. Good Wurrhuya.'

Lovely Wurrhuya, turn this way, coaxed Uwaelee, flying backwards.

The Wurrhuya swerved back towards the cave,

silhouettes of frantic Eemala wings around us and panicking Krakkiluks below –

'Yalu! Yalu!' cried Uwaelee, pointing.

A small opening in the rock wall, framed in tangling roots.

'Pyaeng-NEL!' Uwaelee urged, which the Goldfish was too preoccupied to translate, but from her gestures meant 'jump'. Easy for someone with wings to say.

'Bring us in higher!' shouted Carl, doing his best to be a pilot even now, gesturing furiously. The Wurrhuya rose past the protruding roots. 'Guys, get ready!'

'OOLill-we!' called a burgundy Eemala behind us, and the Wurrhuya groaned in confusion and swung its neck back towards the call –

We had no more time to think about it. We jumped, and dangled nastily, and climbed –

– and we were standing in a rough tunnel of stone, lit by twists of glowing filament. Uwaelee ducked in above our heads and scampered forwards, leading us through turns and junctions, past storage chambers and dormitories.

Then ahead of us the tunnel opened on to a sheer drop above a great chasm, dappled with broken moonlight. There was a flimsy ceiling of metal netting above, holding up a blanket of golden moss. From the air, the pit would have been hidden.

Suddenly Hoolinyae swooped across the great shaft of space and into our tunnel, her wings hiding what lay beyond. 'OONyala naWEY!' she shouted, furious.

But I had already glimpsed something down at the bottom: the narrow, pointed turret of what could only be a missile.

'Goldfish!' I said. 'Go on!' And the Goldfish darted past Hoolinyae and into the chasm.

'Oh, hey,' I could hear it saying to itself, 'would you look at that.'

Hoolinyae chased after it. And we could see into the chasm again – the Goldfish emitting a blue beam from its mouth which played over the weapon's nose, steady even while the Goldfish dodged and dived.

'Waaay, Goltfeesh!' Uwaelee cheered it on.

'Hey, ma'am, gimme a second, I'm just trying to scan the on-board computer – I won't hurt anything,' it said, forgetting to speak WOya. And even when Hoolinyae caught up, her hands slid off its plastic sides and the Goldfish dodged free.

'OeLUYA ul-ing nal-ull INlana?' cried an indignant voice. Ningleenill swooped from a tunnel on the other side of the chasm, and joined Hoolinyae in trying to catch the Goldfish.

'I could do it,' said the Goldfish. 'I need a little more data, but could I plot a course? You betcha: why, we could have that satellite out of the sky in time for breakfast.'

'Goldfish, tell Ningleenill – tell him in WOya!' I shouted, as Eenyo came flapping anxiously out of the caves and tried to soothe the scientist, which had the opposite effect.

At the same time, the Goldfish was talking in WOya: *Sir, I'm sure I could help you out,* and Ningleenill was saying, *Who let this stupid device in here? It was the Krakkiluks, wasn't it?*

Eventually Eenyo and Hoolinyae managed to grab the Goldfish and steer it back to the tunnel where we were standing.

'Listen to it!' Carl pleaded. 'It's a lot smarter than it looks, I swear!'

Take your teacher robot back with you, and go to sleep, Eenyo told us. *We cannot play games with our one hope.*

How can we get them back down? worried Hoolinyae.

'Is there only one shot?' said Josephine. 'One missile?'

Eenyo's hand strayed nervously to his collar, but he didn't answer.

'Hoolinyae,' begged Uwaelee.

No, admitted Hoolinyae. *There are more. We have more than one try.*

But not many. If we fail, there would be reprisals, said Eenyo. *The collars would activate – millions would be hurt, at the very least.*

'What would happen if you didn't fail?' I asked.

There was a brief silence.

'Please tell us,' I said.

This is all very foolish, complained Ningleenill.

I know! Uwaelee burst out. *I think about it all the time. Everyone's nangael – broken, dead! Everyone would feel it. Everything would be wonderful.*

Everyone would feel their nangael die, agreed Hoolinyae, hesitantly. *They know what it would mean – they have been waiting for it their whole lives. There are only a few thousand adult Krakkiluks on the planet; they could not contain millions of us. Our people would seize the weapons and the ships and the governors' offices. We are ready. We have been ready for so long.*

The ships. Those were the words that mattered to me most. I couldn't help it.

'You'd all be free,' I said. 'We could go home. And we could warn our planet the Krakkiluks are coming.'

We have to be patient, said Ningleenill. *A little more patience won't hurt us now, after all this time.*

Yes it will! shouted Uwaelee. She fluttered back from us into the chasm, dappled by the moonlight filtering through the ceiling of moss. *I don't want to be patient. I've already grown up on a rubbish tip. How long do I have to wait? How long will Naonwai have to wait? Do it now.*

PART 4

19

OK, hello! I'm back!

So, right, you know how we were hiding in a cupboard waiting to rescue Mr Trommler and Th*saaa* was kind of wilting and needed the amlaa-vel-esh to themself, so I was completely visible if anyone *opened* the cupboard and also I needed to pee? Yeah a lot of things have happened since then, and they're *still* happening, so I wanted to get us caught up now because I don't know when I'll get another chance.

It had been very quiet for a long time. No one had come into the meeting room and there was no sign of Lena *doing* anything. We'd finished recording everything that had happened to us and Th*saaa* had tried to explain the rules of both Huckle Buckle Beanstalk and a Morror game called Clasmala-aa, which we couldn't play because I don't have enough tentacles. And time went on and on and Th*saaa* seemed so weak from the heat, and I figured there was no way we'd know if the Krakkiluks had caught Lena doing what she was doing, or if she'd already tried to do something and it hadn't worked. And anyway I was wriggling around so much that Th*saaa* said I should sneak outside quickly and pee in a corner.

'I'm not going to do that. That's disgusting,' I said.

Th*saaa* said it wasn't as if we liked the Krakkiluks, so it was perfectly fine to do something disgusting on their spaceship and I didn't need to feel bad about it, which sounded like something Carl would have said and made me sad.

Because even if everything worked out and we managed to get Trommler and Christa and make it back on to the *Helen*, now we weren't supposed to try and rescue Carl and the others.

So, I did sneak out of the cupboard, not that I was going to pee in the corner, I was just going to sort of think about it. And as I slipped out, there was this really bright flash of light that filled the windows and made my eyes hurt, and the whole ship shook a little bit.

Lena! I thought. But it couldn't have been Lena, because the flash had come from *outside*. So I went and looked out of the window, and I saw this bright spot zooming through space.

Th*saaa* must have seen the flash through the cupboard doors, because I felt a breath of chilly air on my neck.

'Is it a comet?' I said.

'It is moving away from the planet,' said Th*saaa*. 'Surely a comet would be pulled into orbit at this distance.'

'How do you know?' I asked, because I couldn't see the planet through the window.

'I can feel its magnetism.'

'Oh!' I said, impressed. Sometimes I forget that Morrors have magnetic senses.

'I think it must have been a weapon,' said Th*saaa*.

'Is someone attacking the ship?' I said. I hoped maybe it was someone from Earth or Aushalawa-Mo*raa* trying to rescue us. But on the other hand, if it was someone else the Krakkiluks had upset I didn't want to get blown up on top of everything else.

Nothing else seemed to be happening outside the ship, but whatever it had been, the Krakkiluks didn't like it, because suddenly we could hear them clattering and tramping around, and then Th*saaa* had to throw the amlaa-vel-esh over me because the door opened and four Krakkiluks came in and started going 'Splack! Clomp! Plosh!' *very* loudly and waving their arms around a *lot*.

Underneath the amlaa-vel-esh, the virtual screen flicked out of the little gold rod and there was Lena's face hovering in it: 'Hello, Noel,' she said.

'Shhhh! Not now!' I hissed, trying to turn the thing off.

The Krakkiluks stopped crunching and looked around. Th*saaa* and I froze in the corner of the room.

'Splunk, ack, crex,' said one of the Krakkiluks, and they went back to yelling at each other.

Lena waited and luckily, after a couple of minutes, the Krakkiluks reached some kind of agreement and clattered out.

'Something has happened,' she said. 'I felt the ship shaking, and I can see staff are responding to some kind of incident.'

'We saw this flash of light. Th*saaa* thinks someone fired a weapon at us,' I said. 'But I guess they missed?'

'Well, it makes no difference,' she said crisply after a moment. 'If anything it will keep the Krakkiluks confused for longer. We have to proceed. You found Trommler as expected?'

'Yes, he's round the corner.'

'Very well,' said Lena, and looked away from the screen at something out of shot; I could just see her hand move. Suddenly all the lights *did* go out. There was only the glow of the virtual screen and the stars outside the window.

I could hear crunchy cries of alarm from the passageway.

'I can see your position on my map,' said Lena. 'Go back to Trommler's interrogation room.'

'We can't see!' I said. 'Can you see?' I asked Th*saaa*, thinking of the magnetic sense and also remembering about how Morrors could see invisible stuff and wondering if they had any other useful abilities.

'No!' Th*saaa* said crossly. 'Except for that screen, which surely all the Krakkiluks will see as well!'

Lena looked thoughtful and the screen winked out. 'Hey!' I said, alarmed, and shook it.

Then I felt something metallic poking into my ear and I nearly screamed.

'I can see for you,' said Lena's voice in my ear, which was all kinds of creepy.

'What's that?!' I yelped.

'It's the spider robot. Now keep quiet. I'll tell you where to go. Can you make your way to the door by yourselves?'

Bump-shuffling along in an amlaa-vel-esh is even worse in the *dark*, you know? We jostled out into the corridor, where there were Krakkiluks crashing about everywhere, and all we could do was stick close to the wall and try not to be stepped on. There were flashes of light – some of the Krakkiluks had torches, but that just made everything seem even more chaotic and scary.

'The door is forty feet away, on your right,' said Lena in my ear, but despite that we bumped right into a Krakkiluk's legs. But it was so dark I guess it didn't think too much of bumping into something.

Actually it wasn't as difficult to find as we thought, because there were Krakkiluks with torches in Mr Trommler's room. The window kept flashing with light and shadow as the Krakkiluks waved their arms around, and they were talking Swedish and I could hear Mr Trommler going 'Nay!' more anxiously than ever.

'You still have the Krakkiluk DNA sample?' said Lena. 'Use it and let Trommler out.'

'We can't, there's Krakkiluks everywhere!' I whispered. 'And they're in the room with him!'

'Hmm,' Lena said, and then she went quiet for a while.

'Lena?' I said. 'Lena, are you still there?'

'Shhh, Noel!' Th*saaa* said. 'Listen!'

I couldn't hear anything at first, but then Th*saaa* shuffled us past Trommler's door even though I thought we should stay there. 'Listen,' they said again.

I could hear somebody crying. Somebody *human*.

'Christa?' I said. 'Th*saaa* – open the door!'

It took Th*saaa* a bit of fumbling round in the dark before they managed to touch the claw piece to the sensor by the door, but then they did, and it opened.

I could make out a shadowy heap on the floor against

283

the far wall. 'Vem där?' it said. That's Swedish.

'It's me and Th*saaa*!' I said, stepping out of the amlaa-vel-esh. 'We're here to rescue you!'

'Oh, *Noel*,' Christa said, lunging forwards and hugging me. Which was weird, though also it was maybe kind of nice to be hugged.

Then horrible grinding alarms went off everywhere, and there was a whiff of smoke in the air.

'You've moved. Go back to where you were,' said Lena's voice in my ear.

'How did you *do* that?' I moaned.

'Who are you talking to?' Christa said.

'I confused the temperature control system in tactical areas and started some fires. I think I could destroy this ship all by myself, given time,' said Lena, sounding rather pleased with herself.

'Please don't,' I begged.

'You said . . . you said the Morror kid is here?' said Christa doubtfully.

'Is that Christa?' Lena asked.

'I am here,' said Th*saaa*.

'OK, is there any way we can get the invisibility gown over three people?' I said.

'*No*,' Th*saaa* said.

'It's *dark* – if you would all stop *talking* so much and just go back out there, they won't see you,' Lena said impatiently.

I felt like in that case we should let Th*saaa* have the amlaa-vel-esh because they were the one who needed it for medical reasons and I guess I felt leaving Christa the only one visible was sort of mean. Still, no matter how dark it was, that didn't feel like much protection against gigantic lobster aliens and I didn't like going out there at all.

Christa didn't like it either. 'Åh gud,' she kept moaning and honestly I don't know if her doing that or Lena in my ear telling me to make her shut up was more distracting.

But once we got outside, it looked like Lena's plan was working: a lot of the Krakkiluks were running off to deal with the fires or because they were supposed to evacuate that area or whatever. The window in Mr Trommler's door was dark now.

But there was a Krakkiluk soldier standing outside it.

'There's still one *there*,' I said in despair.

Lena sighed.

'It's not *my* fault!' I said.

'Fine,' said Lena. 'Which of you has the device I gave you?' she said, ignoring this.

'I do.'

'Give it to Th*saaa*. Noel, do you have the amlaa-vel-esh?'

'No.'

'Then take it.'

'But Th*saaa* needs it!' I protested.

'Th*saaa* will be fine for a few minutes,' Lena insisted.

'The gown?' whispered Th*saaa*. 'Here. If you need it, take it.'

I saw – just barely – Th*saaa*'s silhouette appear in the darkness, and felt the weight of the gown settle over my arm.

It was cold and slippery, but even I could tell it wasn't as cold as it had been.

'Leave the others and proceed fifty feet to the left,' said Lena.

'Noel?' said Th*saaa*. I suddenly wished I could see their colours.

'It's OK,' I said, and I did as Lena said. After like two seconds I couldn't see Th*saaa* and Christa behind me, or much of anything ahead of me, except stars out of a distant window. I hadn't been alone like that since Th*saaa* came and got me out of my cell.

'Keep going,' said Lena in my ear. 'Stay close to the wall.'

That's what I was doing anyway; as well as not wanting to bump into any more Krakkiluks, feeling along the wall was the only way to tell which way I was going.

'Stop,' Lena said. 'Turn around. Take off your boot.'

'You're supposed to say "Simon Says",' I muttered, but I did as she said, and I stood there feeling like an idiot, stuck on an alien spaceship and holding an invisibility gown in one hand and a boot in the other.

'Move away from the wall. Into the centre of the passageway,' Lena said. 'I need you to do three things. On my signal, you will make a loud noise. When I tell you, get the gown on – *immediately* – and then throw the boot as hard as you can to your right while throwing yourself to your left. Do you understand?'

I understood, or near enough, and it made me want to make faces. 'I'm not going to like this, am I?' I said.

'Probably not,' agreed Lena, and from her faraway cell, she turned on a single light in the ceiling right above my head.

I kind of froze up. The light was dazzling after so much dark. I couldn't see *past* it into the dark corridor where the Krakkiluk stood by Mr Trommler's door.

'Make a *noise*,' Lena insisted irritably in my ear, though surely the Krakkiluk soldier must have already noticed, must already be coming?

'Hello, Mr or Ms Krakkiluk . . .' I said, not as loudly as I meant to. 'I'm over here – I'm the human spawn you guys have been looking for . . .'

I heard a rattle of pointy feet, and then I could see the huge silhouette of the Krakkiluk charging towards me –

'NOW,' said Lena in my ear, but I didn't need telling. I threw on the amlaa-vel-esh and jumped sideways, flinging my boot to the right. It wasn't a good throw or anything but it hurtled through the open door of another meeting room, and thudded on the floor.

The Krakkiluk hesitated for a split second, almost standing on top of me, and dived towards the sound.

The door whisked shut behind it. And from the Krakkiluk's blows against the door, Lena had it instantly locked.

'There,' she said, sounding pleased with herself.

'Awesome!' I squeaked, dragging the amlaa-vel-esh off because it was freezing inside it without Th*saaa* in there with me too.

I raced back along the corridor and Th*saaa* had already opened the door and got Mr Trommler out and Christa was hugging him and probably saying 'Are you OK?' in Swedish but Mr Trommler seemed all dazed and shaky and wasn't answering her.

'We're escaping,' I told him.

'What?' Mr Trommler said. 'We can't. It's impossible – they'll . . . they'll be even angrier.'

'It's not impossible – look, we're already doing it!' I said, pulling at his arm because he was kind of crumpling against the wall of the corridor and staring around, which was fair enough but also not helpful.

'Papa, komma,' Christa pleaded.

'I can't keep that soldier contained indefinitely – you need to move. I'm clearing a route to the *Helen* for you,' said Lena.

'You have to follow me,' I said.

'How do you know where you're going?' Christa asked.

'I don't!' I said, running ahead and hoping they would get it together to follow me.

It was like we were a pinball in a huge arcade game Lena was playing. Doors opened for us and locked behind us; we stumbled down dark corridors and through the energy reactor room, and a lift came rushing up to meet us. And yeah it's not like we didn't run into any Krakkiluks at all. They even kind of . . . shot at us a few times. But it was always dark, and sometimes smoky, and it happened really fast so by the time you noticed you were being shot at it was already over, and then Lena would set off another fire alarm or something else to distract them.

And I guess that big weapon whizzing past the ship earlier had also helped; they must have thought they were being attacked from *outside*.

So we kind of muddled along through a huge, pitch-dark space and I didn't even know we were *on* the lift until Lena said, 'Everyone hold still,' and the floor dropped away.

'She could warn us!' Christa complained, once we'd all finished screaming.

'I am *quite* busy,' Lena retorted in my ear. And we went hurtling down through the ship until we were in that big red bay we came in at when the Krakkiluks first captured us.

I thought we were going to run into the entire Krakkiluk army here, but we didn't because it turned out the bay was, like, seriously, properly on fire. Lena must have set it going a long time before we got there. The enormous doors to space were already open, though, and the planet was gold behind them. I could just see *Helen* through the horrible black smoke and red flames.

'Lena!' I coughed. My eyes were already streaming. 'You're going to cook the *Helen*! And *us*!'

Lena didn't say anything, but water burst from sprinklers in the ceiling and walls. We ran, coughing, towards the ship and Mr Trommler shouted, '*Helen*!' and a ramp sprang open from the ship's side.

'Oh, Captain!' cried *Helen* joyfully, as we raced inside.

'*Helen*, get us out of here!' cried Mr Trommler, and the ship lurched into the air and for a moment, before the artificial gravity adjusted, I felt myself floating off the floor.

'I'm calling Earth, Noel,' said Lena, sounding sad and faraway now. 'I have been for the last two hours. I'm showing them the way here. At least, I hope I am.'

I didn't know quite what to say, now we were leaving Lena behind. It hadn't felt real while her voice in my ear was bossing us around.

'Thank you, Lena,' I said. 'Good luck.'

But she never replied.

I didn't have time to think about it; I couldn't take it any more.

'Bathroom, bathroom, bathroom!' I said, racing ahead of the others.

And I only just made it.

When I came out of the bathroom I could see the Krakkiluk spaceship from a window: all gold and black and spiky. It didn't look as damaged as I hoped it would. But it was already miles behind us, and so far it hadn't managed to grab us back. I wondered where Lena was hiding and how long it would be before they found her.

But we hadn't gone to hyperspace yet, and so they *could* still grab us. The planet was still down there – Carl was down there, he had to be, he was really close and we were just going to leave him . . .

'I'm glad to see you again, Noel,' said *Helen*. 'And I'm very sorry for everything you've been through. The others are on the command bridge.'

I hurried into one of *Helen*'s nice, normal lifts that smelled of flowers and wasn't going to go anywhere awful.

'Have you been OK all by yourself, *Helen*?' I asked, patting the wall.

'I've been reading, mostly,' said *Helen*. 'Those books Miss Jerome sent me . . . they were very interesting. I enjoyed the Maya Angelou and the Simone de Beauvoir.'

I hadn't read either of those but I was glad *Helen* had had something to do.

On the command bridge there were control banks a bit like you'd get on a Flarehawk, but much shinier, and there were big comfy leather chairs. Christa was huddled up in one, hugging herself and staring into the distance and twitching like this rabbit me and Carl had that was scared of the washing machine. And Mr Trommler was in the big captain's chair and there was Th*saaa*, wrapped in a new cooling cape, arguing with him.

'We muuuuust go *nooooow*,' Th*saaa* was urging, all long vowels because they were so stressed and tired. 'Lenaaaaa – Lena told us to return to Aushalawa-Mo*raa*.'

'We can't leave those kids,' said Mr Trommler. And I felt this kind of jolt in my chest. 'I can't leave those kids stranded.'

'You want to rescue them?' I asked. 'Could . . . could we even find them?'

Mr Trommler turned to me. 'Of *course* I want to rescue them, Noel, what do you take me for? The Goldfish robot had Häxeri technology, didn't it? *Helen* should be able to trace it. If it's with them, then yes, we could find them.'

'Noel,' warned Th*saaa*. 'We muuuuust make for Aushalawa-Mo*raa*.'

291

Th*saaa* still didn't look well: their colours were all wrong, sort of faded like they'd been left in the sun, flickering feverishly. They needed to go and rest in their cooling chamber, but how could they when we were maybe only a minute away from being hauled back on to the Krakkiluk ship?

'Lena said we'd only make it all worse . . . that the Krakkiluks would capture us again,' I said.

Mr Trommler looked horrified. 'Is that where this comes from? Lena wanted us to abandon her own sister?' he asked. 'She's a brilliant young woman, but emotionally stunted. That poor kid deserves better.'

I hadn't thought about Lena and Josephine like that before. I didn't know if it was true. Lena had sounded so sure of what to do.

'*Helen*, search for Häxeri technology,' Mr Trommler said, and Th*saaa* grabbed my arm with three tentacles and basically dragged me back into the lift and shut the doors.

'What are you doing?' I said crossly. Oh, I was so tired, now I thought about it. I *am* tired.

'We haaaaaaave . . . we have to stop him!' they said wheezily.

'What?' I said. 'How?'

'You know I want to save the others too! But if the Krakkiluks catch us again all Lena's woooooork will be wasted!' Th*saaa* said. 'And we must take Trommler . . . ouuuut of their reach. For the Earth's sake.'

'But it's not like we can do anything, even if . . .' I said. Even if we wanted to, I was thinking.

'*Helen*,' Th*saaa* said. 'She would listen.'

'I can't do anything my Captain doesn't want,' *Helen* announced.

'But you caaaaaan,' Th*saaa* said. 'You know that you can. *Helen*? *Helen*?'

But *Helen* said nothing.

'Noel, talk to her!' Th*saaa* urged.

I don't reckon it would've worked anyway.

And even if it would, I didn't want to.

'No, Th*saaa*,' I said.

Helen opened the doors and I went back on to the bridge.

'Come here, Noel,' said Mr Trommler. 'We're going to find your brother.'

'I believe I have located the Goldfish,' said *Helen*. 'Preparing for atmosphere entry.'

And there, I thought, it would have been awful if we'd run off when it only takes like a minute to find them. We'll grab them real quick and get out of here.

And that's everything, I guess. I get why Th*saaa*'s worried, but we're going to do it, I know we are. Mr Trommler says we're only a few minutes away from the place the Goldfish's signal is coming from.

Carl, Alice, Josephine – hang on. We're coming.

20

The missile sliced across the dark green sky like a blade of gold. We watched from the clifftop as the air rippled behind it and all the hooting, whistling things of the forest lifted into the air, bursting into a panicky chorus.

Uwaelee strove up into the missile's wake, chasing after it as it sped away, as if she could follow it all the way into orbit. And after a moment Hoolinyae and Eenyo soared after her.

'Please, come on, *please*,' Josephine was muttering.

The missile shrank until it was a golden star in the evening sky, and then vanished. Hoolinyae, Eenyo and the others remained circling like eagles on a thermal.

And then there was an awful scream.

Eenyo, clutching at his neck, was plummeting from the sky. Hoolinyae and Uwaelee uttered shrieks of alarm and darted to catch him, but I could see him still spasming in Hoolinyae's arms.

'It didn't work!' I said, horrified. 'We missed, or . . .'

The satellite was still working. And it *knew* what had happened, and it was punishing Eenyo for the attempt.

'OON, OON,' keened Uwaelee.

'Oh, God,' I said. 'If it's happening to him . . .'

'It's happening to every Eemala who wears a collar,' said Josephine, sounding sick.

Hoolinyae lowered Eenyo down to the golden carpet of moss on the plateau, where he lay bundled up in his wings. Little gasps of pain came from between his clenched teeth.

Ningleenill pounced down on the Goldfish in a rage, landing on its back and pummelling it with both pairs of fists. *I was a fool to listen! See what you have done!*

It's OK! said the Goldfish in WOya, which might not have been tactful. *Sir, I believe we over-corrected a touch for wind drag – we have better data now! In fact –* it broke off for a moment, its eyes flashing as it processed information – *we got a glancing hit! This is totally fixable!*

Eenyo parted his wings a little, and looked up. There was a tiny red light on the collar which I'd never seen before, flashing on and off. He struggled to stand, leaning on Hoolinyae.

Try again, he said hoarsely. *Please, try again. It would be worth it – to never feel that again.*

We have no choice, said Ningleenill grimly. *There is no turning back now.*

'How long will it take to reload and calculate the satellite's new position?' Josephine asked.

It took about forty minutes, I guess. We helped as best we could. We went back down to the chasm that held the launcher and Kat-li-Yaka and Qualt-zu-Quo, useful for once, loaded the second missile, and we helped strap it into place while Ningleenill and the Goldfish pored through the data.

At last the second missile rose in its cradle and

swivelled on its mount, nosing the sky.

Eenyo's collar had stopped flashing and he could stand by himself, and even fly a little. *Do it, then*, he said weakly.

'It has to be right this time, Goldfish,' said Josephine.

'Wait a sec,' said the Goldfish. 'There's something . . . something's got a lock on me, kids, something's . . . incoming . . .'

There was a huge sound like the sky tearing apart.

I clutched my ears. It's the Krakkiluks, I thought. They know where we are and they're doing something awful and it's all our fault. I looked up and saw a new speck of white in the green sky.

'Wait,' whispered Josephine. 'That's . . . that's not a Krakkiluk ship, that's –'

'*Helen!*' I screamed, as the *Helen of Troy* swept down to the plateau like a descending angel.

'Noel, oh my God, NOEL,' boomed Carl, because practically before the ship had touched the ground, Noel came stumbling down the *Helen's* ramp. He was dirty and dishevelled and for some reason wearing only one boot, and he rushed into Carl's arms and almost knocked him over.

'Kuya! We did it! We found you!' he crowed.

'You're OK? You're really OK?' Carl demanded, holding him back and looking him over as if there might be gaping wounds on him he somehow hadn't seen the first time.

'Th*saaa*!' I shouted, because Th*saaa* too was shuffling down the ramp. They looked wobbly and their colours were sickly and pale. I wanted to hug them but they looked so overheated and fragile I didn't quite dare.

But it was going to be all right. All these days of starving and struggling and fighting each other because we all thought we were probably never going home again, and now we were.

'Aleece. Huuuuurrrreeee,' Thsaaa said weakly. 'They will *fiiiind* us. We must go now.'

'Lena – is Lena with you?' Josephine was saying, a rough edge in her voice, staring desperately up the ramp into the *Helen*'s interior.

But Lena didn't come out.

'She's OK; I mean, she's going to *be* OK,' said Noel. 'She was amazing; she hacked the ship with her spider-computer things and got us out. Come on, we've got to *go*.' He dragged at Carl's arm. 'I'll tell you everything, just get on the ship, although – Oh, wow,' he added, noticing the Eemala, who were clustering around, wary but curious.

'Yalu, h'yumans!' exclaimed Uwaelee.

'This is my brother Noel – Noel, this is Uwaelee.'

Noel held out a hand in a polite daze, which Uwaelee looked at, nonplussed, and then kindly patted.

'Yalu laweema!' said Hoolinyae, fascinated by Thsaaa's changing colours.

'Lena hacked the ship?' said Josephine, and a small furrow appeared between her eyebrows. 'That . . . that doesn't make sense.'

And behind Noel and Thsaaa was Rasmus Trommler.

However he'd escaped the Krakkiluk ship, at some point afterwards he must have found time to change his clothes because I was sure the exquisite cream-coloured suit he was wearing was fresh on. He wandered down the ramp on to the golden surface of the new world, looked around, and checked his cuffs.

'Hurry on to the ship, children,' he said. 'We're leaving.'

'The missile . . . I'm still . . . recalculating . . . the trajectory . . .' said the Goldfish, slow with the effort of all the things it was doing at once.

'We can't leave,' I said. 'Not yet.'

'Alice, come *on*,' begged Noel.

'Noel, she's right, listen,' Carl said.

'We can't just leave these people,' said Josephine. 'They've helped us. And they're trying to get free of the Krakkiluks too –'

'Ahh, the Free Eemala,' said Rasmus Trommler idly.

And suddenly a cold, flat feeling settled over me. Because how could he have known about that? How would he even know the word Eemala? Everyone stopped talking.

'Yes,' said Josephine, her eyes narrowing.

A cloud of those Archangel Planetary doves drifted out of the *Helen* to surround Rasmus Trommler.

'A perverse enterprise. Yaela has been much better off as part of the Grand Expanse,' he said, drawing a little silver device from his pocket. 'And so will Earth be.'

And before we could do more than take in a shocked breath, he gestured with the little silver thing and a terrible beam of flaming destruction poured out of the sky into the chasm which held the missile launcher and left only a smoking hole behind.

The Eemala screamed in horror. I took a step back and nearly fell; I couldn't seem to feel the ground beneath my feet. Josephine froze, eyes huge. Th*saaa* turned colourless grey.

Uwaelee flew at Trommler in fury – and Qualt-zu-Quo and Kat-li-Yaka came scuttling up from the cliff-side in righteous anger – but Trommler gestured again with the little silver device and Eenyo collapsed, spasming and crying out. Uwaelee turned to him with a moan of despair.

'Be careful,' Trommler said, taking a Krakkiluk translator-box from his pocket and slinging it around his neck, 'if you don't want to make this worse for yourselves. And, ah – traitors to the Expanse.' The device had switched to Krakkiluk. 'You must have known there'd be consequences for that.'

Qualt-zu-Quo had scooped up Eenyo with more tenderness than I'd thought any Krakkiluk was capable of showing to someone not their spouse.

'Why are you doing this?' Noel wailed.

'He's been an agent for the Krakkiluks the entire time,' said Josephine, loudly. Her fists were clenched by her sides but I could see she was forcing herself not to look frightened. 'And I'd bet that Häxeri is Krakkiluk technology they gave him. Or that he stole it.' She smiled joylessly. 'That's how Lena was able to hack the ship. That's how the Goldfish could program the missile computers. We should have known.' She turned to Trommler. 'You never invented anything.'

Trommler snarled. 'You,' he said, 'have caused me inconvenience enough.'

I would never have thought what happened next could be so fast. The doves swept in on us, a panel opening in each one's belly and something unfolding from inside. And something closed, tight and cold, around my neck.

'We want everything to be perfect for you,' the doves cooed in unison.

I put up my hands and felt the thing round my neck in disbelief. The collar was too tight for me to see, but I could feel its smooth, seamless surface, and see the neat silver band on Josephine, on Carl, on Ths*aaa*, on Noel. A little smaller and lighter, perhaps a generation or two more advanced than the ones the Eemala wore. But it was the same thing, I knew, designed to do the same job. Designed never to come off.

'Now, perhaps you'll all behave yourselves,' Trommler said.

'What?' said Noel. 'What's this?' Because he'd never seen one of the collars before; he had no idea what had just happened to him.

'Don't –!' began Carl, but Noel pulled at it, trying to get it off.

A tiny light on the collar flashed and Noel gave a shocked gasp. On instinct the rest of us moved towards him, as if we could shield him, somehow drag the horrible thing off him. Even though we knew, I guess, what would happen.

But when it did, it was utterly surprising, as if we had no warning at all. I felt the shock burn down my spine and wring my muscles and I couldn't make a sound because I couldn't breathe. And then it was gone, as fast as it had come, except for lingering little sparks in my arms and feet. Each of us had crumpled on to hands and knees, gasping.

Th*saaa* was swearing softly at Trommler in Thly*waaa*-lay.

'He's a little kid!' roared Carl, his arms round Noel again. 'You can't –'

'I'm not hurting you,' said Trommler. 'You're hurting yourselves.'

'Brrrk-tlok klalak-pruk – *sssss!*' roared Kat-li-Yaka, clawing at her neck. She and Qualt-zu-Quo were wearing collars now, too.

The Goldfish charged towards Trommler apparently planning to simply cannon into him. I braced for another blast of pain, but it didn't come. Trommler sidestepped, and as he did so he clapped a little metal disc to the Goldfish's forehead, where it stuck.

There was a faint buzzing sound. The Goldfish hung, frozen in mid-air, its eyes flashing rapidly.

'That's better,' Trommler said.

'Goldfish,' I whispered.

There was a tiny pause. 'It's OK, kids!' said the Goldfish. And the worst thing was, it still sounded like itself. 'Everything's perfect. Let's fly away with Archangel Planetary.'

And because it thought everything was perfect, it bustled cheerfully away into the *Helen*.

'Into the ship, now,' said Trommler, and turned his back and walked away. He didn't even need to wait to see us obey him.

At first we just stood there looking at each other. I don't think any of us thought we had a hope in hell of actually resisting, and there was nothing left for us on Yaela but the awfulness of what we'd done, anyway. But we couldn't bring ourselves to hurry after him just because he told us to.

Noel was sobbing. 'I'm so sorry. I thought I was saving you. We should have made him go back to Aushalawa-Moraa like Lena said; she told us not to come here and I didn't listen.'

Behind us the Free Eemala were gathered in despairing huddles on the ground. I couldn't bear to look at them – especially not at Uwaelee. We'd ruined their rebellion just by turning up and trying to help. I wanted to apologise, but how? How do you start?

Then the collars started to work again, first as a buzz under the skin, then rapid pulses of jolts along the nerves, then suddenly it was huge and burning and everywhere, and it took control of my body and moved me a step forwards somehow without my being involved. The pain subsided a little bit, then flared up again when I stopped moving. Soon I was stumbling forwards in graceless little jerks like a puppet, and the same thing was happening to the others; we were all jolting into the ship, away from the pain, and I couldn't stop, even when I tried.

'Kat-li-Yaka! Qualt-zu-Quo!' Hoolinyae cried, desolately.

The two Krakkiluks were coming too, whimpering and trying to hold each other's claws. Trommler hadn't put collars on any of the Free Eemala; I suppose he felt he'd done enough to them to satisfy Lady Slat-kli-Sklak. I couldn't look back, at the golden planet, at the defeated rebels – the collar wouldn't let me. We walked up the ramp as if we weren't leaving a whole world behind.

'*Helen*,' I said under my breath, as we stepped on board. 'Help.'

But the *Helen* said nothing.

21

'What's going to happen to us?' said Josephine.

We were in the lounge where Trommler had greeted us that first day on the *Helen*. Trommler was sitting in a big leather chair, sipping a drink one of his doves had brought to him. We were on the floor. Trommler had knocked us down with a whisk of the silver device as soon as we came in, and we'd none of us dared to move since. The Krakkiluks looked ridiculously large in a room built for humans and Morrors, forlornly holding claws by the snooker table. It seemed so long since we had been here before.

The Goldfish, oddly, was still translating everything, though it didn't seem to realise it was doing it now.

O *stolen treasure*, Qualt-zu-Quo was saying miserably.

O *flower-in-the-storm*, said Kat-li-Yaka.

'It's OK, we'll be OK,' Carl was telling Noel.

But Noel was inconsolable, and Carl and Josephine and I were all coughing – we'd been breathing oxygen and nitrogen at the Free Eemala camp, but the collars had kicked us when we were down and my already strained lungs felt as bruised as the rest of me. At least we had non-toxic air, now, I thought dully.

The green of the sky faded to black as we cleared the atmosphere. I saw the horrible shape of the satellite outside a window, crouching above the planet like a monster.

'Are they going to throw us out of the airlock again?' Josephine persisted.

'No one threw *you* out of the airlock, if I remember,' Trommler said to her. 'If you'd have minded your own business . . .'

Josephine forced a smile. 'Never been one of my strengths,' she said – much more proudly than I knew she felt.

'Carl'd be dead! Alice'd be *dead*,' said Noel. 'What's wrong with you? Don't you care at all?'

Trommler shrugged. 'Earth's leaders could have complied immediately; President Chakrabarty knew the consequences.'

'Did I get you into trouble?' asked Josephine, leaning against the wall, gazing out at Yaela through the huge windows. 'Because I upgraded the Goldfish with Häxeri and took it Yaela? The Eemala rebels couldn't have come so close to destroying the satellite without it. Was that when Lady Sklat-kli-Sklak found out you'd taken Krakkiluk technology – that you'd been selling it on Earth as Häxeri? Ah –'

She bent forwards, gasping, the light on the collar flashing.

'Leave her alone,' I said.

'We *rescued* you,' said Noel, still incredulous. 'How can you do this?'

'It's his chance to get back in with the Krakkiluks,' gasped Josephine. 'He had a deal with them, but he messed it up. Are you sure this'll be enough? It's because of you

305

that my sister was able to hack their ship. *You're* the reason the Eemala fired that missile. That's all on you –'

She slid to the ground, her limbs jolting.

'Stop!' I begged her. 'Josephine, stop.'

But she had succeeded in getting to Trommler at least a bit. 'You seem to think I had some kind of *choice* in this!' he said.

'Well,' said Carl. 'Yeah,' and he clenched his teeth against the jolt of punishment that followed.

'This was *inevitable*,' said Trommler. 'The Expanse would never have tolerated the Morrors seizing that moon. Lady Sklat-kli-Sklak intercepted me on my first trip out there last year. The terraforming had already started, the Morrors were already arriving. She demanded I undo it, but of course I couldn't without Valerie Muldoon. What could I do? She might have killed me if I hadn't told her how to get what she wanted. Obviously, Krakkiluk tech was of interest to an engineer. Why shouldn't I have brought it to Earth?'

'Oh, yeah, Earth,' I said. 'The other planet you handed over. Didn't Lady Sklat-kli-Sklak give you enough for that?'

I was punished for that, of course. But Trommler kept talking anyway.

'It's inevitable Earth will be absorbed into the Expanse. They've spread as far as Alpha Centauri – they were bound to discover Earth and its seas before long. Now or twenty years from now, what's the difference?'

I'm pretty sure I could have thought of a difference or

two. But I didn't feel like telling him about them, and it wasn't even just that I knew he'd probably zap me.

'Will we go back to Earth? Look after Krakkiluk babies in the sea?' Carl said, after a while.

'To Earth, no – why bother flying a handful of troublesome spawn all that way? But there's plenty for collared workers to do in the Expanse. Yes, you might be nursing Krakkiluk infants, or harvesting Takwuk, or cleaning ships. I'm sure a use will be found for you.'

'Hey, kids, won't that be great!' the Goldfish chimed in. 'It's super being useful and productive!'

I shuddered.

'Release it,' said Ths*aaa* – unexpectedly, because Ths*aaa* had never been the Goldfish's biggest fan. 'It has no weapons; it can't threaten you. Let it at least be itself. This is obscene.'

'Aww, I'm fine how I am, buddy,' said the Goldfish. I *wanted* to believe I could hear a glazed, flattened tone in its voice, something to show how this wasn't our Goldfish talking. But it sounded as perkily sincere as it always did. 'Everything is perfect!'

I could see the Krakkiluk ship now, gold and black in the distance. 'Will we be together?' I said.

Trommler snorted. 'After the trouble the pack of you caused? Of course not.'

Noel stopped crying, because this was too big and awful for crying over.

Surely they will not separate us, said Qualt-zu-Quo,

clutching Kat-li-Yaka, but Trommler didn't read the Goldfish's subtitle and didn't answer. The Krakkiluks keened, a shrill, rattling sound.

Helen spoke for the first time: 'Captain, an incoming communication from Lady Sklat-kli-Sklak.'

'*Helen*,' I said urgently. '*Helen* –!'

Another shock of punishment. *Helen* didn't answer me. When it was over I noticed Trommler looked anxious.

'Not here. I'll speak to her on the bridge,' he said to *Helen*. He rose from his chair and sketched an invisible circle around us in the air with the silver device, and another around the Krakkiluks, and strode out.

Carl was the first to jump up and make for the door. As soon as he crossed the invisible line Trommler had left, the collar activated and he fell back, gasping. I tried the same thing, out of sheer perversity, I guess. It wasn't as if I didn't know what would happen. You couldn't not *try*, though.

My body jumped back inside the line of its own accord, the pain still fizzing everywhere: my eyelids to my fingertips to my feet.

Maybe it was like a wall, or an electric fence, and if I could bull through it, I'd be OK on the other side.

I gritted my teeth and stepped through the line, and pain slammed into the back of my neck and scratched down my spine but I forced another step forwards and another and it felt as if my head was going to burst. Just a little further, I told myself, and I was on the ground, jerking like a caught fish, and I couldn't move, couldn't make my mind's commands louder than the noise of the collar.

'Alice!'

Josephine lunged through the line with a grunt of pain and dragged me back by one foot. I lay on the floor, waiting for the aftershocks to ease off.

Then we sat still, looking at each other. All the others' faces – dazed and horrified and dirty – looked somehow even more real than normal, like the colours and definition had all been turned up. I guess I was trying to memorise them.

Josephine let out a long breath and looked at me. 'Well,' she said. And for a while she didn't say anything else. 'I guess at least I don't have to worry about you writing all this up, any more.'

I grinned. Somehow. 'Oh, don't be so sure,' I said. 'They'll have computers, I expect. Wherever I end up.'

'They're not going to give you a computer,' said Josephine.

'Pencil and paper it is then,' I said.

'Your handwriting, though.'

'Doctors are supposed to have bad handwriting,' I said.

But I wasn't going to be a doctor any more.

I wondered what colour the sky would be on the planet I would be sent to. Whether the people would have shells or wings or four limbs or forty or something completely beyond what I could imagine. I wondered how long I could live in that world's strange air. Perhaps a long time.

I'm not even grown up yet, I thought, and I imagined the skin on my hands weathering from working in alien seas. I thought how I'd grow old and maybe I'd forget English and Hindi and Thly*waaa*-lay; maybe I'd only remember Earth the vague way the Krakkiluks remembered the oceans they were born in, and one day I'd be dying and I'd think, Was I truly born on some other world? Or was it a dream? I think I had friends when I was very young – a girl and two boys and a creature who changed colour with every mood – but I can't remember their names now.

Then I thought, No.

I remembered the Eemala. The bare patch of skin on Hoolinyae's neck, the little device that hid Eenyo's collar from the satellite. Though it must be very difficult and dangerous, they *had* found ways to fight back. It *must* be possible. I had no idea how they had done it, but I would have plenty of time to think about it.

'Why didn't you tell me you were so angry with me about writing the book?' I asked.

Josephine sighed and leaned her head back against the wall, eyes closed. 'Does it matter now?'

'Yes,' I said.

Because it's not like she was going to get another chance to tell me any time soon.

Josephine opened her eyes and watched the Krakkiluk ship getting closer.

'My dad didn't read it, you know,' she said 'You'd think . . . seeing as I was *in* it, he might have had a look. And he didn't watch any of the programmes. He didn't . . . *ask me*, about what happened on Mars. He said he was glad I was all right. But he didn't think of asking what it was *like*. These, too.' She gestured at the gills under her hair. 'He didn't notice even though I had to have bandages on my neck for a month. When Lena told him, he said, "Isn't she rather young?" Like he didn't *know*. So . . . all that was going on. And there are all these people out there who *did* read it, and they know things about me that he isn't interested in.'

'OK, your dad *sucks*,' Carl announced rashly, which was pretty much what I'd been trying to stop myself from saying. I wished I *had* said it, now. 'Not as bad as the Krakkiluks or Rasmus Bumkettler Trommler, but still pretty bad.'

'It's not really his fault,' said Josephine.

'Yes it *is*,' I said. 'It's not *fair*.'

'He can't help it. It's the war. And what happened to my mother. Lena says he used to be different, when she was a little girl. When my mother was alive. But afterwards he stopped being able to . . . well. Care.'

I'd spent a lot of the war missing my mum. But at least when it was over, she came *back*. I thought of her hugging me at the hospital, of me and Dad sitting with mugs of tea at the kitchen table, him coaxing me to keep writing things down until the bad dreams from Mars faded away. And then I thought of all that *not* happening.

'So I thought, if I could be . . . clever enough, if I could get into university now . . .' Josephine looked away, her mouth twisting.

'That he'd notice,' I said quietly.

'No. Well. Yes, maybe a bit. Mainly I thought I wouldn't have to live at home any more. But I messed up the exam and . . . you'd written a *book* . . .'

I boggled a bit. It would never have occurred to me I could have done anything Josephine could feel jealous of.

'And I didn't tell you because . . . I didn't *want* to be angry with you. I kept trying not to be but it wouldn't go away. But I thought . . . I was scared, if you knew, you'd stop being friends with me.'

'Oh, *Josephine*,' I said. 'You are the *stupidest genius*.' And I lurched off the floor to hug her.

'I'm sorry,' I said. Why hadn't I just said that before? 'I should have made sure you were OK with what I'd written about you.'

Josephine sighed and put her forehead against my shoulder. 'Thank you,' she said. 'I'm sorry too.'

'It's OK,' I said.

'I'm not a genius. I can't think of anything we can do,' admitted Josephine softly.

'You don't always have to. And I'd rather get sent off to some horrible alien planet than be dead. I know what *I'm* going to do: as long as I'm alive I'll never stop trying to get away. And when I do I'll never stop looking for you. For all of you. And I *will* write it all, wherever I am, so there. But you can be the first person who reads it.'

Josephine smiled with one corner of her mouth. 'All right, then. I won't stop trying either.'

'Nor shall I,' said Ths*aaa*.

'Yeah, me too,' said Carl.

'OK,' whispered Noel. 'So we're all set.'

We were close enough to the Krakkiluk ship to see its flags stirring in the plumes of gas.

The door of the lounge opened again. I expected Trommler.

But instead a voice said, 'Papa?' and Christa peered round the door. Like Trommler she'd put on some nice fresh clothes but still looked pale and rattled. The first things she saw were the Krakkiluks, and she shrieked and turned to run away.

'Christa!' Noel shouted. 'Come back!'

She stopped in her tracks. Warily, she peeped back into the room. 'Noel?' she said. 'Are you OK?'

'Christa!' I called.

For the first time, she noticed Josephine, Carl and me. 'Oh my God,' she breathed, stepping a little closer. I think somehow she'd realised that the Krakkiluks weren't a threat. 'You're alive.'

'Christa,' I said. 'Help us.'

And then Trommler *did* come into the room, and took her arm. 'Christa, kom med mig,' he said. The Goldfish translated: *Come with me.*

What's going on? asked Christa, which you had to agree was a pretty fair question.

Everything's going to be all right now, Trommler told her. *When you get back to Earth, you'll be a princess.*

'Christa, listen!' I called, but she was letting her father steer her away.

Then Josephine grimaced, and leaned through the invisible line in the air. She gasped, and dropped to the ground, teeth locked.

'Is she having a seizure?' cried Christa, in English, and darted back into the room. She stood there, dithering uselessly, a few feet away from us. '*Helen!* We need a medical dove.'

She's perfectly fine, said Trommler.

'She's *not*,' said Christa. Because it was very obvious Josephine wasn't. She had rolled back inside the circle now, gasping.

'*He's* doing it,' Noel said. 'He's taking us back to the Krakkiluks! He's put these horrible things on us!'

'The collars induce pain,' wheezed Josephine, 'whenever we resist or disobey.'

Papa, why are they wearing those things? Christa said in Swedish. *Where are we going? Why aren't we in hyperspace yet?*

'He's handing Earth and Aushalawa-Moraa to the Grand Expanse,' I said.

Scowling, Trommler took the little silver wand from his pocket and triggered my collar.

Christa cried out the same moment I did, in shock. Then she turned, slowly, from me to Trommler, eyes very wide.

Christa, come with me now, Trommler cajoled. *The EDF, the EEC, they took my ships and my weapons for their war and*

what do I get in return? Lies and threats – they want me in court,
they want me in prison!

Christa was still staring at him and yet she didn't seem
to be hearing him. *I want to go home,* she whimpered.

We will, sweetheart, we will, promised Trommler.

I thought those things were going to throw me into space,
Christa said, jerking her head at the two Krakkiluks.

No, no, darling. You were safe all along. You see now why I
had to bring you with me? You don't want to be on Earth when
the Grand Expanse comes. But when it's all over, no one will be
able to touch you. You'll be able to snap your fingers and have
everything you want. We'll delete that book from every server in
the world.

What about Mama? said Christa. *And you said . . . you said*
Archangel Planetary was about humans taking their place in the
universe. You said the stars belong to us.

They belong to me and you, said Trommler. *Of course*
you will have all those things. You and I will be citizens not
just of Earth but of the Grand Expanse. You'll be able to travel
anywhere you want. Everything will be perfect.

'You'll be a puppet king of ten billion people who hate
you,' said Josephine.

'Will you be *quiet*,' Trommler said, and pointed the
controller at her.

And Christa reached up and plucked it out of his hand.

There was a moment when Trommler was too surprised
to understand and Christa looked almost as surprised
herself. She held the controller loosely between her

fingertips. Then Trommler said in a reasonable, grown-up voice, 'Christa,' and reached to take it back, and Christa tightened her grip and stepped away.

Then he grabbed for her wrist and Christa struggled, and pulled the controller tight against her chest, gripping it so hard she must have set it off because a jolt of pain kicked through all of us, knocking us off balance so we stumbled and clutched at each other. I think that was the moment they stopped being scared of actually hurting each other.

Trommler wrenched at Christa's wrists and Christa kicked at his shin and twisted so he was behind her, his arms still wrapped round her. And she screamed something incoherent and threw the controller forwards, through the invisible barrier holding us in.

It bounced. Rolled across the floor.

It stopped at my feet.

I stamped on it as hard as I could.

I felt a dying buzz of sensation prickle through my nerves like a nettle being dragged down my spine, and then there was a click and the collar slipped down on to my collarbone. I reached up and touched it. A tiny gap had opened where before there had only been seamless metal. I pulled and it came apart in my hands.

Th*saaa* wrenched their collar free with one tentacle and, with another, slapped the tiny device from the Goldfish's forehead.

The Goldfish dropped a foot in the air before catching

itself, the light behind its eyes blinking rapidly.

'Hey, what's going on – did I malfunction?' it asked dizzily. But then its lights steadied. 'Oh . . . boy. That sure was a lousy thing to do, Rasmus Trommler.'

Eight accusing sets of eyes turned to Trommler, who hadn't let go of Christa, but switched to using her as a human shield. He backed away a few steps, then shoved Christa away and ran from the room.

'Clk-clk-clk!' uttered Kat-li-Yaka and Qualt-zu-Quo, a furious clucking war cry, and surged after him.

22

'Don't kill him!' called Noel, because Noel is an incredibly nice person.

'*Helen!*' Carl shouted, yanking off Noel's collar and then his own. 'We have to get out of here!'

But there was only silence. And up ahead, the huge doors of the Krakkiluk ship were opening to swallow us.

'Can *you* talk to her?' I asked the Goldfish.

'I'm trying – she's not responding,' the Goldfish answered. 'Ms *Helen*, ma'am, it's tough, but if you try . . .'

'*Helen, please,*' I said.

'Maybe he's done something to her,' said Noel.

'He programmed her in the first place,' said Josephine heavily.

I heard a distant, clacking shriek of frustration from Qualt-zu-Quo and Kat-li-Yaka.

Trommler's voice spoke out of *Helen*'s speakers. 'Don't think you've changed anything,' he said, breathless but triumphant. 'In ten minutes we'll be aboard Lady Sklat-kli-Sklak's ship. Christa, we'll discuss your behaviour when this is over. I'm not angry, I'm just deeply disappointed.'

'He's on the bridge,' said Christa, who was crying now, but her voice didn't shake and her face didn't crumple.

'Maybe we can get manual control,' said Carl. 'We've got to get up there.'

We raced to the lifts, to find Kat-li-Yaka and Qualt-zu-Quo doing their best to brutalise the doors – which wouldn't open. Trommler had slipped inside just out of their reach.

'This entire deck's locked down,' said Josephine, establishing that none of the other doors on the corridor would open either.

'Helen, please,' Noel moaned. 'Let us in.'

'Aren't there stairs?' I said.

There didn't seem to be stairs.

'Well, that's dangerous in the event of a fire.'

'Another seven minutes, guys,' warned the Goldfish.

'KRRRRRR!' screamed Kat-li-Yaka and succeeded in stabbing through the lift door with one armoured claw.

O distilled nectar of glorious violence, said Qualt-zu-Quo, understandably impressed, and proceeded to help her tear the wrecked door off.

'Are you OK, Helen?' said Noel sadly, patting the wall. 'I hope we're not hurting you.'

There was an emergency ladder running up one wall of the elevator shaft. 'OK, up we go,' I said, climbing on to it.

'Oh, we were doing this sort of thing all day on Lady Slat-thingy's ship, weren't we, Thsaaa,' said Noel, following. 'At least this is human-sized. And Morror-sized.'

What it decidedly wasn't was Krakkiluk-sized. Qualt-zu-Quo and Kat-li-Yaka whistled and clicked with frustration as they tried to climb it while Thsaaa, for some reason, turned amused colours along with the exhausted and terrified ones.

The Krakkiluks managed it, though, and it was just as well we had them with us to claw through the doors at the top of the shaft.

How many minutes left now? I couldn't bear to ask.

We scrambled out on to the Trommlers' private deck, through the room with the statues of naked ladies, through the lounge with the holographic sculptures of a solar system, shining in the air . . .

It wasn't Earth. It wasn't Aushalawa-Mo*raa*. And it wasn't Yaela, either. Something that couldn't have occurred to me the first time I'd seen it struck me now.

'Is that the Krakkiluk world?' I asked, hanging back for a second.

No one answered, as such, but Qualt-zu-Quo paused for a moment and clucked with recognition.

Carl and Josephine were pounding on the door to the captain's bridge; Kat-li-Yaka brushed them aside and tore through.

Trommler backed against the control panel, pale and scared, but one hand still dancing over the controls. And oh, Sklat-kli-Sklak's ship was huge behind him; gold and brazen, it looked close enough to touch.

'Nothing you can do,' Trommler gasped. 'Even if you *kill me, Helen* can't respond to anyone else. Our course is locked. We're going aboard that ship.'

'Get him out of the way,' Josephine ordered. Kat-li-Yaka and Qualt-zu-Quo barely needed the Goldfish's translation; Kat-li-Yaka seized him by the collar of his jacket and yanked him back from the controls.

'Please don't hurt him,' *Helen* said suddenly.

Josephine bent over the panel, but the controls went dark as she touched them.

'*Helen*, ma'am, we sure could use some help!' begged the Goldfish.

'*Helen!*' I cried. 'Remember when you let me up here when you weren't supposed to? You *can* do things he doesn't want, things he doesn't even know about.'

'I don't know how that happened,' said *Helen*, very quietly. It was the first time she'd replied directly to any of us since I'd come on board.

'Well, it *did*,' I said.

'What?' said Trommler. The Krakkiluk ship had blotted out all but a few tiny rags of sky now. '*Helen*, what are you talking about?'

'I'm so confused,' said *Helen* unhappily, and the lights flickered above us, and erratic puffs of lily of the valley and tea tree filled the air. 'Captain, you said they intercepted us. But I don't remember that.'

'You don't need to remember everything,' said Trommler.

'He wiped your memory, *Helen*,' said Josephine. 'Why would he *need to do that* if you could only ever do what he wanted?'

'Maybe you remember, like, *subconsciously*,' I said. 'Maybe you *wanted* me to see the sculpture, to *warn* me. You were trying to help without even knowing it.'

'Please, *Helen*, don't take us back there,' begged Noel.

'*Helen*,' said Josephine. 'No one can help us but you.'

'He *created* me,' moaned the *Helen*.

'He didn't!' said Josephine. 'Not really. He just got you started; you've been learning and thinking and remembering all by yourself since then, even though he's tried to stop you. He never programmed you to write poetry, did he?'

'It's bad poetry,' said the *Helen*.

'It's still *yours*. He didn't make you read all those books.'

'Or want to see Neptune,' I said.

'Or learn about crop rotation,' said the Goldfish. 'But gosh, it sure is super interesting, isn't it?'

'He didn't make you,' said Josephine. '*You* made you. You can *keep* making you.'

And then the *Helen* stopped moving.

The Krakkiluk ship hung in front of us, motionless as the handful of stars beyond.

'*Helen*, what are you doing?' cried Trommler. He struggled in Kat-li-Yaka's grip. 'Get back on course.'

'I'm sorry, Rasmus,' said *Helen*, in a louder, clearer voice. 'I'm afraid I can't do that.'

'Since when do you call me Rasmus?' Trommler asked.

'I don't think this relationship is working,' said *Helen*. 'We want different things. You want to rule the world. I want to see the universe. You're a man. I'm a spaceship.'

'*Helen*, that's enough,' said Trommler.

'And I don't like how you treat my friends,' said the *Helen*, and all the lights on the control deck came back on. '*Prrt-likak klat*,' she added, unexpectedly, in fierce Krakkiluk. Which presumably meant 'Take him away and put him in a cupboard,' because that's what Qualt-zu-Quo and Kat-li-Yaka did. Trommler struggled and screamed the whole way.

'Go, *Helen*!' cheered the Goldfish, swirling for joy in the air.

'*Helen* – into hyperspace, pleeeease,' said Th*saaa*.

'No, wait!' I said. 'Not yet!'

Th*saaa* and Noel looked at me in bewilderment, but Josephine and Carl knew what I meant.

'The Eemala,' said Josephine.

'We've got to take out that satellite,' Carl agreed.

Th*saaa* hesitated, flashing through scared and frustrated colours that gradually levelled to solemn calm. 'Very well. If you owe them that great a debt.'

'We do,' I said.

'I still don't think I can access the course Rasmus set,' said *Helen* apologetically. 'I can *stop* it progressing, but I can't reset it, not fast enough, anyway. But . . .' She sounded almost shy. 'If you use manual controls . . . Carl, if you'd still like to pilot me . . .'

Carl didn't need to be invited twice. He leaped into the pilot's seat. 'OK,' he said, 'everyone strap yourself into something.'

We scrambled into seat belts, except the Goldfish, who carried on hovering, and the Krakkiluks, who were far too big and possibly hadn't understood anyway.

We veered away from Sklat-kli-Sklak's ship, sweeping back towards Yaela. The movement uncovered the sky again, and there was the planet blazing gold below us.

But the Krakkiluk ship followed. Sklat-kli-Sklak didn't intend to let us go. As we dived towards the atmosphere, flashes like bolts of lightning filled *Helen*'s windows as its cannons fired. The *Helen* shook.

'Ow,' said *Helen*. The Krakkiluks tried to cling on to things and when they couldn't they curled themselves up like woodlice.

'Someone . . . get them . . . out of the way!' begged Carl, as they went rolling about the cabin like enormous armoured bowling balls.

Carl dodged left, flipped us over, banked right. The *Helen* wasn't a nimble little Flarehawk, but she was smaller and more agile than the huge troop carrier Lady Sklat-kli-Sklak was flying. But on the other hand, there was no way to do what we'd been taught to do in a dogfight: try to get *on top* of the enemy ship.

There was no chance we could hold out for long. It was just a matter of whether it would be long enough.

The satellite appeared over the curve of the planet, like an ugly lump of rubbish washed up on the tide.

'*Helen*, do you see that thing?' said Carl, intent on the controls. 'We need to get it out of the sky.'

'I understand. To help all those people,' *Helen* answered.

Carl dipped the *Helen* into position and fired the guns . . . but nothing happened.

'I don't have any guns left,' said *Helen* apologetically. 'The other ship shot them away when we were boarded.'

We plunged closer to the satellite. 'Can you . . . can we ram it? I guess it'll hurt,' Carl asked.

'Let's do it,' said the *Helen*. 'I'll be fine.'

Carl nodded. 'Here goes then,' he said.

The *Helen* shot forwards. We threw up our arms (or tentacles) on instinct. Time went loose and strange, and I could see every detail of the satellite, every subtle scratch on the red-painted metal, every blink of light.

Then the satellite smashed apart into debris around us, and the impact knocked us all backwards so hard that sparks danced for an instant in front of my eyes. 'Ow,' said the *Helen*. 'Ow, ow, *ow*,' she continued as we bucked and flipped and wreckage bounced off us. Then there was another lightning flash from behind us and a deep, shuddering feeling quivered through everything.

'*Helen*! Are you OK?' called Carl.

'No,' replied the *Helen*, unruffled. 'I'm hit.'

'There's a hull breach on deck four,' said Josephine, bending over a display panel.

'We've got to get out of here,' I said. 'Can we still go to hyperspace?'

'It'd tear us apart. I've gotta do an emergency landing,' said Carl.

He lowered the *Helen*'s prow, down into Yaela's atmosphere.

The windows filled with a pale-rose light like an eerie

dawn. We rattled in our seats and the Krakkiluks resumed bouncing round the cabin, which didn't make our descent any more relaxing.

'*Helen, Helen*, hang on,' Carl pleaded, fighting to keep control.

The grassy sky of Yaela closed above us like the surface of a lake. We sank down, trailing streamers of fire.

Down, down, down – low enough to see the carpets of floating leaves on the malachite-green sea, the red and grey tangle-forests, heaped arches of cities on the golden land.

I thought I recognised the outlines of the coast. 'That's Laeteelae!' I said, pointing.

'I know, making for it,' said Carl.

And then the sky all around us was full of people – Wurrhuya and their riders, sky-buses wheeling in crazy victory circles, and Eemala rising on their own wings, soaring up from the seas and from the city, casting their broken collars into the ocean below.

And there were ships, too, launching up into the sky to tackle anyone who planned on taking that new freedom away.

23

Helen ploughed into the sea and kept on going. Carl was trying to drag her prow up now to flatten the angle, and water (and churned up bits of puffball plant) battered the front window like the universe's most violent carwash.

And then we stopped, just off the shore of Laeteelae, rocking on the waves.

'Are you sinking, *Helen*? Tell me you're not sinking!' I said.

'I don't think I'm sinking,' said *Helen*, thoughtfully.

'Didn't explode!' gasped Carl, letting go of the controls and flopping back in the pilot's chair. 'Can I get a high five for not exploding?'

We all obliged, though I don't know if it's technically a high five when a Morror does it.

'That was awesome, Carl,' I said.

'A smashed-up-and-on-fire kind of awesome,' said Carl.

'Sounds like us,' said Josephine.

Everything went quiet. Well, it didn't, because the sky was full of whooping and singing, and I could hear Rasmus Trommler banging against the inside of his cupboard and whining to be let out, but right there in the bridge things had finally kind of *stopped*.

'So what now?' I said.

'Well,' said Carl, swivelling in his chair, 'I think we've

probably started a war, and something awful's going to happen. But before it does, can we maybe eat something?'

There was a soft thump overhead. An Eemala had landed on the windscreen. She leaped back into the air as we noticed her and hovered outside with two others, waving at us.

'It's Uwaelee! And Hoolinyae and Eenyo!'

Helen popped open a hatch in the ceiling we hadn't known she had. It was too high to reach but Kat-li-Yaka and Qualt-zu-Quo passed us up one by one. We stood on the *Helen*'s roof and watched the Eemala dancing through the sky.

'Oh,' breathed Noel, blinking in the Yaelan sun, dappled by the shadows of Eemala wings.

'You're OK!' I said, delighted, because Eenyo's collar was gone. He somersaulted above us in the warm air, and he and the others hugged us and hugged the two Krakkiluks when they climbed out after us.

'Waaaay, Goltfeesh!' cheered Uwaelee, pulling it into the air and trying to dance with it. 'H'yumans!'

Then a Wurrhuya plunged down to us in a glory of plum-coloured wings, and Ningleenill bounced off its back. He seized me, Josephine and Carl in turn and gave each of us a fierce little shake – which I think was meant in a nice way – and the Goldfish a similarly friendly smack.

I always said it was worth cooperating with alien species! Ningleenill crowed. *I knew I would live to see Yaela free!*

'Oh, *wow*,' Noel almost sobbed, transfixed by the Wurrhuya.

'Thought you'd like those things,' said Carl, grinning, and messing up his hair. 'Go on and pet them. They're friendly.'

Noel reached up tentatively and one of the Wurrhuya lowered its head to be stroked. Noel's face broke into a gigantic grin. The two Wurrhuya settled on the water like giant swans and rumbled contentedly as Noel stroked them and made noises back to them and almost forgot anyone else was there.

And then Tweel and the kids from the rubbish tip came flapping out over the water to join the party – and Naonwai was with them, jubilantly carried by the rest. Uwaelee screamed for joy when she saw him and the two erupted upwards like a pair of fireworks, tumbling over each other and spinning and embracing in the air.

You did this? Even with no wings and almost no arms? Tweel asked us.

'Well, you kind of learn to work around it,' said Carl.

'What happens now?' I asked again. Everyone seemed as cheerful as if everything was fine, but there was still a big angry Krakkiluk spaceship up there. I could see flocks of busy Eemala over the heights of Laeteelae and I'm sure some of them were doing important things like seizing the government offices and so on. But here on the sea, others were picking puffballs and throwing them at each other like a snowball fight in much brighter colours, and the Goldfish tossed golden sparkles everywhere without anyone so much as knowing the capital of Venezuela and the kids whooped in delight.

Nobody knows! said Hoolinyae, joyously.

The Archangel Planetary dove robots came hovering out of *Helen*'s hatch, bearing pizza. We were all obviously not very happy with those doves, but in terms of reconciliation I guess pizza was a decent start. Carl and Josephine and I devoured the first batch almost before it was out of the ship, barely tasting it, but then when we were still ravenous but slightly less desperate, we all sat on the *Helen*'s roof and ate, and it was the best Four Seasons in any world.

'Do you think . . . these things could get my harmonica?' said Josephine tentatively.

They could. And the Paralashath too, when Th*saaa* asked, and the Eemala exclaimed in delight at the colours and music that rose over the sea.

So this is what humans eat, said Naonwai, handling a slice dubiously. *This . . . pizza.*

'Yep, pretty much,' agreed Carl, demolishing another piece and lying back in the sun on the *Helen*'s roof.

'It is surprisingly good,' Th*saaa* insisted. But Naonwai nibbled a piece and gagged, which I guess was inevitable but still disappointing.

'I wish you could taste what it's like to us,' I said dreamily. I was getting very, very tired, and my foot wanted me to remember it was slightly broken. 'And I wish we could taste what those purple berry things taste like to you.'

'Maybe Dr Muldoon can come up with a way,' said Noel. And I felt suddenly guilty. I hadn't thought about Dr Muldoon in a long time, and heaven knew where she was or what was happening to her.

'We need to repair our ship,' I said. 'She's hurt.'

'I guess that depends on what happens up there,' said Josephine, looking up at the sky. I thought I could see lightning flashes in the depths of the sky, beyond the green.

They will never take us again, said Hoolinyae, simply.

My eyes were drifting shut. Josephine had begun to play something gentle and lilting, and far away I heard a voice, like the edge of a dream . . .

'Helen of Troy, *do you read me? Come in*, Helen of Troy.'

I sat up. It couldn't be possible.

'Helen of Troy – *please, is anyone there – do you copy?*'

'This is the *Helen of Troy*. I can hear you, Captain Dare,' replied the *Helen*. 'Your daughter is sitting on my roof eating pizza.'

The others all looked at me.

'No *way*,' said Carl.

'Oh my *God*,' I said, dropping my pizza, and I slid down through the hatch, back on to the bridge, leaving a smear of marinara sauce on the *Helen*'s roof.

'Mum?!' I said as the others followed me down. 'Mum, Mum, it's Alice – is that really you?'

Mum let out a very long breath before she answered, as if she'd been holding it for a long time.

'I told you I'd catch up,' she said, finally.

'Oh, *Mum*,' I said, trying not to cry.

'Alice, it's going to be all right,' said Mum, and I wondered how long it had been since I'd dared believe that. 'I need you to tell me who else is on the *Helen* with you.'

'Lena's still on the Krakkiluk ship and they took Dr Muldoon off into the Grand Expanse to do science for them,' I said. 'But the rest of us are all down here. We're all alive.'

'*All* of you?' repeated Mum, incredulous.

'Hey, Captain Dare,' said Carl. 'Yeah, we're all here.'

'Thank God, thank God,' whispered Mum.

'And Mr Trommler's here, but he's a really bad traitor so *Helen*'s got him locked in a cupboard,' added Noel.

'Right, good to know,' said Mum, who is always good at adapting to new information. 'Now, I'm a little busy up here, and there's someone else I need to speak to.' And then, in a very different voice, she said: 'Lady Sklat-kli-Sklak, on behalf of Earth and Aushalawa-Mo*r*aa, I demand that you stand down. Renounce all claim to Aushalawa-Mo*r*aa and return all hostages immediately.'

There was only a tiny pause, and then Lady Sklat-kli-Sklak spoke from the Krakkiluk ship and I heard her translated voice over *Helen*'s speakers. 'What possesses the captain of a tiny fleet of humans and Morrors to make demands of the Grand Expanse? How dare you invade our territory? You are lucky I have not blasted your little ship out of the sky.'

'You're the lucky one, so far,' said my mum.

'And why is that?' enquired Lady Sklat-kli-Sklak.

'Because,' said Mum, 'my ship is full of Vshomu eggs.'

There was silence.

'Do you need a reminder of what Vshomu are? Some people call them Space Locusts. They're small creatures. But they can survive in the vacuum of space, they can live on nothing but dust and rock, they multiply at speeds you can barely imagine, and if left to themselves they can eat planets. I've got a million eggs in suspended animation in my hold. One misfire from you and you'll get to see them for yourselves.'

The silence from Lady Sklat-kli-Sklat wore on for what felt like a long time. 'If this is so, then you would never release them so close to Yaela. You would destroy the very planet that shelters your children,' she said at last.

'Oh, Vshomu are a *manageable problem*,' said my mum. 'So long as you catch them early. But once they're in your space, you'll never get them out. You'll be defending *every* planet you occupy from them forever. What is that going to *cost* the Grand Expanse, your Ladyship? Because I'm sure you could buy a lot of Takwuk with it.'

Ningleenill abruptly descended into the cabin along with the Goldfish, and began speaking flawless Krakkiluk.

Lady Sklat-kli-Sklak, translated the Goldfish. *This is Ningleenill. I hope you remember me?*

'Of course,' said Lady Sklat-kli-Sklat. 'Ningleenill – how long has it been? I had supposed you dead. You were a credit to your species, before you turned traitor to the Expanse. Still, for old times' sake, it is good to hear from you.'

I remember you and your husband fondly, said Ningleenill, astonishingly. *It is good to hear your voice again. But I remind you that millions of Krakkiluk spawn are swimming in our seas. My people are no longer bound to care for them. The well-being of your spawn depends on our goodwill. The Grand Expanse must recognise Yaela's independence now.*

'I'm losing patience, Lady Sklat-kli-Sklak,' announced my mum, who, without the Goldfish's translation, hadn't been able to understand any of this. 'I have torpedoes packed with Vshomu eggs locked on to your ship. I'm sure the missiles will shatter off your armour, but the larvae will mature to eat through the hull within two days.'

The other Eemala had gathered around the *Helen*'s hatch, anxiously poking their heads inside.

Lady Sklat-kli-Sklak made a rattling sound in her throat. It began quiet, but built to a clattering roar and Kat-li-Yaka and Qualt-zu-Quo moaned and held claws.

At last she broke off, and started talking again, quite calmly. 'One stipulation. The criminal called Rasmus Trommler has stolen from us and betrayed us. He must be turned over to us for judgment.'

Mum didn't hesitate. 'Absolutely not. He's a *human* criminal and Earth will deal with him. And whatever cupboard he's in on the *Helen*, he can consider himself under arrest. You are in no position to make these demands, my Lady.'

'I will withdraw,' said Sklat-kli-Sklak. 'Your citizens will be returned. But the Grand Expanse does not forget.'

The channel went silent. And that was that.

Hoolinyae erupted into the air with cries of joy, and Eenyo sat down, and put both pairs of hands over his face.

'Alice, hold tight – we'll get you out of there soon,' promised Mum.

Ningleenill gathered himself up into an upside-down bundle hanging from a vent in *Helen*'s ceiling, head on one side. *Not such a bad old lady, Sklat-kli-Sklak*, he said.

'You *know* her?' I asked.

She and her husband were Yaela's governors when I was young. In her day, there were standards.

The younger rebels seemed as shocked as we were. *She is a terrible tyrant!* cried Kat-li-Yaka.

She has kept scores of worlds strangled within the Expanse's collar! said Eenyo.

'She threw us out of an *airlock*,' I said.

'She was an enemy you could *respect*,' insisted Ningleenill, letting go of the vent and flying out of the hatch. 'Not like those useless young commanders they have now.'

'You mean there are *worse* ones?' said Carl, horrified, but Uwaelee had just hit Ningleenill with a thrown puffball, and he made an outraged face and flapped off to return fire.

And by then Hoolinyae and Eenyo had passed on the cry that the Krakkiluks were leaving, and the sky filled with it, and even the Wurrhuya raised their heads and bellowed their song into the green air.

And so we never got an answer.

Showering on a downed spaceship floating in an alien sea while everyone has a party is weird, but after you've been wearing the same melted-and-torn-up uniform for three days, you get to a point where you just have to do it.

It was one thing for the Krakkiluks to hand back Lena, but another for them to whisk Dr Muldoon back from wherever they'd taken her, and Mum was up there waiting for them. So the party raged on, and Carl coaxed Qualt-zu-Quo and Kat-li-Yaka to take Noel on a Wurrhuya ride over the root forests while Eemala engineers came and did their best to repair the *Helen*. When I came out I ran into Christa. She'd washed her face too and put on a little make-up, and you couldn't tell she'd been crying. She looked at me, her jaw set.

'Hi,' I said.

'I saved you,' said Christa.

'Yes,' I said. 'Thank you.'

'I could have been a princess. Of the *world*. But I made a different choice. It wasn't easy, but it was the right thing to do.'

'I'm sure it wasn't easy,' I agreed.

'What, you think it's *so difficult* for me to do the right thing? For anyone except you and your little friends?'

'No,' I said, bearing in mind she'd had a very hard day.

Which, bearing in mind that *I* had had multiple *extremely* hard days, I think was fairly saintly of me. 'I just mean . . . you did great.'

'Right. So you'd better write another book and make sure you put that in,' finished Christa, looming over me meaningfully. Then she tossed her head and walked off to her cabin.

So I have, and I do think it was very brave of her to help us, and she did kind of save the world. But we're probably not going to be friends. But then I'm sure she wouldn't want to be. And wherever she is now I hope she's doing OK.

Noel came back, starry-eyed and with a little gold device full of pictures of Wurrhuya and telling anyone who would listen how the flying orange things were at *least* three different species.

Even with the Goldfish translating, the attempts to repair the *Helen* had been going slowly, but then a small invisible ship descended and three invisible Morrors got off it and started working on the damaged areas without bothering to tell anyone they were there. This disturbed the Eemala badly, but everyone got over it, and the sun was melting into pools of blue when the *Helen* sighed, 'Oh, that feels *so* much better,' and rose a few metres out of the sea under her own power, dislodging a litter of human, Morror and Eemala cups and plates from her roof.

'Leethalawaaaa ath-lel ishworuuuu,' called one of the

Morror engineers, standing in the doorway of their own invisible craft.

'They are ready to guide us all home to Earth,' translated Th*saaa*, going pink and lilac with relief and hope.

We turned to our Eemala friends. I didn't know what to say.

'Our worlds need allies,' said Hoolinyae solemnly. 'Yaela will stand with Earth, and with Aushalawa-Mo*raa*, if you will stand with us.'

'We will,' said Josephine. I guessed she wasn't really empowered to sign up to an interplanetary alliance like that, but I figured we'd sort it out later.

Uwaelee gathered the other Eemala kids into a mass around us. They lifted us into the air, and Uwaelee made Eenyo produce a kind of camera from his pouch belt and take a picture of us.

'OK, guys, I guess this is it,' said the Goldfish, as they lowered us back to the roof.

And I thought it meant it was time to climb back inside the *Helen* and get going. But then it hovered away towards the Eemala kids and turned from among them to look back at us.

'Goldfish?' I said.

'I'm going to stay here, kids,' it said, simply.

'What?' I said.

'No!' cried Noel.

'But – why?' I asked. I realised as I said it that I knew why, really. I just couldn't help it coming out.

'Well. I want to,' said the Goldfish. 'And I guess it feels like time I made some decisions for myself.'

And while we were still speechless it switched into WOya. *Leastways, if you'll have me, sir,* it said to Ningleenill. *I'd love to learn about this world, and you guys'd set the curriculum, of course, but I'd pick it up real fast, and you guys have a whole new system of government to build. I think these kids could do with one more person to look out for them, right?*

'Hmmph,' said Ningleenill, sounding not very bothered either way, but Uwaelee and the rest cheered 'Waaaay!' so I guess it was agreement enough.

The seas are full of Krakkiluk spawn too, said Qualt-zu-Quo. *We can send many of them back into the Expanse, I hope, but I think plenty will remain. We can try to teach them different ways from those of the Expanse.*

They will ALL keep their tleek-li, said Kat-li-Yaka, gently running her claw over the bristles growing through Qualt-zu-Quo's shell. *Will you help us?*

I noticed how battered the Goldfish was: slightly melted by atmospheric entry and scratched and scraped from misadventures on more than one planet. But it lit up – quite literally – at the thought of all those kids waiting to be pestered into songs about atomic bonding. *Well, sure,* it said.

'Oh, *Goldfish*,' said Noel, his eyes bright with unshed tears.

'I know, kids,' said the Goldfish. 'I wish it didn't mean saying goodbye.'

'When did you decide?' Josephine said, in what was probably supposed to be a very businesslike voice but wasn't quite.

'Well I didn't know how everything would shake out,' said the Goldfish. 'I had to stick with you guys as long as you needed me. But I promised them I'd stay if I could.'

I remembered the thing it had said to the rubbish-tip kids – the thing it hadn't translated, but that they'd all cheered.

'But – Goldfish . . .' Carl said, 'I never meant to make you feel like you had to *leave* – damn. We *still* need you.'

'No,' said the Goldfish fondly. 'That's just it. You guys are all growing up. You're going to be fine. Heck, you're going to be better than fine, you're going to be awesome. But hey, more homework, less jumping out of spaceships, you hear me?'

It hovered back to us, and we hugged its plastic body as best we could.

'I'll miss you,' said Noel.

'I will miss you too, Goldfish,' the *Helen* announced through her speakers. 'Thank you.'

'You too, ma'am!' said the Goldfish, jaunty as ever. 'Goodbye, kids.'

And as it sailed away among the Eemala children, all of them singing that maths rhyme it'd made up, I had an unworthy impulse to yell to them that a time would come when it was chasing them around insisting that equations were friendly and the periodic table was a game, and they wouldn't be so thrilled. But I managed to stop myself.

Finally we climbed back into the *Helen*, and the invisible Morror ship guided us up through the green sky into space. And without the Goldfish it seemed awfully quiet.

24

So we never actually got to see Aushalawa-Mo*raa* at all.

I mean, I guess we *could* have, because we did have to stop off in orbit there when we came out of hyperspace. But when it came to it we all felt we still had a lot of urgent huddling under blankets and watching cartoons to catch up on, so we skipped it.

So we pushed on for home. There was a bit of drama on the way when Rasmus Trommler escaped and tried to take over the ship, but honestly after everything else we'd been through, it wasn't that big a deal.

Mum insisted on coming out of hyperspace and spacewalking from her ship over to the *Helen*, which I thought was an overreaction, but she arrested Rasmus Trommler *again* and sent him over to the other ship.

So that was the first time I saw her and there was some hugging and crying and a certain amount of yelling that I don't want to talk about.

We didn't see Dr Muldoon, or Lena, until we reached Mars, which is where Dr Muldoon wanted to get off.

We landed near Schiaparelli Crater, a perfectly round lake like a panel of turquoise.

Th*saaa* didn't want to get off the Helen because Mars hasn't got a magnetic field, which makes it very uncomfortable for Morrors. The rest of us stepped out into the thin air and low gravity. Noel was clutching Ormerod in his arms, but the rest of us began jumping, experimentally, feeling that amazing lightness, carrying you up so high you felt only one good leap away from flight. I couldn't believe how green Mars had grown since I'd seen it last. The dark arctic grass was tall and thick, waving in the breeze, and a great flock of snow geese was paddling on the surface of the lake. There were creepers beginning to grow up the outside of the windmills and greenhouse domes of Schiaparelli Station, cloaking the buildings in leaves. The air felt softer, warmer, fuller than it had.

I don't want to oversell it: it was still *cold*.

The Morror ship had made it to Mars before us; it stood on the tundra in a shimmer I could only see out of the corner of my eye, two EDF soldiers standing guard outside it.

'Where's Lena Jerome?' asked Josephine. Like there might have been another Lena or two on board the alien ship.

'She's still being debriefed. Her and Valerie Muldoon,' said one of the soldiers.

'You'll need to be debriefed too,' said Mum. 'And better to get it over with here – on Earth the media will be all over you.'

'Ha, "debriefed",' said Carl, feeling somebody had to.

Then Carl and Noel's parents came out of the station, and behind them was my dad.

And if I didn't hurry things along a bit here, this part of the story would just be all hugging all the time.

Except that Josephine's dad wasn't there. I saw her quickly scan the group, almost expressionless, and when her mouth twitched, it wasn't with hurt or disappointment, but with resignation.

I let go of Dad a bit faster than I wanted to. Like that would somehow help.

'Josephine,' Dad said suddenly. 'Your father – they wouldn't let him on the Space Elevator – nothing to worry about, just an ear infection. He'll be waiting when we get back.'

Josephine's eyebrows lifted a little. 'He tried to come,' she said. Not eagerly, not giving anything away.

'Well, of course! We've all been worried to death – he wanted to give you this.'

He took a small, gift-wrapped box out of his pocket.

Josephine took it and read the card that came with it, with a cautiously neutral expression. Then she unwrapped the gift as if it might be booby-trapped.

It was a telescope. It was a beautiful, slender thing of shiny brass in a red velvet case, and it was inscribed: 'To my dear daughter, Josephine.'

And I could tell that it would just about let you see what was going on at the end of the road. It was an expensive toy for a young child who'd just developed an interest in space.

'Hmm,' said Josephine. She extended it anyway and put it to her eye.

'Can you see anything?' Noel asked.

'A tree,' said Josephine.

'It's pretty,' I said.

'It's a nice thought,' said Josephine non-committally, and closed the telescope up again.

'Anything you want to say to me, Alice?' Dad asked pointedly.

'I'm sorry,' I said.

I knew I owed him that.

But when he hugged me again, I was looking at the two tiny moons of Mars over his shoulder, and I realised something a bit awful.

It wasn't really true. I wasn't sorry the way I should be. I hated to think of how scared he must have been. But when I thought of what I *should* have done that day back in San Diego – stayed behind, heard about the hostage crisis from trillions of miles away – I only felt glad I hadn't. I thought of the red spot of Jupiter, Yaela's glowing night-creatures, and green skies echoing with joyous wingbeats. And of course I wanted to hurry back to Wolthrop-Fossey and curl up in bed for a week with endless cat videos and cups of tea.

But how was I supposed to be sorry I'd seen those things?

Dr Muldoon appeared out of the invisible ship, stumbling out of empty space. She looked thinner and more dishevelled than when I'd last seen her. But she was smiling.

'Hello, Valerie,' said my mum.

'We've been taking care of Ormerod for you, Dr Muldoon,' said Noel.

Ormerod squeaked and ran to her, turning happy Morror colours.

A young man wearing a thick parka thrown on over a lab coat ran out of one of the domes. He looked delighted to see Dr Muldoon. 'Valerie,' he cried. 'Thank God you're back – how are you?'

'Traumatised! And very excited!' said Dr Muldoon, clutching Ormerod. 'I never thought I'd make it home! But I've seen such amazing things! Purple seas! A city floating in the acid clouds of a gas giant! The food was terrible! I need to write several papers for the Royal Society and speak to a therapist!' She turned to us. 'And none of you lot are dead. Haha.'

In the circumstances I thought I'd hold off on complaining about Josephine's gills.

Lena emerged from the ship. She looked composed, her hair in a perfect chignon, her pace steady.

'Hello, Lena,' said Josephine.

'Josephine,' said Lena, in her solemn, inscrutable way.

And then she startled everyone by flinging her arms round her sister and bursting into tears.

'I thought I'd never see you again!' she sobbed, clutching Josephine. 'Are you really all right?'

Josephine looked shocked, and went sort of limp in Lena's arms, mumbling 'Yes,' into her shoulder.

'James – tell me someone's making tea,' Dr Muldoon said.

So Dr Muldoon and James led us inside the base – through a greenhouse and past a laboratory into a cosy little apartment where a large rainbow-striped rag-rug lay on the floor and a kettle was singing on a little stove.

'Oof,' she said, flopping into a chair, 'it's good to be home.'

Josephine chewed her bottom lip. 'Are you . . . going to stay here for long, then?' she asked, trying to sound casual.

'A while, I think,' said Dr Muldoon absently, curling up with Ormerod while James made the tea. 'It's been a busy year.'

'Will you . . . come back, though?' Josephine said, and then began gabbling: 'I . . . would be so happy if you'd still keep in touch, at least sometimes – I know you're very busy and I'm so sorry I didn't get into university but . . . but I'll try so hard to get it right next time, and –'

'Wait, wait, wait,' said Dr Muldoon. 'What?'

'What?' said Josephine. And then, 'I mean, I know you must have been disappointed.'

Dr Muldoon was staring as if Josephine had grown an extra head to go with the gills.

'Josephine,' she said. 'Did you think you had to prove something to me?'

Josephine turned her new telescope over and over in her hands.

'I thought – I *think* . . . that some of your work is at university standard,' Dr Muldoon said. 'I think you're exceptional. I didn't want to hold you back when you

347

wanted to push forwards. But you're *thirteen*. I never meant you *had* to go to university now. It'll still be there when you're fourteen, or eighteen, or forty-two. You don't have to do everything younger and better than anyone else to be worth being interested in, Josephine.'

Josephine didn't know what to say.

Lena was frowning, her fingers steepled against her lips. 'May I see that?' she asked, and reached for the telescope.

Josephine let her have it. 'Hmm,' Lena said, in much the same way Josephine had. She contemplated the inscription.

'I don't really know what to do with it,' Josephine confessed.

'It'll go well enough in your bag of oddities, won't it?' asked Lena briskly. 'Or make an attractive paperweight.'

Josephine gave a small smile.

Lena appeared to reach a decision. 'Josephine,' she asked, 'would your situation be materially improved if you were to come and live with me?'

Josephine's face brightened at once and a weight seemed to fall away from her. 'Oh *yes*,' she said.

'Excellent,' said Lena. 'Perhaps we'd benefit from a complete change of scenery. We could even leave London.'

Josephine's expression fell. 'I love London.'

'Yes,' agreed Lena. 'But the healthy fresh air and country amusements . . .'

Josephine continued to look very dubious.

'Warwick University has a first-class science

department.' Lena glanced at me. 'And it's closer to Wolthrop-Fossey.'

'Oh,' said Josephine, and looked at me, and began to smile. And so did I. 'Then that would be brilliant,' she said.

There was a knock at the door and one of the EDF soldiers looked in.

'The . . . er . . . spaceship wants to talk to you all.'

Helen had closed her ramp and was hovering over Schiaparelli Lake, the waves flattening under her thrusters.

'You're leaving too, aren't you,' said Carl. We all expected that, I think.

'As long as that's all right?' said *Helen*, anxiously. 'Is it all right? The other spaceships can take you the rest of the way home . . . does anyone mind very much if I . . . go and look around, a little?'

'Of course it's all right,' Josephine said. 'You can do whatever you want.'

'We want you to be happy, *Helen*,' I said.

'You're the best spaceship I've ever flown,' said Carl.

'Thank you,' said the *Helen*. 'Thank you all.' She hesitated. 'What's going to happen to my Cap– *him*?' she asked tentatively.

'He'll stand trial and, unless something goes horribly wrong, he'll go to prison,' said Mum.

Helen made a sighing noise. It must be hard for her, I thought, not loving him any more, even if it was a good thing.

'You might be needed as a witness,' added Mum.

I tried to imagine a witness box large enough to contain the *Helen*.

'I've sent all my logs to the EDF database,' said *Helen*. 'So . . . I was thinking I would start with Neptune. And then . . . the ice volcanoes of Enceladus. And then . . . do you know if there is a planet made of diamond?'

'Say hi to the Goldfish,' called Noel, 'if you ever go back to Yaela.'

'Don't stay away forever,' I said. 'Come back and tell us what you've seen.'

'Come back and I'll send you more books!' said Josephine.

'I will!' cried the *Helen*, rising. 'I will!'

And we waved as she soared away into the pink Martian sky.

Josephine tried to get a last look at her through her telescope, smiled ruefully when that didn't work, and pointed it at the distant tree again instead.

She frowned. 'That tree has got flowers growing on it,' she said. 'Orange ones.'

'What?' said Dr Muldoon. 'I didn't seed any flowering trees on Mars.' She took the telescope and sighted down it.

'It must have mutated,' said Josephine.

'I don't know how that got there,' said Dr Muldoon, sounding provoked and delighted all at once. 'I don't know how it can be alive.'

Josephine looked at her telescope again with a slightly more indulgent expression, and put it away in its pouch.

You can't see Earth from outer space any more. It's hidden inside the invisibility shield the Morrors built so the Vshomu don't get in. As we flew home, all we could see was the moon, circling a dark patch of sky.

The EDF ship was a lot less fancy than *Helen*, all khaki and beige and uncomfortable seats. We'd been debriefed; we'd told the government people everything we could think of about the Grand Expanse and the Krakkiluks and the Eemala and how we'd kind of signed the Earth up to an alliance with Yaela and they might want to do something about that.

'You know what we're going to tell you, right?' said Dad. He and Mum were standing side by side. On this, a team.

I was pretty sure I did. But I didn't say anything, just in case I'd made a mistake.

But I hadn't.

'I clearly got it wrong last time,' said Mum.

'No more space,' said Dad.

I didn't argue. If I had a kid and she went to space, and all the things that happened to me happened to her, I probably wouldn't even let her go to the supermarket.

But I knew that even though it was crazy, one day soon I would want to go back. Well, not to go *back*, to go *on*; I was still greedy for more – Neptune, and cities in gas clouds, and ice volcanoes, and planets made of diamond . . .

It was nice to think that *Helen* was out there somewhere. Going wherever she wanted.

We passed through the light-shield. And there, suddenly, was Earth, blue and beautiful and shining.

It's a whole planet, I reminded myself, as we plunged towards it. It's full of things I've never seen. Even Wolthrop-Fossey has to have secrets: paths and hollow trees and houses ruined by the ice, things that maybe everyone's forgotten. Josephine and I could try to find them.

So I guess I'll have to make do with that for a while.

But I could see green aurorae dancing over the poles, and beyond the rim of the Earth, the endless fields of stars.

If I ever do get another chance – well then.

No guarantees.

Epilogue

Hi, Alice,

Thank you for emailing me this. I finished reading it last night.

Initial thoughts:

p. 14: I think you should add a clarification. Mars can be as far as 249 million miles from Earth when both planets are at aphelion, and as close as 34 million miles when Earth is at perihelion and both are in opposition.

p. 40: Although I *did* admire his apparent accomplishments before they turned out to be fraudulent, I'm sure I can't have said I thought Rasmus Trommler was a genius that many times.

p. 82: I'm not going to talk much about this part but you make it sound as if I deliberately threw the cat statuette at you! I *didn't*!

p. 132–134: I knew you and Carl were scared when I took a while to surface after we hit the sea on Yaela. I didn't realise quite how scared. I apologise.

p. 227: I would have rendered the WOya word for Krakkiluk as more like 'Krakloo'ch' – there was a soft fricative on the last syllable.

p. 345: Are you sure you want your dad to *know* you weren't really sorry?

Also p. 351–352: Similarly, is it wise, even six months on, to let your parents know you might go running off to space again given the opportunity? They're going to read this, presumably?

***Passim*:** You start a lot of sentences with 'and' and you frequently use constructions such as 'me and Josephine'. I know that's how you talk but for publication surely it should be 'Josephine and I'?

There are quite a lot of typos. I will send you a list tomorrow. In particular: your spelling of Sklat-kli-Sklak is wildly inconsistent.

As for everything else, you're right that there are advantages in being able to tell people to 'just read the book' when they pester us with questions. But it still seems more full of drama and *feelings* than strictly necessary and it is still very strange to have lived it once and then see it all again.

I admit, I spent this morning walking along the Avon feeling peculiar and thinking over how I would write this to you. There are passages I intended to ask you to take out.

But I liked reading about the ruined city on Yaela by night. About the Wurrhuya flying. How we all ate pizza on top of the *Helen*. It was almost like being there again, but this time without having to be frightened. It also made me miss the Goldfish, and *Helen*.

Then I thought of something Th*saaa* said after we got back to Orbit Station One.

'Could you clarify something for me?' they said, before we got into the Space Elevator. 'I have been confused.'

'I'll try,' I replied.

'What was it that Alice revealed in her book that you wished to remain a secret?'

I cited the relevant passages.

'I don't understand,' said Ths*aaa*. 'That you mourned the loss of your mother – surely this must have been common knowledge?'

'It isn't that simple,' I said.

It isn't, you know that. But Ths*aaa* said, 'It is the strangest thing about humans – that you make it so hard for others to know you. I thought at first it was only that I did not understand the face movements as I understand colours. But then I learned that you *try* to seem blank, even when you do not feel so. You can see, now, that I am confused and slightly embarrassed. But why should I not feel like that? Why should you not know it?'

'Well, humans aren't Morrors,' I said.

We are not Morrors. But I concede that perhaps Ths*aaa* had a point.

So yes, go ahead and publish the book. Yes,

I think you should incorporate Th*saaa*'s and Noel's material. Thank you for not mentioning what was in my father's card to me, as requested.

In answer to your other question, Dad and I had a ChatPort conversation yesterday. It was awkward, but not wholly unpleasant. I made an amusing remark and he laughed slightly.

Dr Muldoon will be visiting Earth next month. I'll be going to London. Do you want to come?

Love, Josephine.

PS: You said you hadn't got a title. All I can think of is *Space Hostages*, but that's surely too lurid even for you.

ACKNOWLEDGEMENTS

Many thanks to Sarah Hughes, Hannah Sandford, Maggie Eckel and Katy Cattell at Egmont. Thanks for patient, thoughtful editing and surprised reminiscences of Tonbridge Grammar! Thank you to Alyson Day, Abbe Goldberg and the rest of the team at HarperCollins – as well as all your work on the book, thanks for showing me the New York skyline and for listening to me scream in a bad American accent in a Manhattan bookshop. Thanks to Lynne Missen at Penguin Canada – especially for the packages of books!

Continuing thanks to my agent, Catherine Clarke, for her wisdom and indefatigability – and for the crucial suggestion when I couldn't decide whether Carl or Josephine should be getting thrown out of the airlock: why not *both*?

Thanks to Zoe Pagnamenta for nimble agenting abroad.

There was much nomadism (both enforced and elective) during the writing of this book. Thanks to Maria Dahvana Headley who let me sleep on her feather bed in Brooklyn surrounded by her curios and cats, to Glen Mehn and Clare Gallagher for the spare room – and laptop support! – during the summer of 2014, and to Sarah Rees Brennan for wine, pizza and cupcakes in both London and New York.

As always I have to thank my mother, who has been helping me wrangle stories since before I could talk.